the Cenote

CHELSEA DYRENG

the Cenote

SWEETWATER
BOOKS
An imprint of Cedar Fort, Inc.
Springville, Utah

This is a work of fiction. The characters, names, incidents, places, and dialogue are products of the author's imagination and are not to be construed as real. The opinions and views expressed herein belong solely to the author and do not necessarily represent the opinions or views of Cedar Fort, Inc. Permission for the use of sources, graphics, and photos is also solely the responsibility of the author.

ISBN 13: 978-1-4621-1728-4

Published by Sweetwater Books, an imprint of Cedar Fort, Inc.
2373 W. 700 S., Springville, UT 84663
Distributed by Cedar Fort, Inc. www.cedarfort.com

LIBRARY OF CONGRESS CATALOGING-IN-PUBLICATION DATA

Dyreng, Chelsea Bagley, 1978- author.
The cenote / by Chelsea Bagley Dyreng.
  pages cm
Summary: "When Sandpiper finds she is pregnant with the baby of a traveling trader, her mother forces her to marry an unattractive (and unsuspecting) chief's son named Lark from a distant jungle tribe. Lark, however, is thrilled. He takes his exotic island bride to his village, built on the ruins of an ancient temple. Lark introduces Sandpiper to the cenote--a mysterious, deep pool and the village's only source of water--and explains that part of her duties as his wife is to haul water from this well for their home and garden. One day, when Sandpiper goes to the cenote, she discovers the body of a young man, face down in the water. Horrified, she runs to tell her sister-in-law who explains that men are often found dead in the cenote. No one knows why, and no one is supposed to talk about it. It baffles Sandpiper that the villagers are reluctant to talk about these tragedies out loud, but she joins the silence since she has her own secret to hide. Before long, another victim is found in the cenote. Cedar, the wife of the chief, fears that her adult sons will be next, so she gathers the women for a secret meeting hoping that if the women talk openly about the cenote, they might be able to find a way to finally put an end to the tragedies. This alarming information transforms the attitudes of the women in the village. They become mistrustful, suspicious and obsessed with their appearance, feeling like they need to compete with the voices of the cenote."--Text from publisher.
ISBN 978-1-4621-1728-4 (perfect bound)
1. Mayas--Fiction. I. Title.
PS3604.Y74C46 2015
813'.6--dc23
                    2015023699

Cover design by Shawnda Craig
Cover design © 2015 by Lyle Mortimer
Edited and typeset by Justin Greer

Printed in the United States of America

10 9 8 7 6 5 4 3 2 1

Printed on acid-free paper

for the star counters

My clarion call
for all to hear
is that we are at war,
and this is my spear.

PROLOGUE

At first the voices are gentle. Gentle as ripples of water. They rise over the forest on the night breeze, whispering, inviting.

Tonight would be the last time. Just once more, and then I would be done with the cenote forever, I promised myself.

I crept down the pathway, passing the huts of my friends. All was quiet and still and dark. I entered the black forest, stumbling over hidden roots and fallen logs as the voices beckoned from beyond the trees. When I reached the clearing I stopped, knowing that the further I went, the harder it would be to turn back. High above me the pointed moon curved like a jaguar claw, illuminating the world in inky indigo. From here I could see my destination in the distance.

Like a wild animal, I crouched. My fingers were already trembling and my heart pounded in my chest with the fevered excitement that can only be compared the thrill of drawing back a bow for the kill. For a moment I felt a twinge of guilt, knowing that my wife might wake and find herself alone and wonder. But I smothered the feeling, because this, after all, would be my last time.

Come, they sang.

I crept into the blue clearing, making my way toward the bushes where the cenote lay hidden. Invisible strings looped around me like spider silk, and I let them pull me forward.

Sometimes when I came to this point I could see the silhouettes of other Listeners approaching the cenote or hiding among the shadows. Others who, like me, had come to listen to the water sing. We never spoke to each other, and we kept our distance. Privacy must be respected.

But tonight there were no others. Only me. Only me and the voices.

A fragrant breeze blew into my face, and with every step the voices grew louder and harder to resist. I was almost there.

Then, like a great mouth in the face of the earth, the cenote appeared before me, inviting, deep and hungry. The voices grew stronger, heavier, rushing out of the pit and pulling me forward with an intensity that made me tremble.

Come! Come down! their voices beckoned, both beautiful and savage.

I stood at the edge. Far below, the vast pool of water glowed with a ghostly light. I closed my eyes as the sounds circled about me in a deafening roar.

Come! Let us show you our secrets!

The voices swirled out from the cavernous hole, echoing against the walls and becoming so intense that I felt as if at any moment I would need to cover my ears, but I did not because I wanted to feel the force of their message. The din soon became a part of me, flashing under my skin, through my heart and brain, filling every part of my body with fire.

Come! Come down to us!

I wanted this feeling to last forever. The overwhelming desire to be one with the rapturous sounds consumed me, and I had no other thought, no other wish, no other desire than to be swept away into the mysterious vortex of their realm, where I could not just hear them but also see and touch them. Nothing else was important. Nothing else mattered. The thought of complete surrender thrilled me to my core and I leaned forward, completely willing to do whatever they asked of me. *Take me*, I breathed. *Take me, I am yours.*

THE DRY SEASON

SANDPIPER

I twirled the crimson feather between my thumb and middle finger, back and forth, back and forth. Had I been wise, and had I known what trouble that feather would cause me in the future, I would have buried it there in the sand and let it rot.

But I was not wise.

I sat with my back up against the mango tree, watching the splendid feather spin and trying to ignore the sound of my name being repeated over and over again in the distance. Sometimes the voice was loud, sometimes it was soft, depending on whether she was shouting into the ocean breezes that constantly blew across our island. She had been calling my name for a long time, but I was not going to leave this spot. If it was important enough, she could find me.

When she did finally find me, her countenance was sour. She put her fists on her wide hips and let out an exasperated sigh, the kind of sigh that mothers make when they are resisting the urge to strangle their offspring.

"There you are," she said, shaking her head, her face glistening with sweat. "You could have answered my calls at least once."

I said nothing, but I obediently stood and followed her out of the mango grove, through the bean milpa, and across the dunes to our hut on the edge of the village. She herded me up the ladder to our home. As I climbed, I looked through the rungs and saw my father sitting under the house in the shade, mending a net. His eyes followed me as I ascended, his countenance drooping with the same disappointed frown that had not left his face since Mother told him my secret.

As we entered the room, the afternoon sunlight filtered through the gaps in the thatched walls, and the floor creaked under my mother's hurried steps. Flinging the lids off baskets, she began to busily search through our clothes, sending fabrics flying around the small room like bright, leaping monkeys.

"What are you doing?" I asked.

"Sulking will not take away your troubles, Sandpiper. Only action will. And today we must act."

"What do you mean?" I asked.

She continued to rummage through the basket. "I am fixing the disaster you made of your future."

I pressed my lips together tightly and folded my arms. My future was not a disaster. It was simply . . . uncertain.

"Canoes arrived today from the mainland," she said, holding up a tan-colored tunic and then tossing it aside.

My heart began to pound. "I told you he would return for me!" I gasped. "Did you see him?"

My mother looked at me, unsmiling. "Not those canoes," she said. "Canoes from a mainland village, with a young man looking for a bride."

My smile died, for I could see where this was going. "No," I said. "I will not be married to a different man. I will wait for him."

"Did he promise you he would come back?" she asked, surveying the mess she had made on the floor.

I opened my mouth and then closed it again.

My mother knelt down and began stuffing the clothing back into the basket. She grabbed a crumpled sarong the color of cooked shrimp. She held it up. "This should do," she muttered. "No time to get out the wrinkles, though." She laid it across her arm as she finished picking up the rest of the clothes. "He was a drifter, Sandpiper; not the kind of man who would take an oath to be your husband. He will never come back. You will never see him again, and if you do, he will not remember who you are."

"Yes, he will. He loves me."

She laughed and shook her head as she struggled to her feet. "You know nothing about love and nothing about men." She held the sarong up to my chest.

"At least I know what it is like to feel passionate about someone," I said, loud enough for my father below us to hear, "unlike you."

I instantly regretted the words. I do not know why I said it, except that I knew it would hurt. My mother lowered her voice. "Careful, child," she warned coldly.

I lifted my chin. "I am not a child."

"Listen to my words," she said. "The son of a chief does not come every day to our island. You should thank the gods for our good fortune."

"The son of a chief?" I asked, trying to keep my voice indifferent.

"Yes, from the mainland," she repeated, "and he is looking for a bride."

"I do not want to be married. I am not ready to be—"

"Then you should have thought about that before," she said. "You do not have a choice anymore, Sandpiper." She clasped my shoulders. "Do you not see? You have no future here. We cannot wait—time is against you. This is the only way and your only chance. If this does not work, no one will ever want you. You will be alone for the rest of your life. You have already disgraced your father and me. At least this way you will not disgrace yourself."

I could not believe this was happening. "If I marry this man, he will eventually find out I deceived him—"

"Only if you tell him. Men do not keep track of these kinds of things."

"But, Mama, he will take me away—"

"Yes. And just in time."

"Did you even see him? What if he is old or ugly or he beats me or—" My question was interrupted by a sharp slap. Shocked, I bit my lip and covered my stinging cheek with my hand. Never had she hit me before. Never.

"And how well did you know that other man?" she hissed, her breath hot in my face. "Did you know anything of his family? His means? Did you even know what kind of food he liked to eat? You knew nothing about him. Stop being stupid, Sandpiper."

I ground my teeth against each other, regretting that I had ever told her anything about him. At first I thought that she would be happy for me, but I was wrong. It was as if overnight she changed into a person I did not recognize. Now she was always yelling, sulking, or crying. How could her heart be so shallow? How could my own mother not understand true love? It must be because she had never known it in the first place.

I narrowed my eyes and looked at the ground. Mother put her face close to mine and her sharp words came out in slow, measured slices, each one making its own wound across my heart. "For every decision there is a consequence. And for some decisions there are many consequences."

I glared at her and she glared back, but a tear trickled onto her cheek. Seeing that tear made me feel shame in my heart but I dared not let it show. She wiped her face and sniffed. "Now . . . put this on."

I flung off my old tunic angrily and shimmied into the new one. As soon as my frizzy head popped out of the top, Mother began raking at the knots in my hair with a fervor that made me yelp. Giving up, she relinquished the comb to me so I could work out the snarls while she rummaged through more baskets. She pulled out a mahogany box. Out of the box she took a necklace of polished shells and strung it around my neck, then looped more strings of shells over and over my wrists and ankles. A wide beaded belt was tied around my waist.

"Where did you get these?" I had never seen these treasures before.

"I wore them for my wedding," she said, her countenance softening. "I saved them for you." Licking her finger, she smoothed my furrowed eyebrows as if I were six years old, and finally, with a trembling hand, she tucked a flower into my hair. "Do try to look pleasant, Sandpiper."

I scowled.

She shook her head hopelessly. Then, removing the coral earrings from her own ears, she gave them to me. She caressed my cheek, the one she had slapped, and murmured softly, "I did see him."

"You did?" I tried to not sound too interested. "And?"

"He is not old," she said with a hesitant smile, "and I do not think he will beat you."

"How can you be sure?"

She paused. "I doubt he is strong enough."

I frowned. This brought little comfort.

"He will not choose me," I said. "There are other girls."

"Not many other girls. And he will choose you. I asked the gods to make it so, and the gods always grant the prayers of desperate mothers."

As we climbed down the ladder we heard the conch shells blow, announcing an assembly.

We joined the other curious islanders at the Gathering Place. My mother ushered me up to the front of the group, near the large stone fire pit, beside our chief. The other girls were there too, and from their startled appearance, I guessed they had had much the same experience as I did, only I was sure my cheeks were the reddest. The number of eligible girls in our small village totaled three, and we stood there in a miserable row, not knowing whether we should smile, cry, or run. Our mothers hovered behind us, arranging our hair and touching our skirts, tears seeping from their crinkled, hope-filled faces.

On the opposite side of the fire pit stood a small group of travel-weary strangers. They were dressed in long tunics, tied at the waist with colorful belts. A stooped man with a fur cape and a headdress of feathers stood at the front. I assumed he was the chief, though he was much older than our Chief Dovetail. But which man was the son and expectant groom? I examined each unfamiliar face as my stomach began to knot.

Chief Dovetail held up his hands and everyone hushed.

"My people!" He boomed. "Today the gods have smiled upon us. They have sent Lark, the young warrior and son of Chief Obsidian from the village of Temple Mound, to choose a wife!"

My people grunted in approval. The chief continued, "The most beautiful daughters from our village have been assembled for his choosing."

I glanced around at the other girls beside me. They looked as if they were preparing themselves for a funeral. I could only hope the chief's son found their dismal countenances more pleasant than mine.

A young man was nudged forward by the group of strangers, and to my dismay, he was by far the shortest and ugliest of them all. He was weak and lanky, with spindly legs and arms that hung down from his shoulders like two limp eels. Every few moments he would take one of the eels and wipe his nose.

He was so obviously nervous about making a choice it pained me. He could not look any of us in the eye, but his lowered gaze darted back and forth among the three of us, as if he were choosing us based on the size of our knees.

Chief Dovetail placed his massive hands on the shoulders of the young man and shuffled him closer to us. But the groom's eyes remained lowered. He wiped his nose again, this time looking to see what he had smeared on his hand.

"Here are the three finest maidens in our village," said the chief, gesturing toward us.

I grimaced inwardly at the word *maiden*.

"My son," the chief said grandly, "you may make your choice." A wave of heat swept through the inside of my body, and I felt sweat gather under my arms. *Please not me. Please not me.* My heart thumped in my ears and my mouth was dry as sand. I could run, I thought. I was fast, and I knew I could outrun them all. But we were on an island, and they would eventually find me. There was nothing to do but remain there, like a bird on a block, miserably awaiting the blade.

The young man's eyes darted up for a moment, scanning our countenances quickly, and then dropped back to the sand.

"Well, son? Take your choice by the hand, and you shall have your wife," urged the young man's father. I bit my lip.

Then, suddenly, three things happened at once.

The girl to my right fainted into her mother's arms.

The girl to my left turned and got sick all over the sand.

And before I could run, the chief's son stretched out his arm and grabbed my hand.

LARK

Going to White Island to marry a Fish girl was not my idea.

It was probably the idea of my brother, Stone. He is the first son of the Chief of Temple Mound. He is the strongest man in our village. His chest is broad and hairless. His chin is angled and square. His eyes are keen and intelligent, his hands are skilled and lethal, and his skill with a bow is matchless.

I am Lark, the second son of the Chief of Temple Mound. Sporadic hairs pop out in various places on my narrow chest. My chin is rounded and slightly recessed. I could not hit an animal unless it walked right into my arrow. I am prone to sudden nosebleeds and I am left-handed—both considered bad omens in our village, predicting a lifetime of misfortune. For after the gods made my brother, I was created out of all that was left over. At least that is what some people in the village say.

He is the jaguar, I am the mouse. He is the morning sun and I am the shadow behind a wall. He is a mighty thunderhead that brings rain and lightning and gives life to everything below, and I am a puff of smoke that makes your eyes water. And that is how it is.

I am used to it. Despite what people in my village might think, I do not mind being in the shadow of my brother. I have no responsibility, no expectations placed on my shoulders. I do not have to worry about becoming chief one day or having to make hard decisions. I hate hard decisions.

Of course my brother married Jade, the most beautiful woman in our village. After that, I became my parents' reluctant new project. My father, who never took me hunting before, now took me several times a week, and even held his temper when I lost his arrows or sneezed and scared away the deer.

At times, when I was daring enough, I would watch the different girls in the village and imagine each one as my wife. Someday I, too, would make the marriage oath with a young woman, and if I wanted to bring honor to my family, she would have to be a girl of substance, a girl who had skills or wealth. Or at least a girl with wide hips who could promise many grandchildren.

But several years went by, and no marriage was ever organized by my parents. The village mothers were starting to use me as an example to encourage their children to get married young so they did not "end up like Lark." Two and a half decades is well past the ideal age to start a family. I was losing hope.

Then one day, they announced that we should strengthen our alliances with the neighboring villages, specifically the Fish People of White Island. To do this they would propose a marriage, with me as the male offering. I knew that an alliance had nothing to do with it. The real reason was that none of the mothers in our village wanted their daughters to make an oath with me, even if I was the son of the chief. That is what happens when you have a god as an older brother. And being the benevolent god that he is, I knew this was all his idea.

Since our villages shared the same language and worshiped the same gods, marrying one of the Fish People was really my only other option.

The wedding gifts were gathered into baskets: peppers, feathers, and beads of every color. My father remembered that the island people are fond of corn, so we brought that too. To them it is a novelty; to us it is life. The women made bracelets and earrings; my sisters wove mats and brightly colored skirts for the islanders. My mother had special jade bracelets fashioned for my bride. My brother donated two handsome jaguar pelts to the cause.

It was unfortunate that my wedding had to come so soon after Crowfoot's . . . incident. But life was slowly getting back to normal, like it always did. It is something we say we are used to, but that is so morbid. No one should get used to death. It always stings. Especially this kind of death that carries with it so much regret.

I hoped that my wedding and the arrival of my bride would help all of us clear our minds and give the village something to celebrate.

Newt and Lizardtail accompanied my father and me to help carry the gifts and baskets and to be our oarsmen. We loaded the gifts on our backs and started the journey that would begin in the forest and end at the sea.

After several days of bushwhacking through the dense, dry forest we emerged on the thundering beaches. We rested a while in the white sand, watching the waves unravel themselves over and over. The ocean was so brilliantly blue it hurt my eyes to look at it and the air filled my nostrils with freshness. I could have sat there for days, simply watching the blue water swell, curl, and crash. I enjoyed the frothy remnants of the waves that hurried up the beach and bubbled harmlessly around my ankles before being summoned back to sea.

We found our canoes in their storage spot. There were four of them, but only two were in good enough condition to attempt the waves, and even those two had cracks from years of disuse. After smearing their cracks with pitch and testing them to make sure they would not take in water, we loaded our supplies. We pushed the canoes into the breaking waves and headed out to sea.

It would take many hours of hard paddling to reach our destination. I peered down into the clear blue water as we glided over the surface, and I wondered how much life swam beneath me. I had been taught to be suspicious of deep water, but this water seemed warm, wonderful and benign. A welcome change.

Finally the island appeared on the horizon, and my heartbeat quickened. She was there, somewhere on that island. My future wife.

Children playing on the beach spotted us first. They turned and started running back to the village, waving their hands and yelling. It is very rare that we visit neighboring villages, so this was an exceptional occasion and an opportunity to strengthen the bonds of friendship between tribes. As our boat neared the beach my father reminded me, "Remember, you are a man, not a boy, Lark."

Soon people of all ages appeared on the beach and splashed into the water, flashing their white teeth as they surrounded our canoes. They pulled us up to the sand, and, as a token of goodwill, we passed out the beads and macaw feathers before we exited the canoes. The children clamored for more gifts until my father held up his hands and told them, "More when we get to the village!" And they took off running.

A large, bald, bare-chested man with a ring through his nose approached.

"Ho, Chief Obsidian!" the man said to my father. "I hope to bring you honor!"

"Ho, Chief Dovetail!" my father answered back. "I, too, hope to bring you honor." Holding my father steady, I helped him step out of the canoe.

"It has been many years. What brings you to our island, bearing such exquisite gifts?" the Fish Chief asked.

"I have brought my son to make an offering of marriage with a maiden of your village." At this I lifted my chest and stood as tall as I could, my chin up.

The Fish Chief surveyed the men in our group and clasped our oarsman, Newt, in a tight, sweaty hug. "Welcome to our village," he said. "We will be honored for you to find a bride here on our island." Newt gave my father an embarrassed glance, and I closed my eyes and shook my head. My father laughed uncomfortably.

"This," my father said, with one arm around my knobby shoulders, shuffling me in front of the chief, "is my son." Artfully, the gallant island chief masked any disappointment and repeated his gracious greeting.

We walked down the beach, and I could make out the village in the distance. My father had told me that during the rainy season White Island is flooded, and for this reason all of their huts are built on high stilts. I had imagined what it might look like, but to actually see the houses suspended in the air with nothing but a framework of sticks for support was miraculous to me.

When we entered the village, my chin gradually dropped lower and lower as I gazed up at the long-legged homes that stood above me like massive storks. *How does one build something like this without it falling to the earth?* I wondered. My father caught my eye. *Be a man*, he mouthed, and tapped the bottom of his chin with the back of his hand. I realized I was gaping. I closed my mouth and looked straight ahead, as if houses on stilts are something I saw every day.

As we walked I glanced at passing faces, looking for any girls who seemed to be of marriageable age, but there were none to be seen. All I saw were old women and children. The Fish Chief read my mind.

"I think word has already spread through our village of your intentions, my young friend," he said to me. "Do not worry, son. For I am sure they are all preparing to greet you."

They are all preparing. How many is "all," I wondered. Twenty? Thirty? The chief led us through the village, and I found myself looking up again at the floors of the huts towering above me. Each hut had a ladder so they could climb up and down to their homes. The huts were at least twice as tall as a man, and I wondered what it would be like to have such a view from your door. "View" was not a word we often used in the jungle.

We stopped at the largest stilt-house, which I assumed was the chief's lodge, and I followed the chief and my father up the ladder. It was larger than I expected and surprisingly comfortable. There were tortoise shells on the walls and layers of woven mats spread out on the floor. We sat on the mats, and the chief gave us water to drink. We were grateful, for we were very thirsty, even though the water tasted bland and stale compared to the water from our village.

We waited while several other official-looking villagers climbed into the lodge and greeted us warmly. When the chief seemed satisfied that everyone was present, we displayed some of our best gifts for the proposal, saving Stone's jaguar skins for last. When my father rolled the skins out onto the floor of the lodge, a reverent hush fell over the room. I could tell from the look on the Fish Chief's face as he ran his fingers through the glossy fur that the arrangement was secure. Thanks to my brother and his pelts, I would have a wife. Once again I was in his debt.

"We shall assemble all of our loveliest daughters for your son's selection," said the chief. I could have any young woman in the village I desired. All I had to do was choose, and the oath would be made in the morning. Then I could take home my bride. I tried to appear calm about this, but inside I felt like a lizard about to lose its tail.

What would they look like? How could I decide? What would I base my choice on? What would she think of me? I tried count it as a blessing that at least she did not have a choice in the matter, but that only made me feel worse.

M y legs wobbled all the way down the ladder. We headed toward the Gathering Place. Already a crowd had assembled. Immediately I felt all of their eyes on me. Watching me. Looking at me. Whispering.

Be a man, I told myself. I tried to smile. *Look confident*. Hello there, Fish People of White Island. Yes, I am the chief's ugliest son. The ugliest man in our whole village, in fact. And now I am here to take away one of your daughters so I can make more ugly people. The only positive emotion I felt was a deep sincere gratitude that my brother was not there. At least no one here could compare me. Perhaps on my own I might seem somewhat desirable.

We approached the assembled villagers. I have a history of ill-timed nosebleeds that always seem to occur in moments of extreme excitement or desperation. I discreetly dabbed my nose while three nervous-looking girls lined up in front of their mothers. Three. I could deal with three.

I tried not to look at them. I was not concerned with their beauty or lack of beauty. I was more concerned with the reaction they might have as they imagined me as their future husband.

The chief was saying something to the people, calming them down, but his voice was only background noise to me, and a lump rose in my throat. I began to perspire, and sweat ran down my skin. I checked my nose again, just to be sure. My hands were moist and I wiped them on my tunic. I tried putting them behind my back, then folding them, then cracking a few knuckles before putting them behind my back again. My eyes stayed on the soft sand, but finally I let them dart over to the bare knees of the three girls, curiosity getting the better of my nervousness.

All of the knees looked the same. Just normal knees, like my knees. Only smaller. And tanner.

"My son," the Fish Chief announced. "You may make your choice."

Choice. Choice. I cannot make choices. I wished my father would just choose one for me. I looked up at the faces of the girls quickly, and looked back down at the white sand. I closed my eyes and prayed to the gods to give me a sign.

Then a miracle happened. When I opened my eyes there was only one girl standing there—the tall one with puffy hair—and before I knew what I was doing, I grabbed her hand and pulled her toward me. The villagers cheered in approval, and with their approbation I felt a tiny sliver of confidence.

I had never been applauded for anything before in my life.

The next morning we gathered on the beach for the wedding. They told me my new bride's name was Sandpiper and pointed out the little bird racing around the salt-white beach, turning over shells. I was named after a bird, too, so at least we had one thing in common. A good omen, I hoped.

She did not speak nor make eye contact with me during the ceremony, which could have been because I had stuffed cotton up one nostril and the excess was hanging out in a white wad. My nose began to bleed that morning and refused to quit so I had to keep it there during the entire ceremony. I will be the first to admit that this was not ideal.

The wedding was brief. In solemnity, before her whole tribe, we made our oaths to each other by drinking from the same cup. She was crying, but I tried to assuage my insecurities by reminding myself that sometimes brides cried because they were so happy. Then, with just a nod of the chief's head, we were married.

When it was all over our empty canoes were loaded with shells, salted fish, and pearls—gifts from the Fish People. We pushed out into the breaking waves again, this time homeward bound.

Sandpiper sat at the bow of the boat while my father and I paddled. Her hair was wild and untamed and looked like a flowing gob of petrified smoke. I liked it. She wore a pale pink sarong that lay over her right shoulder and swooped across her back under her left arm, leaving part of her back and one shoulder bare, a dress that I knew would raise my mother's eyebrows clear up to the clouds.

At first I kept my eyes on the horizon and the waves, afraid to acknowledge what was before me. But it was hopeless. Her face was turned so I could only see the arch of her cheekbones and the tips of her eyelashes. For a while I was hypnotized by her earrings, swaying back and forth. Then, feeling reckless, I dared to examine her neck and shoulder. Her skin was smooth, brown, and flawless. I could see the contours of her back and the exquisite way her body curved in at the waist and widened at the hips.

I looked down at my feet and smiled. This was the happiest day of my life.

SANDPIPER

The wedding took place in the morning, on the sun-washed beach. The whole village gathered around us. My soon-to-be husband gave me jade bracelets for my wrists, and I accepted them and wore them because it gave me something to look at besides the white object sticking out of his bulging nostril.

With everyone watching, Chief Dovetail recited the oath that we would live together, serve each other, stay true to one another for the rest of our lives.

The rest of our lives.

To seal the oath we were to drink from the same cup. My chief held the marriage cup out to him. He took it and drank. Then he handed the cup up to me, making me feel like his big sister. How I despaired that it was not Red I was sharing this cup with! Tears leaked from my eyes and dripped in the cup, but I drank it, tears and all. The chief took the cup from me, placed my hands in the slender, sweating hands of my dismal future, and it was complete. I was now married, and I had not even said a word.

Then they released the dove.

It was a tradition my people did at every wedding, this dove-releasing, and all the people watched it flap up into the sky. The bird was symbolic of something and the chief was explaining what, but the only thing I could think of at that moment was how big my wrists were compared to the wrists of my new husband.

The canoes were loaded with all kinds of treasures and gifts. My mother handed me her little wooden box. "You keep this," she said. I accepted it without saying a word, for my feelings toward her were as tangled as a mass of seaweed. When she hugged me I kept my arms at my sides, but I leaned into her neck, closed my eyes, and breathed her in. I could feel her heart beating against mine as I tried to hold in the tears. Please do not make me leave, I wanted to tell her. Please let me stay with you. Her arms released me too soon.

My father regarded me pitifully and patted my cheek. "You have always been a brave girl, Sandpiper. We hope you will be happy." Then he added, "Just remember, the first year of marriage is always the worst."

I did not speak during the canoe voyage across the turquoise sea, but clutched the wooden box on my lap and watched the flying fish and glossy dolphins chase after the canoes as if they wanted to rescue me. At least I still had the feather, safe in my box where it would not get bent or lost.

When we reached the beach on the mainland, the men emptied the canoes and we camped.

I did not speak at all the next day when we entered the dry forest. The air was hot with no breeze, and the heat sat heavily on my shoulders like a giant vulture. Invisible carnivorous bugs bit my skin, making red, itchy welts. My feet, used to soft white sand, soon blistered and bled as I walked on the hard rocky earth.

It was difficult to stay clean, and there was no ocean to wash off in. There was little shade, for most of the trees were dry and leafless, and the leaves that did exist were scrawny and thin. The sounds were different too. Gone was the comforting repetition of the waves. Instead the air was stagnant and dry and empty except for the shrill crying of birds and the chopping, cutting sounds the men made with their machetes as they cut the way through the dense brush. All the while I followed my new chief and my new husband followed me.

"Temple Mound is a good village," he said behind me.

I did not say anything.

"I think you will be happy there."

We walked in silence.

He tried again. "There are many women in the village. They are kind."

I sniffed.

"We already have a place to live, a small hut at the base of the mound, near the milpa."

I said nothing.

"We will have lots of children," he said.

I began to sob.

We walked for days, pausing often to let the old chief rest. Always the landscape was the same: flat, covered with thick dry brush and skinny-trunked trees, heavily laden with suffocating brown vines. Without any leaves on the trees, the miserable sun beat down on us without mercy. On the rare occasion that we did pass by a tree with leaves, the cool green was like medicine for my eyes.

Twice we passed large deep holes, filled with still blue water and surrounded by leafy green plants and trees with thick trunks, but the men did not give them a second glance and pushed forward as if they were only mirages.

At night the men strung up hammocks from trees. My new husband tied my hammock a respectful distance from him and the rest of the men, and I realized that perhaps I was not the only one who felt awkward with this new union. A normal marriage would have been consummated by now, but he had yet to touch me. Perhaps it was because we were traveling and sleeping in hammocks. Perhaps he was nervous. But it would have to be consummated, and even though the thought was revolting to me, the sooner it happened, the better.

It was on the fourth day, while I was in the bushes attending to a personal errand and trying to avoid mounds of biting ants and several vicious-looking spiked leaves, that I heard one of the men make a joke about me. He told my husband, "You are lucky to have a wife who does not speak. You can do whatever you want and she will never nag you. It is a gift from the gods!"

I could not hear my husband's reply, but those words repeated in my mind.

The idea intrigued me. What if I really could not speak? No one in this new place knew me or my kin; they would not know any better.

I would most likely never see my tribe again. This way I would not be tempted to reveal anything about the seed inside of me until my time came. I could blend in—be an observer and not have to think as much or act. No one needed to know the truth, and I would not have to lie. My silence would protect me and my secret, like a shell protecting an oyster and its pearl.

I told myself that it would just be for a while . . . just until I could get used to this new life.

We arrived in the village the next morning. It was built on a large stony hill. We climbed all the way to the top on a neatly kept trail that passed dozens of huts, and many people smiled and waved to our group. They stared at me, but that was to be expected. I knew I was a walking curiosity.

The top of the hill was long and flat. We passed a great fire pit and a large, shady pavilion thatched with palms. After passing this pavilion, we arrived at the chief's lodge. There I met Lark's mother and grandmother. They wore loose, brightly colored dresses, tied at the waist with embroidered sashes. The dresses covered their arms down to their elbows, and their legs down their knees. Delicate lace slips extended below their skirts and hung to their ankles. It did not take me long to realize my clingy pink sarong left me startlingly underdressed.

I first met Lark's mother. Threads of silver wove through her black hair, and her brown eyes looked tired but kind. She did not seem to care about the way I was dressed, even though I was becoming increasingly self-conscious of my appearance. By now my island dress was soiled and stained, and I was sure I looked like something that had just crawled out from under a log. If my new mother could appreciate me even in this condition, then maybe there might be some hope for my future happiness after all. "I am Cedar," she said, kissing my cheek and embracing me like a daughter. "I hope to bring you peace." It was a greeting common to both our tribes, and I was supposed to answer back. Instead I respectfully bowed my head.

I met the matriarch, Grandmother Vine—old, bent, and blind, with gray, opaque eyes that gazed just over my right shoulder. When

I took her outstretched hand, she smiled, and the wrinkles on her face multiplied like beams of the sun. She reached up high to pat my cheeks, and assure me that I had married into a wonderful family, " . . . and Lark has always been my favorite," she whispered loud enough for everyone to hear.

I was then introduced to Lark's sister. "This is Honeybee, the runt," said Lark, giving her a gentle punch in the arm. Honeybee smiled shyly, her eyes luminous and bright, her brown cheeks dotted with black freckles. Two braids laced with colorful ribbons hung down on each side of her face. She looked only a few years younger than me. I held out my hand to her. She clasped it and pulled me into a hug.

Cedar served us breakfast of warm tortillas and beans generously sprinkled with a red spice, the smell of which was so powerful it singed the hairs in my nostrils. Lark and his father devoured the food by the plateful. I did not want to offend my mother-in-law on my first day so I ate it, but the effort took all of my concentration. Perhaps it was coming to this new place, or perhaps it was the seed inside me that made food so undesirable. Whatever the cause, the feeling of sickness was constant. I wondered if I would ever be able to eat anything again.

Just as we were finishing the food, I saw a couple coming toward the hut.

"Stone! Jade!" called Cedar. "Come meet your new sister-in-law."

As I watched the man called Stone come closer, I felt my legs turn to dust. Could this truly be my husband's brother? There was absolutely no resemblance. In every place that my husband was skin and bones, this man was muscle. In every way that my husband was unattractive, this man was desirable. On one sturdy shoulder hung a bow, and across his great chest was the strap for his quiver. Two machetes swung from a leather belt around his waist, animal claws hung around his neck, and when he stopped his arms folded across his chest like two great pythons.

It was not only his physical strength that captivated me. His countenance was regal. His eyes were lit with intelligence. To me he seemed like the epitome of manhood; the kind of man whose arms were strong enough to protect a village yet gentle enough to cradle a baby. I bit my lip and stifled the tears that threatened to spring from my eyes. This was the kind of man I imagined I would marry. A warrior. A hero. Or at least someone that was taller than I was. I exhaled a long, miserable sigh. It was true, he was not Red, but if this man named Stone had shown up on my island, I would not have been so reluctant to become a bride.

To make things worse, next to him was his perfect match. Jade was the most beautiful person I had ever seen. There were no angles on her, for she was soft and round; curving in all the ways a woman's body should curve. Her skin was smooth, her eyes were large, and her teeth were as white as the caps of breaking waves. Her hair was the kind of hair I dreamt about, supple as water, and in the sunlight it flashed like polished obsidian. I looked back and forth between the man and his wife, and I could not help think that surely this couple must be the happiest people alive.

I wanted a love like this: a love that was legendary, a love that people sang songs about, wrote stories about . . . at the very least a marriage that could be envied.

"There she is! Lark's long-awaited bride!" gushed the beautiful woman as she brushed my cheek with hers. "Let me look at you," she said. She stood back and gazed at everything from my dirty toes to my frizzy crown. "We all knew there had to be someone out there for Lark. How was your journey? When did you arrive?"

I smiled, resisting the urge to speak.

Jade's smile faltered slightly when I did not answer her question. She tried again. "So, when did you arrive?"

I smiled a little harder.

Jade tried once more. This time she spoke louder and enunciated each word like she was speaking to a very small child. "You—have— happy—journey?" She pointed at me and made two of her fingers walk across the air front of her face.

Lark put his arm around my shoulder. "She knows our language, Jade. She just . . . does not speak," he said.

I tapped my throat tragically.

"Oh," she said with a smile and a wink. "I guess that makes you a good secret keeper."

"It will make her a good wife," Stone teased. Jade elbowed him in the side.

"Pay no attention to him, Stork," Jade whispered to me.

"Sandpiper," Lark corrected, "not Stork."

"Well, whatever your name is, we are exceedingly glad you are here," Jade said. "Now, boys, go do your manly things and leave us alone to dress the bride. As you can see, we have a lot of work to do."

Lark seemed reluctant to turn me over to them. "I will see you later this evening," he said, touching my arm.

"Be off with you, Lark, and do not worry," Jade said, putting her arm around me. "We will take good care of your wife. The next time you see your little caterpillar, she will be a glorious butterfly. Come, Sandpiper," she said. "We must get you out of these clothes and into something that does not smell so . . . fishy."

They took me behind the lodge where I could wash my body and hair with water from some gourds. When I finished Jade handed me a large clean cloth to dry myself, and then she and Honeybee began to rub scented oils into my skin. "We do not do this for everyone," the younger one said, smiling. "Just the new brides."

They gave me a long, soft cotton slip of pure white, bordered on the bottom with a wide panel of lace. I pulled it over my head and let it fall down over my body. I looked up to see all three women frowning.

The slip barely passed my knees.

"We did not expect you to be so . . . leggy," Jade commented.

"Do not worry," Cedar said, her frown curving into a gentle smile. "I will have to make you another one. Soon. Here, put this blouse on over it."

The embroidered "blouse" was a billowy rectangle with a hole for my head and holes in the sides for my arms. It fit me like a small tent.

For the skirt, the women took out a very, very long, wide piece of white fabric and wrapped it around my waist three times. "Hold this here," Cedar said pressing the end against my hip.

They all stepped back to view me and Honeybee muffled a giggle. I shifted awkwardly from one foot to another, embarrassed by the disappointed expressions on their faces. Apparently the skirt was too short as well.

"It will have to do for now. Where is the sash?" Cedar asked.

Honeybee unfolded a blue sash and put it in Cedar's hand.

Cedar held it close so that I could see the exquisite birds and flowers embroidered with yellow thread.

"Do you like it?" she asked.

I nodded.

Cedar smiled and gave it to Jade to wrap around my waist. "I dyed it blue," Cedar said significantly. "I thought you might miss the color of the sea."

The thoughtful detail brought unexpected tears to my eyes, for she was right. There were some things I would not miss about my island, but I knew I would miss the sea.

Jade pulled the belt tight, cinching all the fabrics in place, and making me feel like I was locked in a permanent embrace. Now I had on the slip, the blouse, the skirt and the belt. For Fish People, that was three days' worth of clothes.

"We have to do something with her hair," I heard Jade say to Cedar when they turned their backs. "She looks like a palm tree that was just struck by lightning."

So Cedar took a comb and raised it to my head. When she paused, not knowing exactly where to begin, I held up my hand and shook my head, conveying to her that yes, indeed, my hair is unbrushable. She was content and left my hair alone. But Jade was not. She left and appeared a few moments later with a fistful of white flowers, each blossom as big as my thumb, and she gently nestled their stems into my hair. Cedar and Jade stood back and made me spin a little circle. When I turned to face them again, they finally seemed satisfied.

"You look lovely," Cedar said.

"Just like a bride," Honeybee sighed.

"Lark will be thrilled," Jade said.

I was sent to sit in a special place under the shady pavilion next to Grandmother Vine for what Cedar called the "bride's circle." I was told that soon there would be other women arriving with wedding gifts. But they were a long time coming, and I sat there, sweating in my layers of cotton. Had Grandmother Vine been able to see, and had I been willing to speak, we might have had a conversation. Instead we listened to the whirring of the insects and the calls of birds in the trees above us while I smoothed my new dress over my knees and traced the intricate lacework of the white slip.

Eventually the women did arrive, bringing bundles and baskets under their arms, and sometimes babies on their backs. They looked at me with eager curiosity, and I was glad now that I was not wearing my island dress. As it was, I already felt like a flamingo among doves.

One by one the women gathered under the pavilion. They made themselves comfortable, some on benches, some on the floor, some starting to nurse impatient babies, many of them fanning themselves with woven fans, for it was late in the morning and already scorching hot. The women kept coming until there was no room left under the pavilion and some had to sit in the hot sun, squinting.

The women wore brightly colored variations of the same blouse and skirt I had on, some with embroidered designs, some tied at the waist with bright sashes and belts. All of them wore the white lace slip showing beneath. I could not help noticing how covered the women were, even now in the rising heat of the day. Even the women who were nursing their babies found ways to be discreet and modest.

Each woman laid gifts at my feet. I guessed that Cedar had somehow spread the word of my muteness. Although they all greeted and congratulated me, no one asked me any questions that I could not answer with a smile or a nod.

Before long I was surrounded by a growing pile of gifts: baskets of potatoes and squash and onions, woven rugs and sashes, wooden bowls, cakes of soap, pouches of seeds, ornamented pots, smoothly carved spoons, even a metate stone for grinding—all practical and purposeful, but also beautifully crafted, created by women who understand that that even the monotony of everyday work deserves beauty. Their generosity filled me with guilt.

As the women talked together, delicate beads of sweat dappled their foreheads like dew. I was sure they were all lifelong friends. Would there be any way I could find a place here? Who would be my friend?

Jade was passing around a gourd filled with water for the women to drink. I hoped that we could become friends. And if we did, would she ever guess my secret? Could I trust her? No, I thought. No one must ever know. And the best way for me to keep my secret was to not let anyone suspect I had a secret to keep.

"Good morning, everyone. I hope to bring you peace, " said Cedar graciously.

The women returned the greeting.

"I want to welcome everyone who came to celebrate with Sandpiper today," she continued. "Your gifts are thoughtful, and I am sure they will help Sandpiper immensely as she begins her new life in our village." Cedar looked at me with dewy eyes, and I knew that was my moment to smile gratefully.

I smiled gratefully.

"And now, Sandpiper," said Cedar brightly, "at a bride's circle it is the custom in our village for the married women to offer advice." The women perked up. Clearly this was something they all looked forward to. "Who would like to go first?"

The women were politely hesitant, as if waiting for someone else to begin, even though I could sense that their eager tongues crouched just beyond their curved lips, like anxious animals waiting to be released from their cages.

"Very well, I shall begin," said Cedar. She turned to me. "Always be honest with each other."

I swallowed. Already I was a bad wife.

A few thoughts went by while we waited for someone else to release the next animal.

"Always keep your hut organized and clean," suggested a voice in the back, and they all nodded, thoughtfully.

Then an old woman with gray hair spoke up, "Make sure you remind him of his duties and his responsibilities. Men are naturally inclined to be carnally minded. It is up to you to refine him."

Another quickly agreed. "Yes. If you do not like something about your husband, find a way to change him. Just be careful to not let him know you are trying to change him."

There were some nods and laughter, and after that comment all the cages were opened and the animals came pouncing on me at once. I wanted to shield myself.

"Keep your opinions to yourself."

"Never nag."

"Do not complain about the way he eats."

"Do not complain about the way he smells."

"Keep yourself clean and modest."

"The only way to make sure he comes home is to cook good food."

"It is up to you to remember where everything is, since men always lose things." Several women cackled like seagulls and looked at each other knowingly.

"That is right. When it comes to anything domestic, men are helpless."

Even Jade added her words. "Always know where he is," she said, "and whatever you do, do not let him fetch his own water." And to this strange comment all the women solemnly agreed.

Finally everyone had said something. Or so I thought.

"Is there anyone else?" Cedar asked while they all panted, their tongues lying on the floor of their mouths, exhausted.

Grandmother Vine cleared her gravelly throat. "I would like to add something." She was sitting on my right side and she turned her face toward mine, gazing at me with her strange milky eyes that made me feel queasy. "I will give you the most important advice you will ever receive," she paused, "and that is to toss the tassels. Often."

Two teenage girls in the back giggled.

I was confused. Jade leaned over and whispered in my ear, "She means sex."

But the old woman was not finished: "And always remember," she continued, "that when it comes to making love, the most important part of the body is the—"

"Would anyone like more corncakes?" Cedar suddenly said, moving right in front of Grandmother Vine. "I made them this morning, and they will taste better today than tomorrow." She began enthusiastically handing out corncakes to the women.

Meanwhile, the old woman reached over to me, feeling for my arm and then patting my hand. In a low voice she whispered, "Do not worry, honey. I will tell you later."

I blushed, slightly horrified. That was the last thing I wanted to know.

By now the women were chatting and talking among themselves. No one spoke to me after that, and that is how I wanted it. I was grateful for their generous gifts, but the advice was overwhelming.

Right now everything was overwhelming.

SANDPIPER

At sunset the fires were kindled. Torches were lit. Tables were set up under the pavilion and filled with food of all varieties and colors. Jars of honey stood next to piles of corncakes, and baskets overflowed with a rainbow of green, yellow, orange, and red fruits. Tidy banana-leaf packages were stacked in little pyramids and, when opened, revealed steamed cornmeal filled with spicy meat. Over the fires there were spits of roasting fowls with juices that dripped and sizzled on the hot coals. The salted fish and dried seaweed from my village were spread out on platters and garnished with herbs and berries that I had never seen before. I looked at all the food in its abundance and marveled that not one thing looked appetizing to me.

Villagers appeared out of the darkness, entering the pavilion and bringing with them even more food to spread on the tables. Then they broke off into small, intimate circles, laughing and slapping mosquitoes as they ate their food and the torches cast a warm glow over their faces. Children ran through the crowds, playing games and squeezing in and out of the legs of the adults, enjoying the opportunity to stay up past sundown.

I followed Lark around the groups of people to his father's fire, where Obsidian sat in a large chair, looking much more chief-like than he did on our journey. He was dressed regally, wearing gold armbands, a headdress of bright green feathers and a necklace of bones. Over his shoulders draped a luxurious jaguar cape. Next to him sat Cedar, also dressed in fine clothing, her hair braided on the side, and next to her was Grandmother Vine, shriveled, smiling, and humming to herself.

Lark guided me to a seat facing the fire where I could watch three pheasants slowly sweating on a spit. The smell of the roasting meat was nauseating. My greatest desire was find a bush where I could throw up. My mother warned me about this. Why did it seem that mothers were always right?

Lark sat next to me, of course, constantly offering me a wide variety of stomach-churning foods. Eventually he gave up and ate the foods himself, smacking his mouth and licking his lips and making every other unsavory eating noise that could or could not be imagined while he ate.

Then Stone and Jade arrived, followed by two wide-chested men that I presumed to be friends of Stone. I was introduced to Turtleback and Moss. The group sat down opposite us, bantering with each other. I could not help staring at the tightness of the skin over Stone's upper arms . . . it looked as smooth as the skin of a ripe mango.

Feeling guilty, I pried my eyes away from Stone and tried to focus instead on my own husband, who was slurping up some mysterious sauce from a bowl. When he was finished, some of the sauce clung to one cheek. He saw me watching and held the bowl to me. "Want some?" he asked.

"What a feast," declared the chief. "The meat is perfectly prepared, my love."

"The thanks goes to Stone," Cedar said. "I believe he killed most of what we are eating tonight."

Jade leaned her head on her husband's massive, ripe-mango shoulder. "My husband, the humble hunter," she cooed. The "humble hunter" showed his white teeth in a half-smile and then used them to rip the meat off a huge turkey leg. Jade watched him with an expression of exquisite awe, as if she were observing a comet blazing through a starry sky. "Sometimes I think it would be better if he did not hunt so much, though. He brings home so many pelts and furs that I just have no idea what to do with them all."

Stone cast a worshipful glance at Jade who returned a secret smile and they whispered together for a few moments, looking into each other's eyes, and admiring each other's lips. I watched them like a starving child.

"I was with Stone when he shot those three pheasants," the man called Turtleback said.

"Pheasants? That is nothing," said Moss. "You should have been with us when Stone slew that great buck that we butchered this morning. Here, taste it." He passed the dripping meat to his companion, who stuffed it in his mouth. Then they retold in detail how Stone jabbed and stabbed and slashed and skinned and spilled the blood of our dinner until I thought I would pass out. All the while Stone listened with a handsome smile on his face, clearly soaking up every word.

Jade laughed. "To hear you two talk, one would think that there would be no animals left in the forest."

"He leaves some," said Turtleback, grinning. "But just the slow, sick ones. So Lark can catch something."

Lark smiled good-naturedly at the joke and everyone laughed. Everyone, I noticed, but Stone.

"It is a good thing Lark does not rely on hunting as his trade," Jade said to me in a serious tone, "or you would have no food or clothing."

"Yes," agreed Moss, wiping turkey grease from his grin, "hunting is not really Lark's greatest strength."

Stone, who was about to bite into something, put his food down. There was not a hint of amusement on his face.

Obsidian cleared his throat. "Let us not get carried away. I think we are all aware that it is not the hunting that keeps this village alive," said Obsidian, raising a golden tortilla. "It is corn."

Everyone offered a hearty agreement and more tortillas were passed around to the delight of everyone.

"No, it is not," said a low voice. It was Stone who spoke.

"What was that, son?" said the chief, mopping up food from his plate with his tortilla.

"It is not the corn that keeps this village alive. And, as much as I would like to admit it, it is not the hunting, either," he said, eyeing at his companions, who seemed to suddenly shrink from his gaze. Everyone became quiet, waiting for Stone to continue.

"What keeps this village alive is water," he said. "And if we think about it in that sense, no one has done more for this village than Lark."

Stone gazed meaningfully at his brother. No one spoke. Moss moved the food around on his plate uncomfortably, and Turtleback picked at something in his teeth. Even the chief solemnly nodded his head. Meanwhile Lark looked at the ground and dug a small hole in the dirt with his sandal. Stone's statement went unchallenged, but his words brought a strange uneasiness around the fire. After a while Cedar stood and used her apron to turn the spit with the roasting pheasants. "The village needs all our talents," she murmured as the fire snapped and crackled. "We all must seek out what needs to be done and do it."

There were some grunts and mumbles of agreement.

"Shall we speak of something else, then?" Cedar said, taking up her plate again and sitting down with a fresh smile. "Is it not a wonderful evening to celebrate Lark and Sandpiper?"

"That reminds me," said Jade, leaning forward and addressing me, "What is a sandpiper, anyway?"

"It is a seabird," Lark answered, checking my face for confirmation. "It lives on the beach."

I nodded, pleasantly surprised that he knew.

"It is such a pretty name," sighed Honeybee. "I am sure it is a pretty bird too."

I smiled. *No, not really*, I wanted to say.

The chief turned to me. "I am looking forward to learning what you are capable of, Sandpiper," he said loftily. "What skills did you learn on your island? What will you be able to offer our village?"

The question sounded so official and he looked at me with such an unwavering stare that my heart skipped a beat. I was hoping to be invisible and not have to enter the conversation. But this was a direct inquiry, by the chief, one to which a nod or shake of the head would not suffice. Everyone was watching me. I looked around for ideas. How could I explain to them that I made fishing nets?

I put my hands together and had them "swim" forward, like a fish.

"You are a fisher," said Stone brightly, as if delighted that his new sister-in-law also enjoyed killing things.

I shook my head.

I made the sign of the fish again and then, taking both of my hands, I pretended like I was throwing a net.

"She is not fishing," said Jade. "That is a clearly a snake and she is throwing things at it. She is the village snake killer."

I smiled a little and shook my head.

"I am sure Sandpiper will reveal to us in time what she is capable of," said Cedar.

"No, no—this is fun," Jade said. "Just give us some more signals, Sandpiper. And we will decipher them."

With my fingers I pantomimed braiding a rope and then crossing it with other ropes, making a net. I put the "net" to the side. I made the sign for the fish again, picked up the net, and "threw" my net over the fish.

When I was finished everyone was staring at me, slowly chewing their food, their eyes narrowed in concentration. I realized it is hard to explain the concept of fishing with nets when you are speaking to a group of people who have little experience with the ocean. What else could I do? I looked around. Next to me was a gourd with a rope tied around its neck. I held it up so all could see and pointed to the rope.

"Ah . . . you are a rope maker," said Obsidian, nodding.

I hesitated, and then nodded. Good enough. I shall be a rope maker.

My new family cheered, relieved to move on to easier conversations. The men began talking of different types of plants that made the best rope; the women talked about weaving. I relaxed, grateful to not be the center of attention anymore.

This was not as terrible or as hopeless as I had imagined. Even though I had taken the marriage oath with a strange, ugly man, at least his family was kind and pleasant. My eyes studied their illuminated countenances as they talked and laughed, and it was hard to imagine that someday I would know these strangers better than the people on my own island. I wondered if these people were deep-hearted people, people of passion who lived vivid, exciting lives . . . or shallow-hearted people who were content with living a bland, ordinary existence. People like my mother.

While I listened to them, I felt a slight breeze on my skin. I closed my eyes, for this was the first time I had felt anything even remotely like wind since I arrived in the jungle. I relished the warm air as it ruffled the lace slip and wove through my hair. I breathed it in and tried to imagine my island. When I did, I saw Red's face. I held on to that image for a while, drinking in his coal-black eyes and his smile that made my knees tremble. In my mind I reached up to touch his lips when I heard one of the men ask a question. Silence followed.

I opened my eyes, wondering if the reason for the silence was because the question had been directed at me. But when I looked around no one was watching me.

The women were still talking to each other, but all the men had stopped, and the question that someone asked a moment before hung in the air, unanswered and forgotten. Instead, they were oddly still, blinking slowly, all gazing the same direction into the forest. They seemed to be listening for something. None of them spoke or chewed their food. Some were even holding their food midair. From the neck down they looked like they were enjoying a feast in the company of family and friends. From the neck up they looked like they were hunting.

LARK

We sat around the fire and talked late into the night and it was not until I felt the gentle pressure of Sandpiper's head on my shoulder that I realized it was probably time to take my bride home.

It had been a glorious day. My family spoiled Sandpiper with attention, the village buried us in gifts, and I ate so much meat that I felt at least six months pregnant. All evening I tried offering Sandpiper different foods but I was not successful until I gave her a piece of avocado. She touched it, sniffed it, and then devoured it as if she had not been sitting next to me all evening but instead tied to a nearby tree. I am sure she was just nervous about our first night together. I was nervous too, but luckily my nerves never affect my appetite. She enjoyed the avocado so much that she kept me busy peeling two more.

The one awkward moment came when Stone had to defend my contributions to the village in front of everyone. I do not feel I have anything to be proud of, and although I knew he was just trying to be kind, it caused me nothing but embarrassment. I do not mind being the butt of hunting jokes, and I would rather he just let the laughter run its course.

I led Sandpiper down the trail to my new and improved hut. I had been there earlier that day to set out Sandpiper's baskets and to roll out the freshly woven mats made by my mother. Honeybee and Jade must have preceded us, because one wall was lined with gourds full of water and there was a neat row of clay pots bearing Jade's special designs and filled to the top with dried corn and beans. My heart swelled with gratitude for my family and for this new season of my life.

But now Sandpiper and I were at our hut alone, together—in the dark. The awkwardness was palpable. What to do next? I had a fairly good idea of what most men and women did at this point, but that somehow seemed a little too . . . involved for us at the moment, not to mention slightly humiliating on my part since both times I had touched her hand that day she gave an involuntary shudder. I knew that as her husband I could "take" her and make her "mine" as some men in the village say. But, as the odds were not in my favor at winning a girl by brute force or seduction, I decided that the first thing I should do was get her to at least like me.

"Sandpiper," I said as I led her into the hut. "Is there anything else I can do for you tonight to make you feel more comfortable?"

I could barely see her shake her head in the darkness. This no-talking business is going to be tricky at night.

"Here," I said gesturing to the mats on the floor, "is our bed." I paused. "Or, if you feel more comfortable, I could hang up some hammocks. That way you could sleep in one, and I could sleep in the other, and then maybe later on, when you are used to . . . "

But before I even finished, she had taken off her bracelets and anklets, unwrapped her belt and taken off the blouse and skirt, leaving on her long white slip. Then she lay down on the mat. I stood there in the dark for several thoughts, trying to decide my next course of action. Seeing that she did not seem to care where I slept, I took my chances and slid my mat next to hers. I lay down, facing her back, but still a safe distance away.

It was very dark, but I could hear her breathing, soft and low. I closed my eyes but had to open them again to make sure this was real—that I was sleeping next to a real, breathing woman. The night was still and dark, but inside me sparks were flying. I wondered if she could hear the thundering of my heart, for I could hear nothing else.

"Sandpiper?" I whispered.

No answer.

"Sandpiper," I said again, my sincerity swelling in my heart. "Sandpiper, I hope to bring you honor."

SANDPIPER

I was awakened by the chattering of hundreds of birds.

Through the window of our hut, I could see the blackness turning to violet-blue. I rolled over to see my husband sleeping next to me. His mouth was open and drool slid off his lip into a puddle on his mat. I sat up and propped myself up against the wall of the hut. I listened to the frantic screaming and calling of the birds and watched the hut slowly brighten. Dappled light appeared along the walls, making the leaf-shadows dance.

I know what should have happened the night before, but I was so tired and so . . . unenthusiastic. Perhaps we could get it over with this morning. I pulled my knees to my chest, set my chin on my hands, and sighed. This was not how love should be.

In time, Lark stirred and leaned up. His hair was slicked skyward on one side and matted down on the other, making him look like a strange parrot. He wiped his mouth and smiled at me.

"Good morning, Piper," he said with a lazy smile and breath that could have kindled a fire.

He looked so silly I almost forgot and said good morning back, but as soon as my mouth opened I remembered that I was mute and so I bit my lip and gave a little wave with my fingers. He rubbed his eyes. He yawned loudly, stood, stretched, and drank water from one of the gourds. Then he gargled ferociously and spat the water out the open doorway. He crossed his hairy legs and sat down facing me.

"Piper," he began in a very serious tone, "I know there is nothing you want to do more than make love to me this morning, but you will have to wait until I am good and ready."

A complete feeling of relief washed over me I could not stop the genuine smile that spread across my face.

"So instead, I am going to take you on a little journey through our humble village."

Yes. That was a much better idea.

Lark waited outside the hut while I put my blouse and skirt back on and tied it with the blue belt. I splashed water on my face, reached up to touch my hair and paused. Everyone here has sleek black hair that lays straight down their back, and my frizzy head was not helping me blend in with my surroundings. With the help of a long scarf I managed to confine it the best I could until no hair showed. I patted my new look, tucking in any runaway tufts and felt better about myself. I met Lark outside. Together we walked up the path.

"You may think we are walking up a hill, but we are not," he began. A rope hung over his shoulder, and attached to both ends of the rope were large gourds that made hollow, empty sounds as they bumped together. "We are actually walking up an ancient temple. A long time ago, so the story goes, this was the center of a great city built by the Ancient Ones. The city was enormous and spread throughout all of the land surrounding the temple mound. It must have been an amazing time to live. But then something happened. For some reason all the people vanished, and the jungle grew over everything. This was unfortunate for them but good for us, since they left plenty of nicely cut stones for us to use on our own huts and lodges. If you know what to look for, you can still see the remains of the old ruins everywhere. Like here, for instance."

He stopped along the path and pushed away some of the dry foliage. Behind the curtain of climbing vines and thick brush was a stone wall covered in green lichen.

"Our hut is at the base of the temple. Most of the others are built on the platforms that lead up to the top of the temple, which we use as our gathering place. We call it 'the Grassy Top' because it is at the top of the temple and it is, well, grassy." He reached up to move a branch out of my way, a branch he could have walked under without touching.

"From what we can tell, there used to be a staircase on each of the four sides of the temple. Now these stairs are either crumbling or covered with earth, so we built trails to wind up the mound and lined them with white rocks. To make it look decent," he said with a smile. "And also to give the children something productive to do."

Now that I was looking for it, I could imagine the old form of the temple as we climbed up the path, though I never would have guessed if Lark had not told me. The trail soon brought us to a flat area where there were several oval huts. These dwellings had a stone foundation of neat, cut stones—taken from the temple, I presumed—with earth walls and palm-thatched roofs, just like the hut I now shared with Lark. Around the huts were playing children, softly smoking yard fires and rows of colorful laundry strung out on lines, sorted meticulously by color and shape. Villagers waved at Lark and me as we passed their yards, and we walked until we came to another set of earthen steps that led up through a bushy thicket to another platform similar to the first, only smaller, with similar huts, children, fires, and colorful laundry.

I had the continual feeling of rising above the earth around us, but the thick brush and tall trees blocked any view of the land below. I could tell from the height of the forest that grew straight out of the walls and platforms of the rubble that the "Ancient Ones" had been gone a long time.

Halfway up, we passed two large double doors that leaned into the hill. The doors were made of long poles and were held together with straps. Lark stopped in front of the doors. "Years ago, part of the temple caved in and we found a cavity. We dug into the cavity and found a large room. We do not know what the room was used for by the Ancient Ones, but we found our own use for it."

He undid the straps and opened one of the doors wide until it fell back against the side of the hill.

"Behold," he said, "the corn cellar."

The opened door revealed five stone steps that led into a chamber. Lark walked down these steps, and I followed him into the cool darkness.

The roof of the chamber was low, and I had to duck my head

slightly. As my eyes adjusted to the light, I could see huge woven baskets extending back into the darkness, filled with cobs of dried corn. I had never seen so much corn in my life.

"It has only been two months since the harvest, so we still have much corn." Lark explained. "You can take whatever you need, whenever you need it; anyone can. It belongs to all of us because we are all expected to work in the milpa during planting season." He inched back into the darkness until he came to a wall. "The only corn you cannot use is the corn here at the back in these baskets that have lids. This is the seed corn. This is what we use to plant next year's crop." He patted the lids reverently. It was cool in the cellar, and the skin on my arms started to bump up.

"Shall we move on?" Lark said. I turned and headed up the stairs and into the warm morning light while Lark followed and closed the door behind us and secured it with the leather strap. We continued up the hill, and Lark told me the names of the villagers we passed. Each time he proudly announced, "This is my wife, Sandpiper. Have you met her?" even though they had all been at the wedding feast the night before.

Soon we reached the top of the mound and the long, flat field Lark called the Grassy Top. I could hardly believe it was the same place where we had been the night before. Gone were the torches and tables, the food and the people. The only sign that there had a been any gathering at all was the flattened grass and the smoke that rose lazily from the ashes in the great fire pit.

The pavilion was empty except for Lark's mother and grandmother weaving at their looms. At first I thought Lark would go and speak to them but he only smiled and waved, and they nodded their heads, smiling back.

As we passed them, I could hear their soft voices and feel their eyes following me. I knew they were thinking about how I was not a virgin anymore. And they were right, of course, but not in the way they supposed. This thought made me feel uncomfortable, and I was glad that Lark did not stop to speak to them so I did not have to try and fake a blush.

We circled the huge fire pit, which was filled with white ashes and soft smoke. An iguana basking on one of the rocks flicked his tongue at me. "Deceitful," it seemed to hiss.

We stood next to the fire pit, looking at the ashes and listening to the low voices whispering in the pavilion. Absentmindedly, I brushed my foot across the dirt until the ground became smooth and hard. It was not earth after all, but a flat stone. I kept brushing, revealing a seam and another stone. Sure enough, under these patches of grass and dirt were cut stones laid side by side, evidence of an ancient floor.

I looked up to see Lark watching me thoughtfully. "Piper, how are we going to communicate?"

I made my eyes huge and innocent, knowing I could easily just open my mouth right then and answer his question.

"You most likely used some sort of signals to 'speak.' How did you communicate with your family and the others in your village?"

I bit my lip and looked around for ideas. There was a stick poking out of the fire pit. I reached for it and when I did, the accusing iguana flicked its tongue out at me and slunk away to find another sunny spot. Crouching down I brushed the remainder of the dirt away on the stones I had unearthed and tested the end of the stick. It made a perfect black mark on the stone.

"Oh, I see," said Lark, setting down the gourds. "So what if you wanted something—like food—what would you draw?"

Thinking quickly, I drew the first thing that came to my mind: a fish.

Lark squatted next to me. "Fish means food. Good. What else? What if . . . you wanted to tell me our roof was leaking?"

I drew a cloud and I drew our hut underneath it. I had a dotted line coming out of the cloud and through the top of the hut.

"Very nice. I think I could figure that one out." He paused. "What if you wanted to tell me to fix that hole or I would be in big trouble?"

I smiled and thought for a moment. I drew a picture of a stick man next to the hut. Then I stood up and I put my foot over the stick man, rubbing the stick man away with the ball of my foot until his body became a black smear.

Lark laughed. "I think there might be hope for us after all." He stood up. "So we have figured out how to 'talk.'"

I nodded.

"I have shown you the village."

I nodded.

"What is left to do?" he said, thinking. I looked around. We were standing near a tree; one of the only trees growing on the Grassy Top. Its trunk was smooth and green except where thick thorns grew out around the base. The tree was leafless, but some of the branches were decorated with white ribbons that twirled in the breeze. I pointed to the unusual tree, thinking Lark might tell me about its significance, and why it was dressed in ribbons. His eyes followed my finger to the ribbons and a shadow fell across his countenance.

"That is the ceiba tree," he said, his voice suddenly distracted and far away. "It is a sacred tree in our village. Some people call it the Tree-Under-Which-Prayers-Are-Heard." He then sighed.

I gazed thoughtfully at the tree. *And why was it decorated like this?* I wondered.

But he did not offer any more information about the special prayer tree. Instead he pulled his eyes off the ribbons and looked down at the gourds he had brought. In a grim tone he said, "There is something else I need to show you."

LARK

It was inevitable. I had to show her eventually. I picked up the gourds and led Sandpiper down a different trail than we had come up.

The trail on this side of the temple was steep, and at times I offered my hand to help her but she never took it. This was probably just as well, since she climbed down the hill as gracefully as a puma, and had she held my hand, I might have pulled her to her death.

We reached the bottom, and the trail led into the forest. The forest was thick but offered little shade at this time of year because the leaves were shriveled. I wiped the sweat from my forehead. Already it was getting hot, and I was thirsty. I was sure she needed something to drink as well, judging by the tiny beads of sweat that gathered like tears above her lips. We were almost there. I prayed that the voices would behave.

The dense forest ended abruptly, opening up into a large clearing. It had been many months, maybe even a year, since I had last been past this point, and I hesitated, listening. A breeze fingered my hair and carried with it a faint whiff of water. I was sweating more now, but not because of the heat.

I listened a moment longer, feeling a mixture of fear and anxiety, not knowing exactly what I should do if they started to speak to me. I would have to forgo the usual precautions since I was with Sandpiper, and the cotton would have to stay in my pocket. I was sure Sandpiper was wondering why I had taken her here only to stop and stare. Everything seemed safe, though, and except for the insects, the breeze, and the grass brushing against Sandpiper's skirt, I could hear nothing. I took a deep breath and stepped forward, hopeful that today the voices would grant me mercy.

We walked out into the clearing and the dry grass crunched under our feet. To try to relax I started to whistle. I did not want to seem nervous, especially since, for Sandpiper at least, there was no danger.

We made our way toward the center of the meadow, toward the oasis of shrubs and plants, the only plants that stayed lusciously green year-round. Rising from the foliage I could see the top of the scaffold and the ancient banyan tree. A few more steps and we would be there. I slowed my pace. "Watch your step as we come into the trees," I cautioned.

We entered the cool shade of the leafy trees, and there it was: a huge, round hole gaping in the earth. The distance across the hole was as far as a spear could be thrown (if pitched by someone other than myself) and was just as deep. I watched Sandpiper's eyes grow wide and her lips part as she viewed the huge chasm. Steadying herself, she peered over the side. I closed my eyes for a moment, took a deep breath, and forced myself stand next to her. In my pocket I grasped the cotton with my sweaty hand, just in case.

Far below, at least five men down, was the great shadowy pool filled with stagnant water. Leafy plants grew out of the white rock walls, and on the opposite rim the banyan tree clung fiercely to the edge, its branches arching over the cavity and its thick stony roots gripping the side. Other roots cascaded down the rock cliff to the bottom of the pit like petrified giant hair, tapering until their stringy tips caressed the water's pus-green surface. Dead, yellow leaves lay scattered and immobile all across the surface like flies caught in a spongy web. A swampy odor drifted out of the great opening that gaped like a gigantic mouth.

"This is the cenote," I explained. "People have called it many things: the doorway to the underworld, a gateway to the gods, an ancient bathing pool . . . but I am satisfied calling it the place where we get our water. And, unfortunately for us, it is the only place."

Bending down, Sandpiper picked up a rock and tossed it into the pit. Instead of splashing into the water, the rock merely broke through the surface and was absorbed instantly into the soup. The disturbed water rippled outward, like the laughing belly of a well-fed woman.

"I know what you are thinking," I said, pulling my eyes away and forcing a smile. "You are dying to drink from it. Come over here and I will give you a sample." I walked to the scaffold. The sorry state of the structure was proof that it had been a long time since I had been there. It leaned precariously, and some of the boards were warped and needed replacing. I had neglected it for too long, but to come out and repair it by myself was unthinkable.

The scaffold had an "arm" that reached over the cenote, and at the end of this arm was a pulley, through which a fraying rope was threaded. That, too, I noted, would have to be replaced. On one end of the rope dangled a bucket. The other end of the rope came down into the structure and wrapped around large spool with a handle. The handle was held fast by a brake. I lifted the brake and lowered the bucket down into the pit.

Bats fluttered out of the hole from some unseen hiding place as the bucket descended into the cenote. I could not see the water from where I was standing, but Sandpiper watched from the edge.

I felt the rope slack. "Did I hit the water?" I asked her.

She nodded. I gave the bucket time to sink into the pool. When I felt the weight through the rope, I turned the handle the other way, bringing the now-heavy bucket back up. I snuck glances at Sandpiper's face as she observed. When the bucket appeared beyond the rim, it was dripping with water and small plants hung from the sides.

I pulled the bucket higher until it reached the top of the arm of the scaffold and tipped, pouring all of its contents onto a small ramp. The water rushed down the ramp and disappeared into a large ceramic pot nestled inside the framework of the scaffold. I smiled. Even though the scaffold looked as if it were on the verge of collapse, I was pleased that everything was still working smoothly. We listened to the water trickling through the belly of the pot. After a while Sandpiper gave me a "how long is this going to take" look.

"Patience," I said.

The pot was almost three times the size of the bucket, and the bottom of it was cone-shaped with a hole in the end of the cone. I placed one of our gourds on the ground, directly under the end of the cone.

Before long there was a drop, then a dribble, and then a trickle of crystal clear water that rained out of the pot and into the gourd.

"It will take some time to fill," I told her, "so while we wait you can pull up the next bucketful."

I showed her how to release the brake and lower the bucket. By the time she pulled up the next bucketful, the first gourd was full and I replaced it with the second one.

When both gourds were heavy with water I showed her how to lock the bucket in place so it would be ready for the next person.

I picked up one of the gourds and took a long drink. It was crisp and cold. As I swallowed, the freshness spread down my throat, through my chest and under my skin. Closing my eyes, I took another gulp and some water escaped, running down the side of my face. I stopped, issuing a satisfied "Ahhhhhh" and wiped my cheek and chin with my sleeve.

"Taste it," I said, handing her the gourd.

She hesitated, and her eyes traveled a triangle between the cenote, the gourd, and me.

"It is clean," I assured her, patting the large pot. "This is a filter. Inside this pot there are several layers of rock and sand and charcoal. As the unclean water runs through it, all the impurities—the scum, slime, residue, moss, insects and bat guano—is absorbed. When it comes out the bottom it is as clean as the rain. I promise."

She lifted the gourd and drank. When she finished, her lips were wet and shining.

"As you can see, getting water will take up a lot of your time," I said, picking up the other gourd. "Especially since we live far away from the cenote. It will be your responsibility to keep the gourds filled in our hut. Hauling water is the women's job."

Thank the gods that she could not question why.

"Shall we go?" I said, conjuring up a smile. As we turned our backs on that shadowy place and stepped out into the sun, my anxiety disappeared. We were going home now, and I felt more grateful than ever to have Sandpiper by my side. As necessary as the cenote was to our village, I was relieved to have it behind me.

When we were halfway through the meadow, I paused. "Piper," I began, "unless you are here to get water, it is better to stay away from the cenote. It is not a good place to spend a lot of time." I thought of saying more, but I could not. I would have to leave it at that for now.

SANDPIPER

I was just putting the red feather back and closing my box when a voice outside made me jump.

"Sandpiper?" called the voice. "Sandpiper? Are you in there?"

I put the box away, deep in a basket under some clothes. I straightened my skirt and patted the scarf around my head, making sure that all my hair was tucked in. Then I lifted the flap. Honeybee stood outside, holding a small gourd and smiling shyly. "Hello, Sandpiper," she said. "I like your skirt. Is that the new one my mother made for you?"

I nodded. Cedar had made another skirt, longer this time, so now I looked like I really belonged. She dyed it blue, just a little lighter than the belt. She also gave me a new slip, and its pure white lace extended out from beneath my skirt as is proper in this village. Since I had very few things to wear, she told me she would make me another and that she would teach me how to make my own when we had more cotton.

"It is very pretty on you," Honeybee said.

I smiled to thank her.

"I have something for you." She held out the gourd proudly. "It is to help your voice grow back."

My voice grow—?

"You see," she said quickly, "I want to be a healer someday. I already know of many different kinds of plants that can help stomachaches and heal wounds, and I thought there might be something I could do to help with your speaking problem. I do not know what kind of plant heals voices, but then I remembered that there are these lizards that live in the forest. If you try to grab ahold of their tail, they will just let their tail fall off."

50

I tried to look intrigued.

"But then, the lizard grows another tail back in its place," she said significantly. "I have been thinking about your problem a lot, trying to decide what would be the best salve, when I remembered the lizards. It took a long time for me to find a lizard, and then I had to catch it—that was not easy—but I finally did, and I pulled off its tail and cut it up in pieces. Then I mixed it with honey—because I always put honey in my salves—then some crushed sweetsop leaves, water from the cenote of course, and some cornmeal to make a paste. See?" She pulled the wood spoon out to reveal a grainy yellow sludge, speckled and lumpy.

I took a step back.

"Oh, do not worry; you are not supposed to eat it. What you need to do is keep it in your hut until the next full moon. Then, put it in a place where the moon can shine on it for at least part of the night. Sprinkle some ashes from the fire into the salve and then apply it."

Where? I mimed.

She tapped her throat. "Right here." You need to apply it once every day until it is all used up. And when it is all used up, your voice should be as good as a new lizard tail."

She handed me the salve like a birthday present. "I cannot wait to see if it works," she said. "Last spring when Lark got a black eye, I made him a salve. Lark told me it made his black eye disappeared three days earlier than normal. I keep telling Grandmother Vine that I will make her one for her eyes, but she says she would rather be blind than put my salve on her eyes," she said sadly. She looked up at me and shook her head slowly. "Some people just cannot believe. Will you try it, Sandpiper?" she asked, her big eyes round and hopeful.

I gave her a warm smile. *For you, Honeybee, I will try anything.*

"I knew you would try it. You will not regret it, Sandpiper." She turned to go but then whirled around and asked, "I am going up to Jade's hut to paint pots. Would you like to come?"

I shrugged. I had nothing else to do at the moment, so I put her special salve inside my hut, and together we walked up the mound.

Jade's home was by far the most festive of all the huts. She had woven ribbons through her fence, and there were lines of multi-colored flags strung from tree to tree. Inside her yard, there was a kiln with shelves of pots on either side in various stages of completion. Jade herself was there, wearing a different dress than I had seen her in before and a garland of red flowers in her hair. She seemed sincerely happy that I had come. She gave me an apron to cover my new skirt and invited us each to select a pot and then sit at a little table cluttered with paint-brushes and small pots of paint.

Honeybee and I dipped our brushes and began painting while Jade chose a pot. When she finally decided on one, she smoothed it off and joined us at the little table. Just as she sat down, Cedar came walking into the yard, carrying a baby.

The moment Jade saw the baby, she set down her paintbrush and groaned. "Again?" she asked.

Cedar smiled. "But you did such a good job taking care of him last time, Jade."

Jade held out her hands with reluctance. "When is Fern going to recover?" she said, "I cannot take care of her baby every day."

"You know she has no other family, Jade. But I am hopeful that she will be better soon. I know Fern appreciates your help very much, and when she gets better she will thank you a thousand times."

Jade gave Cedar a look of tortured anguish, but Cedar simply smiled and left. Jade held the baby up and looked into his face. "Behave this time, and please keep your nose jellies and regurgitated milk on your own clothes."

I wanted to know who Fern was and what was wrong with her. Honeybee must have read my mind.

"Fern's husband died last week," she explained.

I nodded, sympathetically. I wished they would elaborate and tell me how he died.

"And there is no need for us all to be sad," Jade said, turning the baby around and sitting him on her lap. "No one really liked Crowfoot anyway."

"That was not very nice," said Honeybee.

"But it is true," said Jade.

"Yes, but we still should not speak ill of the dead. Especially those who die in the—" Just then baby started to cry.

"Ooooo," muttered Jade to the wailing child. "Why did you have to come and spoil a perfectly good morning?" She reached for a gourd and dipped a cloth in to the water. She held the cloth close to the baby's mouth and he began sucking eagerly.

"He looks like he is starving," observed Honeybee.

"He is starving. Do you think that woman gives him enough milk? Cedar says Fern has not eaten a bite in three days. Mark my words, this baby is going to die."

Jade dipped the cloth in the water again and the baby sucked with vigor, looking at each of us with his huge, black, tear-filled eyes and grasping Jade's wrist with his tiny hands. It would have been cute if the circumstances were not so dismal.

"I do not know why, out of all the women in the village, Cedar wants me to take care of him."

"I think it is because he likes you best," said Honeybee. Jade ignored her comment.

"I just hope Fern will get well soon so she will take the little monster back."

"He is not a monster," Honeybee said.

"True," replied Jade thoughtfully as she watched him suck, "he is more of a parasite."

"You should not call him names." Honeybee sighed as she dabbled paint on her pot. "What is his name, anyway?"

"Mushroom," Jade said, dipping the cloth in the water again and giving it to the baby to suck. "Is that not the worst name? No wonder he is languishing. But he is nothing like a mushroom. Look at the way he sucks and his huge insect eyes. I do not care what his mother calls him, I am calling him Mosquito."

LARK

Every day, life seemed to get harder and harder for Crowfoot's family. Fern was not in a state of mind to take care of her many children, and my mother spent much time tending them or trying to find others to tend them. Beetle, the oldest son, now had no father to guide him into manhood, so my father asked Stone to take him hunting. I tagged along too, thinking that it would not be a bad thing for me to learn a little more about manhood myself.

"You are young, Beetle, but I can already see that you will have Crowfoot's strong arms and keen eyes," my brother told the boy as he filled his quiver with new arrows. "Your father was fortunate to have a son who can take the man's place in the family."

We spent the entire day with him, trying to distract his thoughts from his family's problems. We saw a snake, a squirrel, and at least three rabbits, but he had no interest in them. Stone killed four birds and a turkey before Beetle even pulled an arrow from his quiver. When he did finally raise his bow and aim, his attempt was only half-hearted and he missed every single time. By late afternoon we decided to turn for home, and Stone gave Beetle all of his kills. Before parting at the base of the village, the boy finally spoke.

"You were both good friends to my father," he said. "Do you know why he . . . why he went to the cenote that night?"

Stone and I glanced at each other, and I could feel the tingling of a nosebleed coming on. This was one of those moments when I was glad I was the younger brother and was not expected to answer difficult questions.

"I do not," Stone said.

"I do," Beetle said, looking down. A rush of dread spread through my core. *Already?* I thought. *He is just a boy.*

Stone answered gently, "Beetle, it is forbidden to talk of these things. It is best to not speak of it."

"But I heard there was a legend . . ."

"It is a myth," said Stone.

"Then . . . what is it that eats through the—"

"Vultures," Stone said.

The boy nodded. He dried his tears on his tunic and did not say another word for the rest of the time we were together.

It was the first time I had ever heard my brother lie.

SANDPIPER

I woke with an intense craving for fresh fish. My desire would go unsatisfied, of course, and my stomach burned for something to fill it.

But nothing else sounded appetizing to me, and to make things worse, I did not know how to cook very many foods for myself. I could make soup, though. Perhaps if I made a very light soup with only onions and potatoes my stomach could hold it down.

I filled a bowl with potatoes, onions, and an unusual-looking pepper I had found growing in the garden. Then I sat down with the bowl in my lap, took the pepper, and began to cut it into chunks.

As I sliced, I thought about that pool everyone called the cenote. It was like a little paradise compared to the rest of the dry, rocky landscape, and I savored the shade and the smell of water. Since that first day when Lark had showed me how to get water, I had returned several times to fill up my gourds, and could not help lingering at the edge, listening to the birds and watching the dappled sunlight dance across the surface. Every time I visited, the water seemed to be a different shade of jade or turquoise, like a great liquid opal. I soon concluded that this pool was not a stagnant pond, but living and flowing well from somewhere deep underground. Most tantalizing of all was that the water looked deliciously cool. The temptation to strip off my suffocating clothes and go for a swim was great, but I decided against it since I was not sure how easy it would be to climb out. Someday, though, if I had a rope or a ladder, it might make for an exciting adventure. I finished the pepper and picked up an onion.

Yet there was something about the cenote that seemed odd, I

thought, as I sliced into the onion and my eyes filled with stinging tears. For example, if we depended on the cenote for water, why had the village been built so far away from it? I cut again, wiped away a tear, and sniffed.

And why was it "a woman's job" to haul the water? If men and women worked together, much more water could be collected and brought back for the homes and gardens. It did not make very much sense to me. Three more slices and my cheeks were wet with tears and my nose was a river.

The most puzzling thing was what Lark had said when we left the cenote. He said that it was "not a good place to spend time." What did he mean by that? And if that was true, why was there a trail beaten all around its rim? It was definitely frequented by someone. My teary eyes widened. Or some*thing*.

Finishing the first onion was a tremendous accomplishment. To celebrate, I cried a little more and wiped my face on my apron. Then I picked up another and continued to weep and wonder about the cenote. By the time Lark came walking out of the forest, I was crying like my best friend had died.

"Piper?" he said, his voice concerned.

I could barely see him through my tears. Without thinking I rubbed my eyes with my hands. A huge mistake.

Now I was crying in earnest, for the onion fumes and the pepper juices were searing my eyes with fire. I feared I had permanently blinded myself. Liquids seeped from every cavity of my face. Lark dropped the bag he was holding and was soon at my side, putting his arm around my shoulders, trapping me over the poisonous chunks of onions and peppers.

"Sandpiper, what is wrong? Was it something I did?" He said anxiously.

Having my face over the bowl like this was torture.

"I know this has not been easy for you. It must be hard to be so far away from your family."

He handed me a cloth and I mopped my face the best I could.

Lark squatted down and looked up into my eyes as I blew my nose.

He put his hand on my knee. "I know this was not your choice, Piper, but please, please do not cry."

Tears were gathering in his own eyes. This was ridiculous.

"Perhaps there is something I could do for you that would make you feel more at home. Is it the hut? Do you not like it? Would you like me to change it somehow?"

I smiled weakly and shook my head. I patted his hand. *No, Lark, it is not the hut. It is the onions. Please, let me go. I am suffering. I am about to die.*

"It is me then." Lark said, his expression forlorn and miserable. "I know I might not be what you dreamed of, but Piper, I will try to be the best husband I can be for you. I promise you that."

Lark's words were so kind, but I could not take this any more. I had to get away before my eyes liquefied.

Dropping the knife in the bowl, I pushed it into his chest and stood, holding my toxic hands away from my face and rubbing my tears away with my shoulders. Removing myself from the bowl helped a little, but I was desperate for water to wash the pepper juice off my hands. I frantically searched for a gourd.

Lark stood and watched me, holding the bowl and looking forsaken as I rattled the empty gourds. Why had I not filled these up earlier?

Finally I grabbed an empty gourd, sneezed, and with an apologetic wave to Lark, I took a gourd and staggered into the forest.

On the way to the cenote, my eyes slowly returned to normal, though I still kept my hands far away from my face, just in case. I finally reached the clearing. In the distance I could see the scaffold, stiff and stoic, standing in the midst of the sanctuary of green plants.

The air was hot and heavy. I walked into the grasses, the searing sunlight on my shoulders. Out here, in the open, it was strangely quiet, and even the rustling of my skirt seemed loud. Above the bushes that concealed the cenote, large birds made lazy circles in the sky. As I watched them, a soft breeze blew, ruffling my skirt and smelling faintly of water. I thought how welcoming the shade of the plants would feel once I arrived at the cenote.

I entered the leafy shade and instantly felt relief from the scorching sun. I was glad to be back in this beautiful, mysterious place. I approached the scaffold and I put my hand on the handle. Releasing the brake, I lowered the bucket down into the huge hole. Down, down, down it went and I listened for it to dip in the water.

But it did not.

Instead it stopped with a "thud" and I could feel the rope slack. Something was wrong. I turned the handle the opposite direction, lifting the bucket up and then tried lowering it again.

Thud.

That was not the sound of a bucket dipping in water. *How odd*, I thought. Perhaps there was a log or something in the way. I put on the brake and walked the few steps to the edge to see what was wrong. When I saw it, I screamed.

After taking a few deep breaths I made myself look again, and again I screamed.

There, floating face up in the water, was a dead body, and my bucket was resting on its bloated chest.

I staggered backwards and grasped the scaffold. A wave of repulsion rippled through me, and I crumpled to the ground. Huddling against the scaffold, with my eyes as big as pumpkins, I tried to decide what to do. Should I run? Should I find someone and tell what I saw? Should I say nothing and let someone else find the body? Could there be a chance he was still alive? And worst of all—was it someone that I knew?

I decided that I had to look again, to make sure it was not someone in Lark's family. Then I would go and get help. I stood, still trembling, and inched my way to the edge, keeping one hand on my heaving chest. I peered over and looked at the body.

It was a man. His skin had turned pasty white, and his tunic and skirt floated about him. I could not tell who he was, but he looked young. Most disturbing, though, was his head. It lay, tilted back and partially submerged, with its mouth gaping in a silent scream. His eyelids were open wide, but where his eyes should have been there was nothing but the glimmer of water. It was as if everything within the young man's head had been scooped out, and now water filled the void.

I ran through the forest, vomiting in two different bushes before making it back to my hut. I looked around for Lark, but Lark was gone. I ran up the mound trail, passing the huts of the people I did not know until I came to Jade's. She was there in her yard, finishing the pot she had started on the day before. Honeybee was there too, holding the large-eyed baby that Jade named Mosquito.

"Hello, Sandpiper," Jade said, without looking away from the pot.

Honeybee saw my countenance. "Sandpiper, you look sick. Are you all right?"

I shook my head. *No.*

"What is wrong?"

I pointed behind me. *There is a dead man in the cenote*, I wanted to say. How was I supposed to work that out with only actions? I squatted on the ground next to Jade so that she would look into my face. I pointed down the trail. Reluctantly she put down her brush to look at me.

"Do you need something?" she asked.

Yes. I want you to come with me to see something horrible.

"Oh-oh-oh! Let me guess!" Honeybee said, as if I were playing a game. "You are being chased by something."

I shook my head and looked desperately at Jade. I continued to thrust my finger toward the jungle. Jade pursed her lips and cocked her head to the side, while Honeybee continued guessing.

"You just saw something terrifying," she said.

I nodded.

"A snake."

I shook my head no.

"A jaguar?"

No.

"A naked man."

NO.

She put one hand on her hip and tilted her head. "You know, this would be so much easier if you could just talk."

I looked back at Jade, and pointed down the trail once more. I grabbed her hand and gently tugged. Come! Come with me! I pleaded.

"I am guessing want me to come with you somewhere?" Jade sighed, reluctant to leave her project.

I nodded earnestly. Was it possible to make my face look any more desperate? I tried, but I could not get my eyes to go any wider than they already were.

"Very well. Honeybee, you stay here. I am going to see what is going on."

"Oh, can I please come, too?" Honeybee begged.

"Whether it is a snake or a jaguar or a naked man, I am sure Cedar would not want you to see it. Besides, I need you to watch Mosquito until I get back."

Taking her time, she rinsed out her brushes, while I paced back and forth. I worried that if we took too long someone else might also make the grim discovery. Finally, when she was ready, I took her by the hand and led her down the trail, pulling her like a child pulls a mother.

We came to where the trail splits. When I beckoned her onto the trail to the cenote she suddenly stopped and would not move another step.

"Sandpiper—" she asked, lowering her voice. "Does this have to do with the cenote?"

I nodded eagerly.

Jade broke out into a run.

Through the tunnel of trees I followed her, and it was not until we reached the clearing that she stopped.

"Now," she panted, holding one hand to her chest and looking out at the leafy trees in the distance. "Before I look in the cenote I want to be prepared." Her eyes were filled with worry and I suddenly I wondered if she already knew what was in there.

"Is there . . . is there a man in the cenote?" she asked.

I nodded, astonished at her good guess.

She closed her eyes and exhaled slowly. Then she asked, "Is the man . . . Stone?"

I was confused at her question. Why would she think that? I shook my head, no.

Jade exhaled and rolled her eyes to the sky. "Thank the gods," she whispered. "Then let us go see who it was this time," she said, walking past me toward the cenote.

This time?

I walked as far as I dared, stopping so that I could see the bone-white walls of the opposite side of the cenote but not the surface of the water. Jade walked right to the edge and after hesitating for just a moment, looked in. Her hand came to her mouth. As she gazed I studied her countenance, wishing I could hear her thoughts.

"This is not good," she said, finally turning from the cenote. "We must go and tell the others."

We walked back into the clearing, my mind exploding with questions. Who was that boy? What had happened? How do we get him out? Who are we going to tell? Jade's unsurprised acceptance was so perplexing that I almost gave up my commitment to mutehood right then and there. I opened my mouth and was about to utter my first word in days when Jade began to explain.

"I am sorry that you had to be the one to find him," she said as we walked back toward the village. "You, being new and everything." She sighed.

I looked at her, wondering for a moment if she might have something to do with the boy's death.

She continued, "I found a man in there once too. Only I was much younger. It is an exceedingly unpleasant memory. You never forget an experience like that. That boy—" she nodded back in the direction of the cenote, "is—or was—Beetle. He was the son of Crowfoot and the older brother of the baby that Cedar makes me take care of. Crowfoot died by falling in the cenote too. Just before you came to our village."

Her explanation just baffled me even more.

"I know you must have questions," Jade said, seeing my expression. "And so do I. We all do. This is what I can tell you: every now and then a man from the village will drown himself in the cenote. And no one knows why."

A man will drown himself in the cenote. Is that what she said?

"We do not know if it is an accident, or a suicide, or a murder—or just stupidity. And the men—they will not talk about it. They act like there is nothing wrong, and they always come up with some kind of excuse for the accident. If we ever try to talk to them about it, they change the subject or become exceedingly grouchy. It used to be that the men would help haul the water, but there were too many of these "accidents." So that is why the women do it all. We have lived this way for as long as I can remember. We have to. Where else are we going to get water?"

She looked over her shoulder at the birds circling above the cenote. "It is probably not a good idea to get water for the next little while . . . at least until the vultures break up the body. They like to start with the head and eat it hollow. Once the skull fills with water it does not take long for the rest of it to sink. In the meantime, you can borrow some water from me. We will tell Cedar about the boy, and she will inform everyone else. If I were you, I would always have a few gourds filled with water for the next time."

LARK

Every man is required to come to the meeting.

It is held at night, deep in the forest, far from the ears of mothers, wives, and daughters, and far from the reach of the cenote. We are supposed to take a different route each time we come so that we do not make a trail.

I reached the meeting place just as the sun was going down and decided that since I was the first one there I might as well start the fire. As I prepared the kindling, Stone arrived, silent and brooding. He sat on one of the dozens of log seats that surrounded the fire pit.

He watched me strike the stone for sparks. The brittle tinder and dry sticks did not take long to ignite, and once I was sure the flames could survive without my coaxing, I took a seat next to my brother.

"I know what you are thinking," Stone said, rubbing the calluses on his hands with his thumb. "I should have told him the truth."

"Actually, I was not thinking that," I said. "But you are right. You should have told him the truth."

"What were you thinking?"

"I was thinking that if the gods could have granted me one wish it would be that Piper *not* find a body in the cenote in her first week of being here."

Stone groaned.

"It is not your fault," I told him. "Well, not completely. Telling Beetle the truth could have made a difference."

"I thought Beetle was too young," he said. "I thought it was too early to tell him. I take all the blame."

"You cannot save everybody all by yourself."

"I could have saved him."

"Maybe. But some would still find a way to go, even if you staked them to the ground."

With his elbows on his knees he ran his hands into his hair and stared at the dirt. "We are doing this all wrong, you know," he muttered.

"Doing what wrong?"

"Keeping it a secret."

I did not know exactly what he meant by "it" since "it" had many possibilities, but I kept my mouth shut since Stone was making his way to saying something profound and I did not want to interrupt him, lest he think I thought "it" was something other than the "it" he was think-ing of. I only have enough brain space for one secret at a time.

But he did not elaborate, so to fill the silence I just gave a low grunt which he could take as either "yes, I agree, brother, 'it' should not be a secret" or a "no, that is a bad idea, brother, 'it' should stay a secret." That way, he could at least know I was listening and he could choose whichever interpretation pleased him. So in the end, I never really knew which "it" he meant, and I was left to instead study the colors of the sky as they deepened and we waited for the others.

Soon there came a rustling in the grasses and a snapping of twigs, and one by one, from every direction, figures came out of the forest. Eventually, almost every log around the fire had an occupant. Since there are exactly the same amount of logs as there are men in the vil-lage, we all knew if someone was missing. Those who did not come to the meeting received a personal visit from my father the next morning.

Tonight, as he stood before us, my father leaned upon a staff. He seemed older and more fragile than I had ever seen him before. I knew the trip to White Island had been hard for him and that since he returned he had been plagued with a constant cough, but this evening was the first time I had noticed how weak he had become.

Despite all this, with great and trembling passion he began the speech that we all have memorized. He reminded us of our duty to our families and to the village. He told us to stay away from the cenote. Then, he retold the legend. As we listened, our faces grew long and grim. Besides the brief interruptions by his cough, it was the same meeting.

Just like last time. And the time before that. Until Stone roused us from our depressed stupor by standing up.

"I request to speak, Father."

Father looked surprised but granted Stone's request. Our ears pricked.

"With respect to you, Father, we have done this over and over again and nothing has improved. I believe we need to tell the truth."

"My son," he said solemnly, "I am telling you the truth."

"No, Father, we need to tell them the truth about the cenote."

Oh, I thought. So this is the "it" he was talking about.

"Tell who?" asked my father. "Tell the women? Stone, you know that is unthinkable."

"Why not? They deserve to know."

"Deserve to know?" my father said with an expression that would have withered any other man. "Stone, we are protecting them. It is our duty. Their hearts are too precious and fragile. If they knew, it would only cause more suffering."

Stone was firm. "I think they can help us. And Lark agrees with me."

My eyes widened in panic. *I do?*

"Stone, I am still the chief of this village, and as long as—" He was interrupted by a coughing fit and was unable to continue. I had a gourd with me and I took it to him. With trembling hands he grasped it and drank. We all waited. When he composed himself he said in a low, graveled voice, "As long as I am chief, I forbid anyone to tell the women what we know. We are finished speaking of this tonight."

Stone bowed his head and sat down. A cool breeze blew through the group, making a tremor run up my spine.

After the meeting, we all took our separate, somber paths back to the village. I tried not to think about the legend as I stepped through the dark forest, for every time I hear it the hairs on the back of my neck prick, and I feel as if two years of my life have been sucked away.

I tried to think instead of Sandpiper. We had been married for quite a while—over a week now—and I still felt like I knew hardly anything about her besides the fact that she liked avocados.

I was coming to experience for myself what I had heard many older men complain about: the mystery of a woman's mind. I could not tell if she was happy, curious, angry, lonely, or miserable. I could not tell if she was doing something for me because she liked me or because she felt like it was her duty. I was not sure how best to please her. The only thing I knew for sure was that I would not give up.

Every night she brushed her hair and took off her jewelry, her belt, her blouse, and her skirt, and lay down in only her slip to sleep while I stayed awake and listened to her breathe. At least she did not cry anymore like she did on our journey. She snored, though.

I wondered how I would feel if some ugly girl came to my village, told me I was going to be her husband, and took me away to a strange faraway place. I pondered that for a few moments and decided that any girl—ugly or not—who would take me to a strange faraway place would be a fantasy come true. So I tried to think of this the way Piper might think of it:

I am a girl. (Already this was difficult.) I live on an island. I have everything I want and need, a family I love, andfriends who adore me. Suddenly a boy comes from far away. He is not handsome. He is not strong. He is not anything extraordinary except that he is the son of a chief. He takes me to a strange place where I know no one, I have to eat foods I am not used to, and I find dead bodies floating in my drinking water.

I shook my head. I would be miserable too.

When I arrived at my hut, I stood outside for a few thoughts, savoring the light in the window placed there just for me, and imagined the warm womanly body that I would soon be resting beside. There had to be something I could do for her that would make her feel safe and happy. Something that she understood, something that would show her how grateful I was that she was here.

As I entered the hut and lay down next to her, I had the idea. The idea that would change everything.

SANDPIPER

It took several days before I could close my eyes without seeing the image of the boy floating in the cenote. His death created ripples of whispers in the village, but no explanation was given for the accident, no warnings were issued, and strangest of all, there was no funeral.

"It has happened before," Jade said, "and it will happen again. You just hope that it does not happen to someone you love."

That explanation was not good enough for me. Someone should do something. Someone should say something.

But then, who was I to demand that of these people when I, too, refused to speak? But I have good reasons, I said to myself. I have good reasons to be silent.

I did not want to drink the water. I did not want to touch it. I did not want to smell it. I did not want to wash my clothes with it or bathe in it. I did not want to even go near the cenote again. Ever. But there was no choice. Until the rains came, I had to keep making the long journey to the cenote with my gourds. I had to keep pulling up the bucket and pouring the foul water through the filter. I often found myself wishing I were a plant and could suck water out of the ground or absorb it out of the morning mist. But even the plants were dry now, and the villagers said they would be dry until the rains came in the spring.

I spent most of my time near my hut, trying to avoid any cooking smells from other yard fires. Besides the wonderful avocados that Lark found for me, the only other thing I could stomach was corn. But corn required more work. One had to grind it, soften it, and cook it into something edible, unlike avocados, which were enveloped in a thin skin that was easily peeled away and the fruit was there, ripe and green and luscious, a gift from the earth.

Word spread quickly that I could make rope, and I was already receiving requests. I spent much time walking through the forest looking for different types of plants that would make good fibers.

One day I was outside my hut, experimenting with strips of corn husks to see if I could weave them together and make something strong enough to be useful, when I heard a baby crying.

The cry became louder and louder until Jade appeared, walking quickly down the trail, with Mosquito in her outstretched arms. Her hands were cupped under his shoulders and she held him as far away from her as she could, his legs dangling, his arms flapping, and his mouth screaming. I could see the baby's rump was soiled. She slowed when she saw me.

"Sandpiper, do you have water?"

I handed her a gourd and, turning the baby backwards and holding him with one arm, she splashed water over his spanking place. His screams intensified when the cool water first touched his skin, but he slowly calmed as Jade gently washed over his skin with her hand. When he was clean and smooth, she dried him off in her apron. The baby's face and eyes were red and tears still glistened on his cheeks, but his cries were only whimpers now, and there was a look of relief on his face. I put my husks down and held out my arms and Jade eagerly handed me the baby and then slumped down next to me. The baby was soft and warm and I kissed his head.

"That thing sucks the life out of me," she panted, nodding to the child.

I smiled and bounced him a couple times on my knee. He giggled. He was a beautiful baby, with skin as brown as a coconut shell. His hair swirled out of the spot on the back of his head like a little black whirlpool. He had the biggest eyes and the thickest eyelashes I had ever seen.

"Do you like babies?"

I nodded. I loved babies. Panic fluttered inside me as I remembered what was in my future and how there was still something very important I needed to do.

"Stone likes them too," she said, "though you would never know it. He is always so serious." She laughed. "He is always trying to get me to have a baby. He will become the chief one day, did you know that? And he will need sons to become chief after him. But no babies ever come."

I sighed and marveled at the ironies of life.

"You know, you can put these husks under your mats to make your bed softer at night," she said.

I nodded. That was good to know.

I kissed the top of the baby's head again before handing him back to his caretaker. Like it or not, he reminded me that I had to give the seed a legitimate reason to grow.

It had to happen.

That night.

Lark lay with his back toward me. The night was dark. I was nervous. This was so different than the way it had happened before. But it had to happen or I would be shunned from two villages and have no place to call home. Taking a deep breath, I reached up and put my fingertips on Lark's bare skin. His muscles tensed. I slowly ran my hand up and down his back. His skin was smoother than I expected. I worked my way up to his neck and traced my fingers down the slope of his shoulder and back up into his hair. I could feel his pulse quicken beneath his skin.

Then, in a loud crackle of corn husks, he turned over and pulled me into his arms.

LARK

If I were to gather up all of the most sublime moments of my life and push them together like a great ball of clay, it would not equal the happiness I experienced last night. I cannot help thinking that if every man could have nights like that, all the world's problems would be solved.

SANDPIPER

When I woke in the morning Lark was gone, but in the doorway there were four ripe avocados, lined up in a row. I had just finished eating the last one when Lark appeared, breathing hard and dumping a pile of long, thick agave leaves outside the hut.

"Good morning, Sandpiper."

I smiled and nodded.

"What do you think of this?" he said, gesturing to the pile he had just created. "Can you make this into rope?"

I examined the bluish-green spears. They were long and stiff with a sharp thorn on each tip. When I broke them apart, they were filled with wet, yellow fibers. Perhaps if I could separate these fibers from the rest of the plant they might be useable. It looked like a lot of work, but I would try.

I nodded my head.

"Good," said Lark happily. "I will get more."

Later that day, Honeybee came walking down the path, dragging her feet and looking very troubled. She said she had come to see if I had been using her salve for my voice. I told her I had, and justified the lie by promising myself I would dab some on my neck right after she left.

She did not leave, however, but sat on a stool, gloomily studying her toes. Finally she told me there was another reason she came to see me, and that was to tell me that the woman named Fern had died.

"Mother said that she died because she refused to eat," Honeybee said. "But I know she died of a broken heart."

All I could do was shake my head. What kind of place had I come to? I was depressed the rest of the day. I could not stop thinking about that little Mosquito and how he, too, would soon die without his mother.

LARK

I found some agave plants for Sandpiper to make into rope. First she pounded the plant leaves with rocks until the fibers separated from the wet pulp. Then she dried the fibers in the sun. Once they were dried she could braid them into any thickness I desired. The rope was strong and had no give and was perfect for my project.

I was constantly amazed at my good fortune to have acquired such a wife. Not only was she hardworking and skilled, but she had a great power over me. I could hardly concentrate when she was around, and every day it seemed the gods poured on her an extra measure of beauty. I watched her when she walked, I watched her when she slept, I watched her when she cooked, I watched her when she burned what she was cooking—and all the while I wanted to constantly be touching her. She could not make any movement without stirring my heart in some way. I restrained myself only because I did not want her to think I was crazy.

Then I made a great discovery. I knew she had the ability to speak, for she spoke in her dreams. She said the word "red," though I am not sure what that means. Perhaps it is her favorite color. I decided it would be a wise thing to remember.

Now that I knew that the reason she did not speak was because she had decided not to, I was sure that eventually I could find a way to change her mind.

In the meantime, I still worked on my project in the forest, on the other side of the milpa. I cut and dried the wood and lashed the pieces together with Sandpiper's rope. Soon all the parts would be ready to assemble.

Eventually I would win her trust. One cannot ignore love forever.

I found Stone sitting in his yard, chipping on an arrowhead.

"Ho, brother," I said. "I could use your help with something."

"Will it take long?" He put down the arrowhead, picked up a shaft, and looked down it to see if it was straight.

"With your help? No," I said.

He notched the end of the shaft and slid the arrowhead inside. "Have you seen Father lately?"

I looked at the ground and pushed a pebble with my toe. "No," I admitted. I had been too busy with the Project of Love.

"You should go see him. He is not doing well. He needs to talk to someone who . . . will not make him angry."

I gave a weak smile. "In the past that has always been my job. What did you do? Talk to him about the cenote again?"

He flashed his dark eyes at me. I took that to be Stone-language for "yes I did, and I do not want to talk about it."

I sat beside him as he lashed the arrowhead to the shaft. "He is an old man," I said. "Why do you trouble his heart about these things?"

"Because things need to change."

"He is too old to change," I said. "Besides, he is just doing what he thinks is best for the village."

"That is why, when I am chief . . ." he began, and then stopped, for we both knew it was not respectful to speak in such a way. "Forgive me," he murmured.

"When you are chief things will be different," I said, completing his thought.

"Yes," he said, holding the finished arrow out for both of us to admire. The black arrowhead fit snugly at the top. The shaft was flawless and smooth and the yellow feathers at the end would undoubtedly guide it to its mark. It was magnificent, strong and straight. Just like him.

"Well, at least come with me. I want to show you what I am making and would appreciate some advice."

At the word "advice," my brother agreed. He slid the new arrow into his quiver, and we walked down the temple mound, past the milpa, and into a small grove.

"So what is this for again?" Stone asked, surveying my work site and squinting up into the trees.

"A surprise," I said.

"A surprise, eh?" I knew he could tell what I was making, and I also knew he thought I was a lunatic for making it. He did not mock me though. "Are you sure you want to use this tree? That one over there is bigger."

I looked at the tree he pointed to. It was bigger, but it was not in the right location. "This is the one I want. It needs to have a view."

"Very well then," said Stone. "I will help for a while, but then I have other duties to attend to."

That is what he said, but that is not what he did. He worked the entire morning with me, helping me hoist logs and platforms into the tree and lash them into place. With Stone's help I accomplished in one morning what would have taken me at least ten years to do by myself.

While we worked, I thought of Piper. The day before I had watched her carry a melon into the hut. She held it in front of her with both hands, right over her belly. I smiled when I thought of what she might look like someday when instead of a melon she was carrying my child.

In the afternoon I checked my snares, finding I had somehow captured an ocelot. My happiness was growing inside of me like a well-watered plant, and my future lay before me like a golden path. Life had never held so much promise.

SANDPIPER

The only positive thing about a drought is that one can always find dry wood to burn. I came back from the forest with my arms loaded with wood and saw something on the ground, near the doorway. As I got closer I could see that there were at least twenty avocados, piled on top of each other and circled by dozens of freshly picked flowers. I dropped the sticks by the side of the hut and bent down to pick up the splendid fruit. I smiled when I noticed other markings in the earth. I tried to decipher what Lark had written. It was a picture of a man with a spear killing an impossibly large snake. I guessed that Lark had gone hunting.

Capturing the ocelot increased Lark's confidence so much that now he was always hunting. The ocelot pelt was stretched out and drying in a sunny spot near the door. He was very proud of that pelt, and every now and then I caught him staring at it or running his hands through the fur.

I sat on the ground with the avocados and ate three on the spot. They were delicious. I savored every smooth, luscious bit of the yellow-green meat inside and licked the rest off my fingers.

After that, the day went by quickly. I swept out the hut. I watered the pepper plants and yams in our small garden. I filled the gourds with water, cut up potatoes, made some tortillas (burning all but two), searched for more dry wood, lit a fire, boiled and washed some clothes, and hung them as neatly on my line as any other woman in the village. My abdomen was beginning to swell under my dress, but no one yet noticed, and in the evenings I became more tired than usual. When I was with the family, I often felt the eyes of Cedar resting on me, and

I wondered if she knew. I considered traveling up to the praying tree to plead with the gods that my mother-in-law would not count the months, but I doubted the gods answered those kinds of prayers.

In the afternoon, I sat to rest for a moment on the bench outside the hut. I heard the snap of twigs and saw Lark coming out of the forest. He had a leather bag over his shoulder.

"Ho, Piper! I hope to bring you honor!"

I waved. *I hope to bring you peace.*

"How was your morning?"

I smiled and nodded. *Thank you for the avocados*, I wanted to say.

"Good. Would you like to see my kill?" he said.

I tried to look interested.

He lowered his bag to the ground and reached in.

He kept reaching, reaching. He looked in the bag.

"Ah, there it is." He stretched his arm deep into his bag. He pulled out a small iguana by the tail.

My eyebrows raised.

"Not too impressive, is it?" he sighed, and sat next to me on the bench. "Ah, well. I do not hunt like the others, you know."

No, I shook my head. *How do you hunt?*

"You see, we have a lot of great hunters in our village. They bring home jaguars, monkeys—all kinds of big animals. I was never good at that, though. My eyesight is not good. Plus I am always too noisy, and I scare them away. But I am good at setting snares. I catch a lot of turkeys, usually. It looks as though my snares were not very effective today. But do not let this little lizard fool you. Iguana soup is delicious."

I stuck out my tongue.

He sighed and let the iguana wriggle free. "You are right. I do not care for iguana either."

I should tell him now, I thought. I took a stick and waved it.

"You have something to say?" he said, his countenance brightening.

I placed the tip of the stick in the dirt and drew a stick woman. I looked at him.

"You want me to guess who this is?"

I nodded.

"My mother?"

No.

"Jade?"

No.

"You?"

I nodded. Then, I picked up an avocado and set it down on the waist of the stick woman.

Lark squatted and stared at the picture for a long time, stroking his chin. Then he swallowed, his eyes met mine, and a slow smile spread from one ear to the other.

"You would like me to find a really, really big avocado."

I shook my head.

"No?" Lark scrunched up his mouth and tapped one finger on his lips. "Hmm . . . I cannot figure this one out. It almost looks as though you are going to give birth to an avocado."

I brightened.

He raised an eyebrow and repeated dubiously, "You are going to give birth to an avocado?"

I nodded my head and then shook it then nodded it again, all the while my smile was hurting my cheeks and ungraceful snorting sounds were coming from my nose as I tried to keep from laughing.

But Lark was more baffled than when we began. Very slowly, as if he were trying to comprehend a new language he repeated, "You, Sandpiper," he looked at me for confirmation, "are going to give birth to"—and then, as if someone had splashed him with cold water, his face froze in the most peculiar expression of agony and surprise, and a teeny-tiny whisper came from his mouth. "A baby. We are going to have . . . a baby? As in a little person baby?"

I nodded, triumph on my face.

He reached out and grabbed me. "A baby! We are going to have a baby!" he said into my neck.

I could not keep from smiling. *Yes, Lark. A baby,* I thought, closing my eyes and relaxing into his arms. *Not an avocado.*

LARK

I could not believe it. We were pregnant.

Well, she was pregnant, not me, but since she could not have done it without my help, it was almost like I was pregnant too, only not as much.

I probably should have figured it out earlier, but I was new at this. I had not realized it could happen so quickly. After all, Stone and Jade had been married for years, and they did not have children.

I was nervous already about the baby. How would we take care of it? Would it learn to walk? How would we teach it to speak? How would we keep it away from the fire and safe from snakes? Just thinking about how many things could go wrong made me sweat.

It especially made me worry about the surprise I had planned for Piper. But since the Fish People also raise babies, I knew there must be ways to keep children safe. I was sure Piper would know what to do.

Later that day when Stone came to see my finished creation, he was speechless. Finally he rubbed the back of his neck, shook his head, and said, "It is not very practical."

"I know," I said, grinning, "but she is going to love it."

SANDPIPER

It was water day. I gathered all of the gourds I could find and strapped them to my body, using ropes I had made myself. Lark said my rope was excellent, and he had me make piles of it, but what he used it for, he never told me, and I, of course, never asked. In the village I could trade my rope with almost anyone for anything. I made rope for sandals, rope for clotheslines, and I also made hammocks, which were not hard because they are almost the same as fishing nets. It pleased me to have value.

On this particular, blazing hot day, I walked to the cenote, bedecked with a half dozen empty gourds and my budding abdomen, making it look as if I had tumors growing out of my body on every side.

As always, when I arrived at the cenote, I first checked for dead bodies.

I lowered and raised the bucket three times to get the amount of water I needed. I spent several long thoughts next to the scaffold, listening to the water percolate through the filter, waiting as it filled my gourds. I strapped each gourd to my body so that I was balanced on both sides, and then I walked back on the forest trail, going slowly, careful to not spill a single drop.

By the time I got back to the hut, I was exhausted, and my pelvis began to cramp slightly—a signal that I was overdoing things. I wanted to sit down to rest and pour some of the cool water to drink, but the bench that was usually sitting outside the hut was gone. Setting the gourds down, I walked inside to find our hut completely empty.

My broom was gone. My pots were gone, the curtains were missing and the baskets where Lark and I kept our clothing were gone. Lark's ocelot pelt was gone. With a burning ache I saw that even my wooden box was gone.

I wondered if I was dreaming. Did someone steal from us? But who would do that? And why? There was nothing that Lark and I had that was more than what anyone else in the village had.

Dazed and confused, I walked out of the hut, wondering if I had lost my mind. That was when I saw it. It was an arrow, drawn in the ground. Was this Lark's doing? I started to walk in the direction of the arrow but then paused to look at the gourds near the door of my empty home. Perhaps someone would come back and take them too. Sighing, I loaded all the gourds back on to my body and followed the mysterious arrow.

Before long I came to another arrow, and then another. It led into the forest on a trail I had never been on. I stopped frequently to rest and to steal sips of my precious water. The path started inclining gradually, and I trudged up it, sloth-like, the water seeming heavier with each step, the rope cutting into my shoulders. Then the trail leveled a little and led into the open sunlight.

I squinted my eyes against the bright light and looked around. On one side there was a large, wide field, bordered by a stone wall and over-grown with dry weeds. *This must be the milpa, where they plant their corn in the rainy season.*

The sun stared hard at me as I followed the arrows around the milpa, and by the time I reached the trees on the opposite side, sweat had soaked through the back of my blouse. It was shady here, but heat still radiated around me like an oven. Had I not been pregnant it would not have been so hard, but as the situation was, with the suffocating heat and the weight of the gourds, there was nothing I wanted more than to sit right there and start pouring all of the water I had collected over my head. How wonderful it would feel, to have it wash over my shoulders and run down my back . . .

The trail came to a small open area in the center of which stood several large, thick-trunked trees growing out of the earth. The tempta-tion of pouring the water on my body was still on my mind, but just before I could give in, something caught my eye.

It was a ladder. A long ladder hanging from one of the trees. I stopped and stared at it for a moment. Then I looked up. And when I did, I dropped the gourds, spilling the precious water all over the earth. But I cared no longer for the water. It was forgotten to me. For there, in the top of the tree, was the most unbelievable sight. It was a house.

A head poked over the edge.

"Hello, Piper!" Lark said.

Even if I were not pretending to be mute I would not have been able to say a word, for my tongue became as limp as a banana peel.

"Are you going to stand there all day or are you going to come up and see your new home?"

I walked to the ladder and gently shook it with both hands. It seemed sturdy and strong, and it was lashed with my own rope. So this was what he had been doing all of this time. I climbed up, rung by rung, and lifted myself into the hut.

It was slightly larger than our old place, and everything that I thought had been stolen was put in perfect order here. My baskets, my broom, my pots—and there was even a shelf for my wooden box. I stood there, not knowing what do, while Lark stood back in the corner with his arms folded, grinning.

"Look at this," he said, drawing aside a curtain to reveal a large open window. I stepped to look out, and for the first time since I had come to this place, I could see a *view*. It was nothing extraordinary; it was just a view of the brown milpa, but it was a view.

"Of course, we will mostly sleep up here. I will make a cooking area for you down below."

I turned toward him, shaking my head in wonder.

"Do you like it?" he asked eagerly. "Does it . . . does it remind you of the home you left on your island?"

The tears came quickly to my eyes. I did not care if my home was on stilts or in a tree or in a hole in the ground. But the fact that Lark would desire to work so hard just to please me took my breath away. I was overwhelmed with his generosity. No one had ever done something so kind for me, even though I was just one big lie. I hid my face in my hands and started to weep. I felt Lark pull me close to him and wrap his arms around my waist. His skin was warm and his hair smelled of wood and tree sap.

After a while he took my face in his hands and wiped away my tears. He pulled my face down so that our foreheads were touching.

"Sandpiper, I love you. You are the best thing that has ever happened to me. I want you to feel at home here in our village. I will do whatever you want if only I can make you happy."

And so began what I would later call the happiest time of my life. In the evenings after our work, Lark and I would climb the ladder to our home and lie close to each other while we listened to the insects and birds outside. On these nights Lark would talk and talk. He told me what he thought of the world. He told me stories that made it nearly impossible to muffle my laughter. He would contemplate solutions to problems out loud and ask, "Do you think I should do this or that, Piper?" and I would nod or shake my head, according to my opinion. He would consider my answer thoughtfully and say, "Yes, I think you are right."

He always ended these ramblings by turning his shoulders toward me and stroking my cheek with his thumb, telling me how good I was to listen to him go on and on about nothing.

But I loved to hear him talk, for to see things through Lark's eyes was to see everything sunlit. When he ran out of words and stories and questions to fill the air, he would pull me close to him. And I did not mind. I did not mind at all.

There were still some nights, however, that when I closed my eyes I could see the coal-black eyes of someone else. And when that happened I would turn away from Lark and roll to the cool side of the mat. Lark never said a word about it, but I could hear him sigh like the sea.

LARK

"I want to speak to my sons," my father said the night that he died.

Mother, who had not left his side for three days, solemnly ushered Honeybee, Jade, and Sandpiper out of the lodge so that we could be alone with the chief.

As custom dictated, with Stone on the right and me on the left, we knelt beside our father. My heart grew heavy as we watched him struggle with the coughs that shook his fragile body. We helped him drink and waited for the fit to subside.

"You have been good sons," he began. "Lark, I am not unaware of the great sacrifices you have made for the village, for which I am very grateful. Stone, soon you shall be chief, and I am confident that in your hands the village will thrive. It gives me great comfort that you are both married to honorable women." Then father paused. He took several delicate breaths, trying to avoid another fit. "But there is one thing that gives me much anxiety as I go my grave. Before I go on, I want you both to give me your hands."

I put my hand in the hand of my father's, but Stone hesitated, knowing what our father was about to ask of us.

"Stone," my father commanded.

With great reluctance, Stone gave his hand.

"I want you both to make me an oath."

"Father, I—" Stone began. His words faltered and he could not finish. His face pinched and quivered as he tried to control his emotions.

"First, take care of your mother," Father said as tears filled his eyes. "The women are what keep our village alive. Always honor them, for they do more for you than you will ever know, and treating them with kindness will bring great happiness to your families and health to the entire village. Nothing matters more than the marriages in our village, and it is this love, above all, that we must protect." Then he placed my hand over his heart, followed by Stone's hand and then covered our hands with his own. I could feel the tremors in his chest as he breathed. "Now, promise me, as the last thing you do for your father, that you will never tell them what we hear."

Stone winced. "But father—"

Father closed his eyes. "Promise me," he whispered.

"I promise," I said, and looked at Stone.

Stone met my eyes and I could see the frustration burning behind them. Finally, after what seemed an eternity, he surrendered.

"I promise," he said.

A few days after the funeral, the air shifted. Sandpiper and I breathed it in one morning as we awoke. It came in from the east and blew over our skin, fresh and damp. Rain was coming. It was still far away, but it was coming, and the thought of it filled my heart with hope. This had been a hard year for my village, but soon it would be time to plant the corn. The work would be a balm.

Planting is the same every year, and has been since the beginning of time. First we set fire to the milpa. We burn over the weeds and remnants of last years crop. The ashes make the earth dark and fertile.

We wait three days for the fires to burn out and the soil to cool enough to walk in. Then we come with our hands and our tools to turn the soil, mixing the soft gray ash with last year's soil. It is hot, dirty work, and I can taste the grit and ashes in my mouth all night as I sleep.

Once we have turned the soil, we make rows and mounds. Then the children and women bring bags heavy with seed corn that has been soaked and softened and we strap them across our chests. Men and women spend an entire day gently pressing the seeds into the soft earth, singing growing songs to each and every seed:

You will grow, little seed
You will grow.
Tall as me, little seed
Tall as me.

It is a sacred time. A time that brings peace and hope and helps heal all the heartache that we have suffered during the dry season. Once all the seeds are planted, we wait for the rains to come.

THE RAINY SEASON

LARK

There was no first drop of the season, no gentle sprinkling of water that gradually thickened into a shower. No, this year the rains came crashing down on us from the beginning, flooding everything with white walls of water. It was as if the gods finally remembered us at the last moment and poured down all their water for the entire season at once. It rained for three days without ceasing. The drops seemed as big as eggs and felt as hard as nuts on my head and shoulders. At times the pouring rain was so loud that having a normal conversation was impossible.

Sandpiper and I kept to the tree house for those first few days. The house swayed back and forth in the torrents, and I felt at any moment we would surely die. But Sandpiper was exuberant. She thought it was exciting.

When the sun came out and the rains slowed to a sparkling drizzle, we all rushed down to the steaming milpa to view the damage. It was as we suspected; the mounds had been obliterated, and all of the seeds we had sown the week before had been washed out of their beds. Together we replanted the seeds, patiently singing the growing songs once again so each seed would know what was expected of it.

Then it began to rain again; we trudged back up to our huts through the rivers of water that were already eroding our trails into slippery slopes and muddy sinkholes.

The rains brought relief from a variety of woes, the first being that I did not have to worry so much about getting a bloody nose. But the greatest blessing came from the fact that there was no need for anyone to go to the cenote. For Piper's convenience I created ways for water to drain off the tree house roof and into a large pot near her cooking place. If the rains were consistent, then she would have more than enough water for weeks to come.

Now began a new and welcome routine. In the mornings, when the rain was only a mist, I would go out to check my snares. Then I helped in the milpa, looking forward to when the corn plants would pierce through the earth like little green knives.

After the first big storms, the rains rolled in predictably every afternoon. I always marveled that there was no need to filter it, and without any effort on our part it fell in clean, pure abundance.

SANDPIPER

The rains transformed our world. What was once a brown desert was now filled with green plants lifting up their fronds and branches toward the clouds in graceful gratitude. Water-loving creatures like frogs and turtles emerged out of their hiding places. Delicate orchids and irises and other flowers that I had never before seen graced the forest floor with vibrant color. It seemed that fruit blossomed, ripened and dropped from trees in the span of only a few days. The world around me became unrecognizably lush, and the arching leaf-covered branches and creeping vines transformed the trails into jade-green tunnels. This place, which was once a forest of dry sticks and thorny trees, had now become a deep, wild jungle.

Not only did the rains work miracles in the forest, but they also cured my sour stomach. The stagnant, repulsive smells disappeared and I could finally smell goodness again. I stopped vomiting into bushes. I could tolerate my own cooking and I devoured anything Jade or Cedar put in front of me. For the first time in a long time, I felt like I actually had a future.

I could count a dozen different shades of green when I looked out my tree house window, and the sun lit up the leaves like emeralds. One morning I looked out the window and noticed a tree next to ours was filled with huge, brilliantly lit red flowers the size of my head, waving in the breeze. As I looked closer, I realized that they were not flowers at all, but birds.

I watched them for a long time and tried to coax them to my window with some seeds. When Lark asked what I was doing I pointed at them.

"That is a rare sight," he said coming over to the window and gazing at the birds. "Those are scarlet ibises. We see them for only a few weeks when the rains first begin, if we see them at all. Their feathers are very valuable."

Scarlet ibis, I repeated in my mind. I had seen many unusual birds here in the forest so far—there were the rainbow-colored macaws and the toucans. I even spied a shy quetzal bird once with its tail feathers hanging down like streamers.

But the scarlet ibises—they looked like passion. Just the sight of them kindled a fire in my heart.

They are not at all like the birds from the seashore. Those birds are drab and boring, painted by the gods in the muted colors to match the sand and rocks and shells. The gulls, the pelicans, the kits and hawks . . . and then there is the sandpiper, the plainest bird of all. I never felt like I resembled a sandpiper. I watched the scarlet ibis birds fluffing their feathers. That is how I felt on the inside—full of passion and desire.

But men do not look at the inside. They only look at the outside. The men on my island never paid attention to me. That is why, when *he* came, everything was different, and why I let him do what I would not have let anyone do before.

He came as part of a party of traders. They were only going to be on our island for a few days, selling and trading things we could not get on the island, like knives, jade, pelts, jewelry, and mainland fruits. He was hard not to notice—he was taller than the other traders, and he was handsome. Not handsome like the boys on my island, but handsome in a dangerous sort of way that made my heart trip over itself. He had intense, coal-black eyes and scarlet feathers tied in his dark glossy hair. I had never seen feathers that color before. I thought perhaps he had somehow dyed them. But now I knew that birds that color do exist.

We had a large feast, and even though it was noisy and crowded with people, I was aware of his every movement. I felt as if there were an invisible rope between us, and that it was my destiny to be near him. When he was not looking, I watched him, admiring the contours of his face and shoulders and arms. At one point our eyes met. Feeling embarrassed I bit my lip and quickly looked away. But that one look changed everything. He was now watching me, and even when I looked away or turned my head I could feel his eyes following me.

I sat down with my food and ate, trying to act normal but always keenly aware of his presence. At one point I thought perhaps he had stopped looking at me, but when I raised my head to see, his eyes were waiting for mine, and he watched me with an intensity in his countenance that made it hard for me to breathe. This time I did not look away. I stared back at him and slowly blinked. A half-smile formed on his lips.

When night fell, I lost him in the crowds of dancing, feasting people. Eventually I gave up and sat glumly with the group of listeners around the fire while the old men told stories I had heard a thousand times. I watched the dancing flames and all I could think about was that a handsome dark stranger that had shown interest in me. I kept reviewing his face in my mind and I yearned for another glimpse before his group left the island, but I knew that anything beyond that would only be a fantasy.

Just when I felt that I would dissolve in to a grain of sand if I never saw him again, I felt a touch on my shoulder. For a brief moment I turned to stone. I sat, unable to blink or breathe, and my heart grew hot and pounded like the red heat that throbs beneath a volcano. I knew it was him. The touch slowly moved across my back, from one shoulder to the other, and then it was gone. That touch rippled through my skin and entered my body like liquid lightning. I turned and saw him backing away into the darkness, beckoning to me with one hand, holding a finger over his lips with the other. He wanted me. He wanted *me*. For the first time in my life I had become desirable. I had to follow.

"Where can we go to be alone?" he asked me when we were far enough away from the group.

I took him to the beach, and he dared me to swim in the dark lagoon. His challenge made me laugh because I did not think that was scary at all. I bragged and told him I was braver than all the other girls and I pulled him into the water with me.

When we were tired of swimming, I took him to the mango grove.

The moon was full and bright, and I brushed my thumb against the deep cleft in his chin. When he held me in his arms, I felt small and feminine. For a long time we just sat and talked. Then he pulled my face toward him and melted his lips into mine. His boldness made me shy, and I drew back like a crab into its shell. *This is dangerous*, I thought. *Wonderful but dangerous.*

"It is getting late," I told him. "We should go back."

But he said I made his heart burn. He told me my lips tasted like honey. Then a slow, handsome smile spread across his face. "Besides," he said. "I thought you were braver than the other girls . . ."

And because he said that, I stayed.

When I woke in the mango grove the next morning, I was a different person. He had to leave early, just as the sun blinked over the waves. His companions were already in the canoes, waiting for him. He kissed my forehead and took a scarlet feather from his hair, a feather that was as crimson as the early morning clouds, and he brushed it across my lips. Then, solemnly, he took my hand and placed the feather on my palm and closed my fingers around it as if it were something sacred.

"Never forget me," he breathed in my ear.

I stood on the beach and watched their boats leave, and I felt like my young heart was being sifted into the sand.

It was then I realized that he had never told me his name . . . or if he had, I had forgotten it. I needed to call him something in my mind when I thought of him, so I took to calling him Red.

Often, when I closed my eyes at night, I relived those moments of passion all over again, even when I was in Lark's arms. At times when I wondered if it had all been some amazing dream I would open up my wooden box and take out the scarlet feather. Then I would brush it against my lips and whisper, "I will never forget."

SANDPIPER

Sandpiper? Sandpiper, are you awake?" Cedar called.

I rubbed my eyes and yawned. Lark was still asleep, and the sky was dark. The day before, Cedar mentioned that it might be easier to weed if we woke earlier and worked in the cool of the morning. I did not expect her to follow through with her plan. I should have known better. It had been hard for Cedar since Obsidian's death, but she put her all of her energy into the milpa, working harder than anyone except for Stone.

I pulled myself to my feet, wrapped my headscarf around my hair, and forced myself down the ladder, holding on tightly. My belly now brushed the rungs, and I had to be more cautious.

I met Cedar at the bottom and together we walked to the milpa. It had just rained and the ground was as soft as a sponge. The day before, we had planted the cotton, and they told me we would be seeing their little green leaves in about a week. In the meantime, we put our focus back on the growing corn, which was now knee-high.

We finished two entire rows before the men started to arrive. We continued all morning, through the rows of corn, removing every little plant that did not belong.

It was a beautiful, bright morning, and the sun shown through the white mist, crystalizing the water droplets in the air and whitewashing the world in glittering light. A rainbow arched over the milpa as we worked, and the air smelled sweet.

For a long time Cedar and I worked a row together in silence. Mosquito was walking now, and he toddled beside us through the rows of young corn stalks, testing out his limbs. He tried to step over a dirt clod and fell onto his spanking place. Then he picked up the clod and started to eat it. Cedar chuckled and gently removed the clod from the boy's hands, replacing it with a wooden spoon from her apron.

At that moment Stone walked by. "Back to work," he said to us as he passed. Cedar eyed him and looked as if she were going to say something, but he was already far down the row, no doubt telling the next group of weeders to get back to work.

Cedar playfully shook a fist full of weeds at him. "Do you think he knows that we were here two hours before he was?" she said, smiling at me as she squatted down to pull more weeds. She gave a soft chuckle and then a slow sigh. "I always knew he would be a great chief. Sandpiper, I wish you could have seen Stone when he was a baby. He could have been chief when he was two years old, ordering people to do this and that, correcting even me when I did not do something exactly the way he thought it should be done. He is as confident as the rising sun; as if his very presence will drive darkness from the earth and beckon green things to rise. He demands much out of the people in this village, and there are some who complain. But no one challenges him, because he works alongside us, doing twice as much as any other man or woman. He was born to lead. It is an honor to have a son like him."

By now Stone was far off on the opposite side of the milpa, approaching Lark, who was staring at the fading rainbow. We watched while Stone said something to Lark and Lark reluctantly resumed weeding. We looked at each other and smiled. No one was free from the long arm of Stone.

"Now Lark," continued Cedar as she yanked an extra tall weed from the earth, "is completely different."

I agreed.

"He is a dreamer. He will always do what is expected of him, but while he does he will notice the way the sun lights the edges of the clouds like golden garlands. He will pull the weeds, but he will examine each one, wondering if there were some good use it could be put to. He will till the earth, but he will find a moment to run his hands through the soil, enjoying its texture, aroma, and temperature. He will stop to watch his pregnant wife brush the hair from her face and wait for her to notice his gaze."

I looked up and sure enough, Lark was gazing at me from across the rows. I felt my face flush, and I raised my hand and he raised his.

"And it is an honor to have a son like him," Cedar said. "I am thankful I have both kinds of sons."

By midday the rainbow and the shimmering mist had disappeared and the sun was high and fierce. We all sat together as a family in the thin shade of the rock wall, enjoying a lunch of juicy papaya that stuck to our fingers and dripped off our chins as we gazed into the greenness of our thriving plants.

The squash plants had spread out their tendrils on the floor of the milpa and were blossoming with vibrant orange flowers. Jade fingered the petals of a squash blossom and lamented out loud, "They are so pretty now. If only the blossoms would stay longer." She plucked one and tucked it behind her ear.

Cedar leaned her head against the rock wall and closed her eyes. "Yes, It is lamentable, that such bright youthful blossoms only last a few days," she said. "But if it did not eventually wither, we would never have the fruit at the end of the season." She rubbed her neck and shifted her knees to a different position.

I knew she was probably very sore, yet she never complained. I wondered what she looked like when she was young. I wished that I could have seen her and known her then. I rested my head back on the rock and closed my eyes. Why do we have to grow old? Why can we not stay young and beautiful, like the squash blossoms?

Cedar's chest sagged, her ankles had thickened, and her hair was almost gray. It had probably been years since anyone had called her beautiful. Yet she was kind and wise and patient. Her flower was long gone, and she was now like the fruit of the squash, constantly giving of herself and nourishing others. Her wrinkles and aches and sunspots were simply signs of experience and understanding.

If it were not possible to have both the flower and the fruit at the same time, I could see why the gods in their wisdom would save the best for last. There is a beauty in old women that is deeper than the beauty that is in the young. It gives and comforts and nourishes and passes its nourishment unselfishly to the next generation. I rubbed my growing belly. Already my flower was fading and my fruit was beginning to grow.

I had begun to drift into a warm, delicious semiconscious slumber when I was woken by Mosquito tripping over my legs. I opened my heavy eyelids halfway and watched him balance back up on his wobbly fat legs and toddle to Jade. He plopped down next to her and stuck the corner of her apron in his mouth and began to suck. I closed my eyes again and smiled.

This was a funny habit that he must have learned when she was trying to feed him after Fern died. He did this every time Jade stopped her work, and the corner of her apron was constantly twisted and stained with his mouth juices. I know it made Jade embarrassed, but Cedar told her that if it brought Mosquito comfort she should let him do it.

"Do you really think he will be a grown man and still sucking on your apron?" she said once. "Enjoy it while it lasts, for someday he may not want to have anything to do with you."

Jade gave me a look of utter bleakness, and we watched as the child peacefully sucked. When Mosquito noticed she was looking at him he stopped for a moment, took the apron out of his mouth and gave her a shining grin. Jade rolled her eyes.

When Fern died, we all thought that baby was doomed, but Jade worked tirelessly to make sure he would eat and grow, and in her care he thrived. I noticed many times the way she brought hot foods to her lips to test them before giving them to him and how she always stood close to him when it was sunny, covering him in her shade. Not only that, but she dressed him in little tunics that matched whatever she was wearing. We all knew her moans and complaints were only a mask to hide how much she worshiped the child.

One time I watched her as she was bent over with one arm around him, the other was cupping water to his face to clean away the dirt. Mosquito would vocalize a sustained "ah," and Jade would pat her hand on his lips so that his voice came out "bah-bah-bah-bah," making a comical drumming sound. They kept this up until the sound would deteriorate into fits of giggling from both individuals. It was clearly a game they both enjoyed. One day I wanted do the same thing with my child.

I heard Stone calling us to get back to work, and I reluctantly opened my eyes. I stood first and stretched, then I helped Cedar to her feet.

SANDPIPER

A few days later Stone surprised us all and let us go home early. Jade trotted up beside me. "I am so sick of weeding. I am sick of walking through the miserable, muddy milpa, sick of pulling insects off corn plants, sick of doing things for the good of the group. How about you?"

I shrugged, not wanting to seem too excited in case Stone were around, but inside my heart agreed with her a thousand times over. *I would love a change.*

Jade smiled. "How would you like to do some exploring? I want to show you something."

I nodded. *Yes, yes, yes!*

Jade loaded Mosquito on her back. She had dressed him in a green tunic to match her blouse and tied a blue headband—which he kept pulling off—around his forehead. We each took a gourd of water, a mat, and some food and headed around the Temple Mound to a part of the forest I had never been to.

Ever since the rains came, it seemed there was always something in bloom. On this day we walked through tunnels of trees sagging with so many red flowers that we had to dodge the hummingbirds as they zigzagged from one blossom to the other. Light rain misted our hair, and all around us the plants dripped with water. The air smelled green.

I treaded carefully behind Jade, skirting mud pits and ducking under black, half-fallen trees covered with bright-green moss. All around us was the constant tap-tap-tap of water dripping from leaf to leaf. The plants that sprawled out on either side of the trail were so wet I could have washed my hair in them. Their leafy hands and ferny arms reached out across the seldom-used trail, brushing against my knees, dampening my skirt.

"Oh no," Jade cursed abruptly, making me think that something terrible had just happened.

"My slip is getting dirty," she said in dismay. I smiled, relieved that that was all it was. Scandalously I gathered up my skirt hems, folded them back over my big belly and tucked them into my belt. Jade laughed and copied me without hesitation.

It was not a short hike, and the trail had not been used for a long time. We had to step over tumbled pillars and around crumbling walls, all the while listening to Mosquito babble contentedly in his own language. Frogs were everywhere, and I saw a blue one, a black one, and three green ones on a branch, watching me with red eyes. We must have seemed like strange creatures, what with Jade's baby on her back, my baby in my belly, and both of us revealing our brown knees to the world.

We came to a grove of statues, some fallen over, some half-sunk in the earth, and stopped to take a breath. "Long ago, someone told me that these were statues of the gods of the Ancient Ones," Jade said, panting. "The Ancient Ones had gods for everything. Gods for corn, gods for death, gods for war, gods for the rising sun . . . they were a strange people with strange customs."

Strange but fascinating. What happened to these Ancient Ones? Did they leave? Were they all killed? Did they die of a disease? Maybe it had to do with these gods they worshiped. Perhaps they believed too much in them . . . or perhaps they did not believe in them enough.

I paused to examine one particularly gruesome-looking god. He wore a large headdress sprouting with feathers. He looked mischievous, with his narrow eyes and twisted mouth. His tongue hung out of his open jaw in the form of a snake, and in his clawlike hands he clutched something that was the same size and shape of a human heart.

"Perhaps the purpose of these gods was simply to scare their children into obedience," Jade said. She turned so that Mosquito could see the statue. "See that, Mosquito? If you are naughty, that scary snakeman will come and eat you up."

Mosquito pointed to the statue and laughed. We both smiled at his irreverence.

We left the toppled gods in their dilapidated graveyard and continued on, around the back of the temple.

This side of the temple was covered with plants, but I could still make out the old staircase that once led to the top. It must have been magnificent. Now obstinate trees grew up out of the steps, making them crack and buckle like broken clay.

Jade pointed to the misshapen staircase, "That is what happens when you stand in one place too long in the jungle. The jungle will grow right up through your body."

We crossed the rocky stairs, taking care to avoid the large iguana that sunned himself on a flat stone, and came down a small hill to a crumbling walled courtyard. "Here we are. I call this the Picture Gallery. The Ancient Ones were talented artists. This must have been a special place because there are many paintings on the walls here, some uncovered, some still hidden." She took the mat she had brought and unrolled it onto the dewy, moist earth. I helped her take the Mosquito off her back and she placed him, spanking-place down, on the mat. She took a corn cake from her apron and handed it to him.

"Stay right here like a good little boy and eat your cake while Jade and Aunt Sandpiper do some exploring."

"Bagle-blable," he said, looking up at her.

"And if we are lucky, maybe a jaguar will come and drag you away."

He giggled and smiled at her adoringly. She kissed him, and he clapped his pudgy hands and began drooling on his cake.

We turned and walked around the courtyard. All around us, on every exposed wall there were pictures of crows and snakes and copper-skinned people wearing colorful clothing and jewelry. They had jade nose rings, earrings, golden breastplates, collars of turquoise, jaguar capes, and huge feathered headdresses that arched over their heads in great fans. A person could spend days looking at all of the artwork.

"It amazes me that the paints on the walls have weathered the years better the wall itself. The colors are as vivid as the day they were painted." Jade mused, running her finger along a red zigzag border.

There were several bright-red handprints, and I fit my hand over one of them.

Then we came to a wall painted with very unusual scenes. They depicted images of people cutting into the faces of other people with knives and pictures of children with boards fastened on their heads. "They believed in self-mutilation," Jade explained. "They tied boards to the foreheads of their babies to make them grow long and flat, and that is why all of the people in the pictures have sloped heads. They also believed in cutting themselves with knives and scarring their skin with designs. They did this just to become more beautiful. The Ancient Ones were obsessed with beauty. . . and they were willing to do anything for it."

Jade moved on, but I stood studying the images, wondering how people could put so much value on beauty that they would deform their bodies.

"Look here, Sandpiper," Jade called. "This is my favorite one."

I walked through the grass and stood beside her.

"I call it 'the Three Maidens.' "

It was a large picture of three beautiful young women decorated with jewels and turquoise. They had long elegant robes and bright sashes crossing their chests. Paint, expertly applied to their faces, gave their expressions a look of intelligence and power. Earrings the size of small fruits hung from their ears, and their hair was coifed and piled on their heads, each in a different style, and crowned with brightly colored feathers.

"Are they not beautiful?" Jade said. "I do not understand their gods, nor their writing, but they did have an exceedingly fine sense of style."

I agreed.

Jade looked over her shoulder to check on Mosquito, who was happily studying the crumbs on his fingers. We walked along the wall to a place where the plant growth was thicker. Jade took out a knife and began cutting through the slippery plants and tossing them aside. I helped her pull the vines and clinging plants from the wall. Slowly we uncovered a mural. "Look!" Jade said, excitedly. "It is the Three Maidens again!"

Jade was exultant at first, but as she removed more vines she soon frowned.

"This is not what I expected to find."

I looked up to see the Three Maidens depicted, as lovely as ever, but this time they had spears sticking out of their bodies. We cleared away more vines and peeled off the moss and uncovered other pictures of the maidens, only this time there were many, many more maidens, and there were men in white robes were doing terrible things to them: some were being tied to poles and burned; others were lying on altars with their chests open, with a priest over them holding a knife in one hand and the maiden's heart in the other. The images made me feel uncomfortable.

"There is one more panel," Jade said, pointing. We both looked at each other, wondering if we should uncover it.

I did not want to see the last panel, but I could tell that Jade was going to reveal it no matter what I thought. She took the knife and struck down the concealing vines. I stepped away, letting her do this one herself, and slowly, vine by vine, the picture was exposed.

When she was finished, I felt prickles down my back, and for a small moment I could not breathe. Jade stood back, and after taking in the entire picture, dropped her knife into the grass.

It was another mural of the maidens. Only this time the men in the white robes were herding them toward a large blue-green pool. Near the side of the pool was a man with his hands on one maiden, looking as though he were pushing her into the pool. Another maiden was already in the pool, upside down, with her head and arms sinking beneath the blue water.

There is only one pool of water around here that is that big.

In spite of the sweltering heat, I shivered. I felt as if we had stumbled upon a secret we were not supposed to know. I looked around to see if we were alone.

Jade picked up her knife and backed away from the wall. She sat down on the mat, next to Mosquito, who reached for the corner of her apron and began to suck. Sitting next to them, I wiped the sweat from my forehead while Jade flapped the front of her blouse in an effort to cool off. We both glanced at the two gourds, filled with water, but neither of us touched them.

"Sandpiper," Jade said, staring at the painted wall, "I think I am beginning to understand something that I do not want to understand."

Thunder sounded, and the mist turned to rain. Jade scooped up Mosquito and started to run. We took shelter by stooping under the overhang of huge boulder. It was dry there, and there was plenty of room for the three of us to crouch. Thunder rolled and rain poured down from the edge of the boulder like a flashing white curtain.

We watched the rain, Jade, Mosquito, and I, savoring the cool spray on our faces.

We watched the rain for many thoughts.

SANDPIPER

I stared wide-eyed at the dark ceiling of the tree house, feeling the muscles tighten around my abdomen. All night long it had been like this, this intense knotting under my skin, and I knew that something was about to give. I had never been scared of anything before, but it terrified me to think that there was only one way for this baby to come out of my body. It seemed more believable that I could cut down a tree with my teeth or that I could drink up the ocean than accomplish the final scenario that was to be my destiny: making something as big as a coconut fit through a hole the size of a bean.

I could still climb up and down the tree house ladder like a monkey, a skill that never ceased to bring mutterings of amazement from Lark. He said I was a marvel and that many women by this time in their pregnancy would not even leave their hut. It made me feel very proud when he said that.

In the still gray of morning, Lark and I rose from our mats to begin work for the day. Honeybee joined us on the trail, and we started in sleepy-eyed silence, trying to walk ourselves awake.

We arrived at the milpa under a grim, gray sky. The corn was taller than Lark now and almost taller than me. Stone was already there, strutting through the milpa like a tom turkey, and already his shirt had come off, for the sultry morning was unusually warm. With wet brow and brown skin shining, he gave out assignments to each villager as they arrived, pointing a muscled finger to the place they were to go.

I try my best to describe my brother-in-law as strikingly as he appeared, yet I must confess that by that time his impressive figure was merely notable. Gone were the days that I thought of him as a thrilling masterpiece of male perfection. I had learned from working with him in the milpa that he was more of a slave driver than anything else. All day long he barked at us to work harder, weed more thoroughly, and take shorter breaks. It was clear that he loved corn more than people.

He despised complainers. If anyone grumbled or acted like there was nothing left to do, he made them go through the milpa picking up stones to add to the rock wall. All of us served on "stone duty" at least once, and even when we felt like we had picked up every rock in the field and added it to the wall, we always came back the next morning to find more. Lark said he thought Stone came out at night and threw the rocks back into the milpa just so that there was always something for everyone to do. Of course he was joking. No one admires Stone more than Lark does.

I watched Stone walk from plant to plant, gently shaking each stalk. I nudged Honeybee and pointed to her brother, a question on my face.

"You want to know what Stone is doing?" she asked, eyebrows raised. I nodded.

"He is tossing tassels. The tassel is the boy part of the plant. He shakes them so that the pollen falls down to the silks and ears which are the girl parts of the plant."

Ah. So that is where that phrase comes from.

We worked in the milpa all morning, Cedar stayed near my side, ever watchful and eyeing me every time I touched my abdomen or wiped the sweat off my forehead. We were supposed to be pulling weeds, but to me, bending over felt dangerously unhealthy, so I spent my time pinching the insects off the blades, hoping that Stone would see that I was being useful so he would not make me remove stones.

We made our way slowly down the row, Honeybee ahead of us by a few paces. At one point she stopped and peered through the plants. Then she started to giggle.

"What are you looking at, Honeybee?" Cedar asked.

Honeybee's smile grew and she beckoned to us. "I am watching them kiss," she whispered.

Cedar and I were there in an instant. We crowded around on each side of Honeybee and peered through the corn.

"Right there," she said, pointing through the stalks. "Do you see them?"

A few rows away there was Jade, holding Mosquito in her arms. She was tipping him upside down and burying her face in the crook of his neck, kissing him and making him laugh so hard he could barely breathe. Then she would bring him right side up, let him take a big breath and do it again. They were both enjoying it so much they did not even notice the three of us watching until Honeybee sneezed.

When Jade saw us she immediately stopped, sat Mosquito on her hip and mumbled, "I can never get any work done with this little pest."

We were sad to see the beautiful scene end, especially me, for as I watched I felt my baby kick inside me and I hoped many wonderful scenes like that were in my future.

After a while Stone checked on us. As I suspected, he was not satisfied with my efforts at debugging the leaves, so he gave me the job of pouring fertilizer on each plant, a task he usually reserves for himself since, he says, it requires accuracy. The black, soupy fertilizer was a mixture up of water, cooking scraps and bat droppings from a nearby cave, and I ladled it out of a large gourd on my shoulder. The gourd was heavy, and I thought perhaps it would be better if I weeded after all, but Stone slapped me on the back and told me to get to it. So I did.

Pouring fertilizer did not take as much time as weeding and it was not long before I was soon alone, walking through the corn. Every now and then I would see another black head of someone pop up over the corn to stretch, and then the head would duck back down into the waving green sea.

I waddled from plant to plant, pouring the specified amount of fertilizer around each stalk. I found that each time I came to the end of the row, my lower body would harden and press together, forcing me to stop and catch my breath. I thought to myself, perhaps I am having the baby now. But the pain would ease, and I would straighten up again, and I would turn onto the next row.

Today the gods did not send the fluffy white clouds to shield us from the sun but heavy, dark, gray ones that pressed over us like a giant lid, trapping the dense air over the milpa and steaming us like tamales. The heat was unbearable. Sweat dampened my blouse. Sweat dribbled down my forehead, down my neck, and around my bulging belly. Sweat made my thighs rub against each other unpleasantly as I walked. It took deliberate effort to breathe the thick, moist air through my lungs that were already restricted by my unborn baby's size. Every now and then a warm wind, heavy with the scent of rain swept by, rustling the corn leaves, flapping my skirt and pushing me forward like a giant hand.

I knew Stone would want to have all of the corn fertilized before the afternoon rains, so I kept walking and emptying my ladle, feeling sluggish whenever the wind died down and I was left to my own muscles to move me forward. As I expected, when I reached the end of the row the pains returned and I wrapped my hand around my belly, as if that vain gesture would help keep me from being ripped apart. I breathed hard and fast and I bit my lip so hard I tasted blood.

After a moment the pain eased, and I turned down the next row as if nothing had happened. I continued in this way, going through the milpa, row by row, sweating and eyeing the end of each row with a dreadful anticipation. My task was almost finished, though, and I would finish even if I had to crawl to get it done, for in this village the worst thing a woman could be called was lazy, and I was not a lazy woman.

Suddenly a searing white pain cut through me, and this time I knew I would never make it to the end of the row. The pain was so terrible I felt I was surely about to die and could feel my spirit trying to rip away out of my body to save itself from the crushing agony. A sound came out from my lungs—it was not a scream or a moan or a shout, but something frightening and inhuman, and it terrified even myself. Then I crumbled to the earth.

LARK

We all heard it.

It was a sound of great distress or pain—from an animal or a human I could not tell—and it made every hair on my body stand on edge. I lifted my head to see what it was, but all I saw were dozens of other heads poking up around the cornfield with the same bewildered expression.

"What was that?" someone asked. A warm wind blew over the milpa, and the corn plants bowed their tassels like the ancient worshipers in the drawings on the temple walls. My nostrils filled with the smell of rain and the air was so thick you could chew it. When I cast my eyes upwards I saw the boiling sky, looking as if it was being stirred by a giant spoon.

I was standing next to my mother and we listened in silence, wondering if the sound would come again.

When it did, I still did not know what creature could make a sound like that. Then my mother murmured, as she stared out into the waving field, "Lark . . . where is Sandpiper?" The tone of her voice made my blood stop.

"Piper," I whispered. Pushing stalks of corn out of my way, I weaved through the plants in the direction I had heard the sound. "Piper!" I called out into the wind.

From the far end of the field there was another scream and I started to run, crashing over the stalks.

"I am coming, Sandpiper!" I shouted.

Thunder sounded in the distance as I searched. I was not quite tall enough to see over the tops of the tassels, so I peered through the spaces for my wife, weaving and bobbing my head. My heart was so far up in my throat I felt like it was choking me. Where was she? Finally I saw something blue hidden in the stalks of corn. I trampled through three rows of corn to get to her.

She was lying on her side in the dirt, and I knelt next to her, placing my hand on her back. Immediately she turned and clutched my hand with a grip so tight I thought she would break every one of my fingers. Her entire body was stiff and tense, and her long legs sprawled out in the dirt, twisting and contracting in pain.

"I am here, Piper," I said. But now what? I did not know what to do. "Can you move? Can you stand?" I asked, thinking of the impeding rain that would soon fall upon us.

She gave no indication that she heard me and her eyes and mouth and nose were scrunched together in a tight knot. Her face was turning red and no air was flowing in or out of her body.

"It would make me feel so much better if you would breathe, Piper." I suggested anxiously.

She let out a long stream of air through her mouth and the natural color of her face returned.

"Sandpiper! Lark!" said my mother's heavenly voice. Her skirt brushed past my face as she crouched down at Piper's side. She guided Piper on to her back and grasped her other hand. "Do not worry, Sandpiper, I am here."

"I am here too," said Honeybee coming up behind her.

"I am here too," I added, in case she forgot.

My mother put her hand on my shoulder. "No, you can go, Lark. We will take care of her."

"She is going to have the baby here?" I asked.

My mother moved her hands around Sandpiper's lower abdomen. She pressed on a spot and Piper cried out. She nodded and looked up at me. "Here and now," she said. "Lark, it is time for you to go."

But I did not want to go. I could not leave Sandpiper here, in a muddy field, sounding as if she was about to die. Was I not the one responsible for her condition in the first place? And what use would I be anywhere else? This is where I wanted to be, where I needed to be, and I was not going to leave.

"I will stay," I said as the wind whipped my hair. I could feel the clouds so low over our heads I thought they would press us into the earth. Thunder rumbled and drops of rain fell on my mother's face.

"This is women's work, Lark."

"There must be something I can do," I said.

Sandpiper screamed again, and I could actually see new wrinkles sprout on my mother's forehead. I wondered how many wrinkles a woman gets every time a child is brought into the world.

"Very well. Stay," she said. "You might be of some use. Honey, run and get me some clean, dry cloths from the nearest hut." Honeybee disappeared into the corn.

"Now, Lark," my mother said to me, "I want you to sit behind Sandpiper with your legs spread apart. Raise up her body and pull her up to you so she can lean against your chest." There was a loud clap of deafening thunder and it shook the earth.

I did exactly what I was told. I pulled Piper toward me and rested her against me and as I did I felt her relax. This made me feel a little better, for at least I was somewhat useful. The drops were coming faster now, patting like thousands of beads against the corn blades.

I watched my mother's hair melt as the rain fell onto her head and streams of water dripped from her eyebrows and nose as she kneeled on the other side of Sandpiper. "Move your knees apart, Sandpiper," she directed, raising her voice over the ever-increasing drops.

Another surge of pain swept through Sandpiper's body and she began to cry.

I stroked her arms, but my mother was not so sympathetic. "Do not waste your energy on tears, Sandpiper," she said, peering between Sandpiper's legs. "You are going to need everything you have to get this baby out." That was the last thing I heard my mother say before the sky fell upon us.

It beat us like clubs. It flowed over my mouth and nose until I felt I would drown. I hunched my body over Piper's face as much as I could to shield her from the downpour. Lightening bleached the sky. Through the sheets of water my mother was just a moving gray shape. I wondered where Jade had gone and if Honeybee ever found those clean dry cloths and if she did, what would we do with them now?

Sandpiper's body stiffened again, and then there was a sudden shift and her body completely relaxed in my arms.

My mother was yelling something to me, but I could not understand.

"Knife!" she shouted through a cupped hand. "Lark, give me your knife." I reached behind me and pulled my knife from my belt and handed it to her handle first, praying that it was normal to need a knife during a child's birth.

Moving her arms swiftly, she performed a series of tasks. Then she held up an oblong object that, through the rain, looked purple, wet, and anything but human.

"It is a girl!" she shouted, and I could see my mother's white teeth smiling through the blur. She wrapped the baby in her apron and slowly worked her way to her feet. She bent down close to my face, holding the bundle to her chest. "You must carry her, Lark," she said. I held out my arms to receive my new daughter. "No, not the baby, Lark. Sandpiper. You need to carry Sandpiper. We will take them to Stone's."

I nodded. *Of course, of course*, I thought, still amazed that my mother said "them." We were going to take *them*.

I put my arms under Sandpiper's body and tried to lift her out of the mud. She was heavy and wet, and she slipped out of my arms. She moaned as I readjusted my hold and lifted her again, using every muscle in my body. I trudged through the rows of corn toward the temple mound, and I thought my arms were going to rip out of their sockets. I do not know how I carried Piper so far. All I knew was that I was so happy I could have carried the world.

SANDPIPER

I brought you flowers," Lark announced, beaming as he entered the hut.

Jade and Stone were kind to let us stay in their home for a few days while I recovered, for just thinking about climbing the ladder to the tree house made me wince.

Lark put the bouquet of bright orange blossoms next to me and kissed my forehead. "You should hear what people in the village are saying," he said. "Everyone is shocked that I helped deliver the baby. The men think it was reckless. The women think it was romantic. It is a huge scandal."

With great animation he told me all about the reactions of the people in the village and how mad Stone was that he had trampled some of the corn stalks. I noticed that while he spoke he kept massaging his hand. It made me smile.

"What is so funny?" he asked.

He would never guess, but I smiled because I was wondering if I had injured him when I took hold of his hand in the field. Nothing was so terrible as being alone, my body in pain, my face against the dirt, not knowing if anyone would come to me or know where I was. When I finally felt his touch on my back I was just so grateful I wanted to hold on to him and never let go, even if I had to crush every bone in his hand.

With perfect clarity I could remember all that happened in the cornfield. Even though my eyes were closed and my body was being pelted and crushed and half drowned, I could recall every word spoken between Cedar and Lark with perfect accuracy, for, I discovered, the birth of a baby is a singular experience. Over and over I relived the details in my mind, for now they were a part of my history and of this baby's history. It was the bravest thing I had ever done, and I could not help feeling like a conqueror. It was an experience I will remember until I am an old, wrinkled woman, and I do not know how I could have done it without Lark. I will forever be grateful to him for staying with me in that muddy field.

He narrowed his eyes at me, "What are you thinking about?" he asked again.

I smiled and looked away.

"Were you thinking of how handsome I am?" he said.

My smile grew wider and I shook my head.

"I wish I knew what you were thinking, Sandpiper," he said thoughtfully. "I always wish I knew."

He regarded me with his gentle eyes for a long time until finally he sighed. "Piper, there is something I want to talk to you about. Something that has made my spirit uneasy."

My heart started to beat.

"On your island . . . did you ever . . ."

Now my heart was thundering. I felt the blood drain from my face. It was the moment I had been dreading. I was not ready for this, not now. For some reason I had thought that once the baby was out of me, the truth would come out of me too. But now that she was in my arms, a real breathing person, I realized that the truth would be even harder to explain.

"Did you ever . . . worry about children falling from your stilt homes?" he said. "Because I am so nervous about having a little baby so high up in the trees. Maybe we should put up a net or something."

I closed my eyes and let the relief flood my body. I drew in a long breath and smiled.

Lark measured my reaction. "So this does not worry you?"

No, I reassured him. *It is just a matter of vigilance. In all my life I had never heard of any baby falling in my village.*

"Well," Lark said hesitantly, "If you are not worried, I am not worried."

Not worried at all, I thought, thinking more about the arrow I just dodged.

"Now, we have another important matter to discuss: her name. I was thinking we could name her Milpa."

I winced and stuck out my tongue.

"You do not like it?" he smiled. "Something tells me you already have a name picked out."

I nodded.

"And? What is it?"

I paused, biting my lip. How would I tell him? I scanned the room. We were in the hut of a hunter. Knives hung on rack on the wall. Pelts lined the floor. Bows and arrows clustered in the corners. Slowly, so I did not disturb the sleeping joy in my lap, I pulled out one arm. I pointed to the corner.

Lark strode over to the corner and picked up a bow.

"You want to name her Bow?"

No, I shook my head.

He put the bow down and picked up a machete.

"You want to name her Machete."

I gave him a do-not-be-stupid look.

He found an arrow and pulled it out. I nodded.

"You want to name her Arrow?" he said, still doubtful.

I held out my hand for the arrow. He brought it to me and laid it in my hand. I scooted my fingers up the shaft until I came to the top of the arrow where Stone had affixed red feathers at the end. I stroked the feathers with my thumb.

Lark's countenance brightened. "You want to name her Feather," he said, looking relieved.

I nodded admiringly at my sleeping baby.

"Feather," Lark repeated, as if trying out a new taste on his lips. "Feather. That is the perfect name." He bent down to kiss her head, his eyes brimming with love. "Feather," he whispered. "I am so glad you are ours."

I blinked. *Ours?*

Lark took my hand in his as I forced a smile.

LARK

There is a shaded platform in the center of the milpa where the village men take turns guarding the crops. My punishment for destroying half a dozen corn stalks was serving on guard duty for three days and three nights. But I felt no bitterness as I sat on there, watching the green leaves bend in the breeze. The angry faces of the men in my village did not affect me, for I was a normal man no longer. Now I was a father.

I had fulfilled my purpose for existing. Only a few days ago Sandpiper and I were two people, and now we were three. Overnight I became wiser, stronger, and significant. A king of creation. A god of fertility. I had multiplied. I had peopled the earth. My blood and the blood of the woman I loved had mingled and would now continue into the future. I viewed my place in the world around me with new meaning . . . the corn growing so green and tall, the thick thunderheads that floated across the sky like great pyramids, the rain that so freely dropped from the generous gods, bringing life to all living things . . . now I, too, was a giver of life. I sang songs all day. I sang to the rain, I sang to the dirt, I sang to the stalks of corn, I sang to the spotted red beetles that protect the corn from insects.

As the sky darkened and fireflies bobbed in the field around me, I continued my songs. At night when the sky was a great black dome above me and the stars filled it up, as thick as spots on the back of a baby deer, I still sang. Sometimes I could hear a baby's cry coming from the direction of the tree house and my heart would swell with such a deep happiness that I would sing even louder.

I am a father of a beautiful child!
I will sing with power and a clear voice!
I am part of the miracle of life!
I am a father and I will sing!

In the morning Stone came to visit. In truth he came to scold me again, but I prefer to think he came to visit.

He climbed the steps to the platform and sat down next to me.

"Lark," he said fatherly, "at every stage of the corn's growth we are trying to protect it from some kind of creature. When we first plant the seeds, we add fertilizer with the seed to nourish it as it grows. Then, when the seedlings appear, they must be guarded all day and all night from rabbits, deer, and other animals."

"This is true," I said.

"And then, when the corn tassels are tall and the corn begins to ripen, it is the birds that are the hardest to fend off the plants, for they are difficult to shoot with arrows, and they come in dozens to destroy our hard work."

"Also true," I said.

"But little did we know that our crops' worst enemy this year would be you."

"I told you I was sorry."

"Your rampage through the field damaged many plants."

"I know. We have been through this already."

"We have a right to be angry, for without corn we will starve."

I smiled. "I know that, but I had a very good reason."

Stone raised his voice, "You cannot just trample the plants because your wife is having a baby!"

"Stone, it is not going to happen again."

Stone issued a low growl and tossed a small, warm package into my lap. Tamales.

"From Mother."

I closed my eyes and smelled the package. "May the gods forever bless her."

He unhooked a gourd from his belt. "And here is some water."

He noticed the small piece of wood next to me. "What have you been doing?"

"This? This will soon be a jaguar. And this," I said, reaching in my bag and pulling out the carvings one by one, "is a rabbit. This is a turkey. This is a tapir. This is a deer . . . and this one is supposed to be a coati but it looks more like a skunk." I frowned and scratched the insect bite on the back of my neck. "The tail gave me a lot of trouble. I am making them for Feather. When she gets older, of course."

"Splendid," Stone muttered. "But you are supposed to be watching out for birds."

"Oh, I took care of them."

"What do you mean, you took care of them?"

"I will show you." I put down the wooden animals and got to my feet. "I strung it up the first day because the birds just ignored me when I yelled at them."

I stepped to the corner of the platform, toward one of the four poles that supports the roof. Tied to each pole was a thin braided rope that extended out into the corn rows.

I pointed out to the far end of the field. "See those stalks out there? Pretend a bird lands on one of them." Grasping the rope I jerked it.

There was a rustling sound and far out in the field a few stalks shook.

"See? When I move this end, it makes the stalks rustle and scares the birds away."

My brother folded his arms and nodded, trying to not look impressed. "Where did you get the rope? Is this Sandpiper's work?" he asked.

"Yes," I said, untying the rope and handing him the end. "Here, you try."

Stone tugged the rope and again the stalks rattled out in the field. He gestured to other four poles. "And all of these other lines, they do the same thing?"

I nodded.

"I see now how you had time to make your toys."

"Thank you, brother. I thought it was a good idea too."

"A simple idea. Anyone could have come up with it."

"Yes, but no one did."

He knew I was right. We stood there for a few moments, saying nothing. Then he spoke, his voice low. "Have you been to check on the scaffold?"

"Once," I said softly, looking down and kicking some wood shavings off the platform. "It needs repairing."

"Can you do it?"

"Yes. But . . . I do not want to."

I waited for him to say something. A couple of crows cawed and flew over the milpa. We watched them pass and fly into the jungle.

"I understand," he said finally. "You have more at stake now. You are wise to stay away, even though we must find a way to repair it soon."

"How is it on your end?" I asked.

"There is one giving me trouble."

I wondered who it was. I thought of asking, but I knew he would not tell me. So instead I said, "You cannot save those who do not wish to be saved."

"They all wish to be saved," he growled. "Although some do not deserve it."

We chewed on this thought for a moment.

When Stone spoke again his tone changed and I knew the discussion about the cenote was finished. "You have one more night."

"Yes," I said, slapping a mosquito. "One more night of bug bites and uncontrollable shivering."

I got no sympathy. "Just do not sing any more. Your singing hurts our ears and you will make the plants shrivel and die."

I laughed.

He put his hand on my shoulder, his one gesture of affection. "Have a good watch," he said. Then he turned, climbed down the platform, and disappeared into the green blades.

SANDPIPER

A few weeks after Feather was born, the corn tassels turned from yellow to brown. It was finally harvest time. Lark told me that on the next full moon we would harvest all night because, he said, harvesting when it was cool locked in the corn's sweetness. While we waited for the moon to fill, we emptied and cleaned the corn cellar, repaired the harvest bags, and made everything ready to receive the new crop. The afternoon before the full moon, everyone tried to sleep.

With Feather curled up in a ball and strapped to my chest, we walked down paths fragrant with night-blooming flowers and met others on the way to the milpa. It seemed so dark in the jungle that I wondered if there would be enough light to harvest by. But when we emerged from the trees I could see that the great moon hung low and large over the milpa, generously illuminating the entire field with her soft silver light.

With Honeybee as my partner, we broke up into pairs and went down the rows, pulling each ear downwards from the stalk and twisting it until it snapped off. I smelled the wet juices from the plant as they seeped from the stalk and it made me think of the color green, even though everything around me was in shades of blue and gray. I put the ear in the large, empty cotton bag that hung on my back. All around me there were quiet conversations from the others in the field, and every now and then I heard someone laugh.

Eventually Honeybee and the young man named Newt found each other in the darkness. I remembered Newt. He was one of the handsome oarsmen who came with Lark to my island. The two picked side by side, whispering quiet words and giggling in between the snaps and rustles of the stalks. I slowed and let them have space to be alone.

When my bag was so heavy that the strap cut into my shoulder and pained my back, I turned and slowly trudged back up the trail to the corn cellar. Cedar found me, and we walked together up the hill. Others, moving at faster paces, passed us in the moonlight. I could hear Stone coming up behind us.

"Good evening, Mother, Sandpiper," he said.

"Good evening, Stone," Cedar said.

"Where is Honeybee?"

"Picking with Newt. You know, Stone, I think Newt will choose her when it is time to pick a bride. It would make me happy to see her marry soon," Cedar said.

Stone made no comment.

"Well? What do you think?" she asked.

There was a long pause as we walked. "I think," he began, "that Newt is not worthy to share the same air as Honeybee. Do not encourage her, Mother. I would rather that she remained alone than to take the oath with someone like Newt."

"Then it is a good thing you are not her father," Cedar replied.

"I am close enough. You asked what I thought." Stone picked up his pace and traveled up the hill, leaving us to walk alone.

LARK

With the harvested corn quickly filling the baskets and more corn still ripening in the fields, we were ready to celebrate. Tonight we would have fresh, milky sweet corn for the first time in months, but shucking this much corn could sometimes be a long, tedious task.

"And that is why we have the contest," I said to Sandpiper as we hiked side by side up to the Grassy Top.

I explained to her the custom: First we gather all the unshucked blue and yellow corn into a huge pile. When the signal is given, all the young men in the village begin shucking the corn as fast as they can. Whoever can find the single ear of red corn hidden in the pile gets to kiss the maiden of his choice.

Sandpiper lit up. She raised her eyebrows inquiringly and mimed two braids coming down her shoulders.

"Yes, Honeybee will be part of the contest."

Her lips pursed in a hopeful smile and she gave a little skip, bouncing Feather, who was strapped to her back.

To show I was not unaware of the village love life, I lamented with a half-smile, "And, unfortunately, so will Newt."

With a swift swing of her hips Sandpiper bumped me off the trail and left me to exit a bush without help.

When we arrived at the Grassy Top, the huge pile of corn was taking shape. The stools that the maidens would sit upon were distributed in a circle around the pile. The young maidens themselves, dressed in white with garlands of popcorn in their hair, milled demurely about the crowd holding large empty baskets. The baskets were for the shucked corn, but for now they made a good shield to hide their blushes when they heard their name mentioned from the pack of young men eyeing them from beside the corn pile.

The call was made for the maidens to be seated around the pile. There were more this year, almost three girls for every boy, and every one of them was smiling like it was her birthday. All except Honeybee, who clutched her basket with white knuckles, looking slightly terrified beneath her white popcorn crown. In my opinion she was by far the prettiest, and I was certain that no matter who unsheathed the red ear, she would be the one who was kissed. Perhaps that was why she was nervous.

It was almost time. The young men paced around the pile, cracking their knuckles, and playfully nudging each other with their shoulders while the last of the villagers finished making their bets. This year there were five hopefuls: Cache, Branch, Spider, Hawk, and, of course my family's favorite, Newt. They tried in vain to subdue the hopeful grins that kept sneaking out on their handsome faces. Everyone was smiling. Everyone was laughing. Sandpiper laced her arm through mine and could barely keep still.

There once was a time when I looked forward to this game too. I shucked the ears with the other boys, enjoying the competition and the cheering of the crowd. I never thought much about winning, though, until one year when I realized that this might be my only hope of ever kissing a girl.

That year I tore through the husks like a hurricane, determined to win at least one thing in my life. My mother said that my basket was almost overflowing before the other young men had filled theirs halfway, but I was not watching my basket. All of my concentration was focused on discovering that first glint of red corn. People were cheering my name. It was an amazing feeling. Somewhere in that great pile was the red ear, and I felt that it wanted me as much as I wanted it. I knew I would win—it was only a matter of diligence. I could feel what I thought was sweat dripping down my face but I was so determined that I did not even stop to wipe it away. I wish I had.

One might have thought that in all my zeal in looking for the color red that I would have noticed the droplets of blood dappling the discarded husks that were piling up around my knees. But I was a boy on a glorious quest and I knew no distraction. I did not even notice when the crowd stopped cheering my name and looked at me with mouths wide open. All I was thinking of was that pure, sweet kiss that was almost mine.

And then, I had it.

I had not opened it yet, but when I picked it up I knew what it was.

I took a deep breath, tore open the leaves and almost began crying tears of joy when I beheld the red corn kernels gleaming in the sun like rows of rubies. I jumped up and down, waving the red corn in my hand. I had no idea that in my fierce determination to shuck the world to pieces, my nose had started to bleed. Not only did I have blood streaming down the lower part of my face, but in my enthusiasm I was splattering it on everyone in my vicinity. The maidens recoiled in horror and fled, screaming. By the time I had wiped my bloody nose and realized what had happened, they had all disappeared, leaving behind overturned baskets of freshly shucked corn and torn popcorn crowns.

It was one of those experiences I was glad Piper did not know about.

We were waiting for the contest to begin when Turtleback came up behind me, slapping me on the shoulder and putting his face in between Piper and me. "Hello, Lark. Hello Sandpiper. Sandpiper, did you know that one year Lark found the red ear of corn and all the girls ran away screaming?" He left, laughing like it was the funniest thing that had ever happened in our village. Sandpiper glanced at me with gentle mockery, as if to say, "Is that so?" I just closed my eyes and shook my head. *Thank you, Turtleback. Thank you, kind friend.*

Finally everything was ready. Stone gave the signal, and the silk started flying. The rule was that the corn had to be shucked completely and put into a maiden's basket before the young man was allowed to open another ear of corn. Newt was moving through the corn quickly, tossing the peeled corn into the baskets behind him and digging through the pile like a fox after a mouse.

Amid the rustling sounds of the tearing husks, families cheered for their favorites and my mother shouted, "Yes, Newt! You can do it, Newt!" into my ear.

The pile started to shrink as the baskets filled with the yellow corn. The boys started to sweat. The ground around their ankles had turned into a small sea of green and white that shuffled when they stepped. Several boys had corn silk floating in their hair.

Suddenly an arm shot up in the air, holding the gleaming red ear of corn, still partly sheathed in husk.

"I found it!" shouted Newt, smiling so big I could see every one of his white teeth. Many cheered and some groaned as Newt stripped off the remaining husk, and the other boys hung their shoulders and kicked at the loose husks on the ground.

The people quieted as Newt took his time, meticulously pulling off the remaining strands of silk. I glanced at Honeybee. She did not seem nervous anymore. She was illuminated.

Newt strutted around the circle of girls, wading through the ankle-deep husks and patting the red ear of corn against the palm of one hand, pretending that he was faced with a difficult decision. Each girl smiled hopefully, biting her lip or batting her eyes as he passed, and I could see why my mother had mentioned that there was some hysteria among the girls when it came to Newt and his dumb smile. He did not stop until he stood in front of Honeybee's basket. She looked up at him, her eyes bright as stars. Everyone hushed. The children stood on tiptoes.

Newt, without looking away from Honeybee's face, took the red corn by the ends and, with a flourish (which I thought was a bit over-dramatic) gently lowered it into Honeybee's basket. Then he leaned over, cupped her chin with one hand, and kissed her.

All the girls swooned, all the people cheered, and I looked away and winced. There are few things as disgusting as seeing your baby sister kissed on the mouth.

Later that evening, refreshed after a long and much deserved after-noon nap, we gathered outside my mother's lodge, reliving the events of the morning and enjoying the spoils of the harvest. Newt had joined us, and as we sat around the fire Honeybee announced that she had "harvest gifts" for us all. She produced a bag, and one by one drew out a bead bracelet for each member of the family, each a different color—mine was yellow. Even Newt was given a bracelet as if he were already part of the family. His was white and we all noticed it matched the bracelet Honeybee slid onto her own wrist. I had to force myself to not smile. Or gag.

Newt stayed with us for a long while, charming his way into the hearts of the female members of my family. Even Sandpiper seemed to fall under his spell.

I was unmoved, however, for I had known Newt since he was two, running around the village naked with a constant flow of opaque nose jellies streaming from his nostrils that dripped onto his potbelly. That image of him in my mind was hard to replace, and even now, whenever anyone said the word "Newt," that is what came to my mind.

So, as Mother and Jade, Honeybee and Sandpiper enjoyed his stories and semi-hilarious humor, I chewed my food, wishing he would disappear so it could just be our family for a while before it was time for Sandpiper and me to head home to the tree house.

Stone sat scowling in the shadows behind us, sharpening a stick with his knife. His half-present presence, looming like a thunderhead on the horizon of our family circle, was disconcerting, for he neither contributed to the conversation nor did he leave, but hovered, vulture-like, on the fringe. His mood was as black as the beads on his new bracelet.

I could not tell if Newt could feel Stone's coldness, even though to me it was as palpable as a fist. Eventually Newt gave a long, artificial-looking yawn and said he better be getting home. He stood, bowed his head regally and said he hoped to bring us honor. All of the women answered back as one, hoping to bring him peace. Stone stood and folded his flexed arms across his chest, clearly hoping to bring the young man something more painful.

The women did nothing to hide their disappointment of Newt's departure, moaning and sighing, and my mother made him linger longer while she packed his arms with bundles of food to bring to his family and insisted that Honeybee walk with him to where the trail began.

All during this tedious, never-ending good-bye Stone hovered around them, taking small, ominous steps toward Newt and still holding the knife and sharpening the stick in a menacing sort of way, as if he would gladly trade his stick for one of Newt's fingers. Finally Honeybee and Newt left the circle of fire, holding hands, leaning into each other, white bracelets touching.

Stone slowly sauntered into the circle around the fire, confiscating Newt's vacant spot. His dark mood was so tangible that by now even my mother could feel it. She looked at him suspiciously as he resumed his stick sharpening.

Jade's face was a story of disapproval, and finally, when the silence was unbearable, she glared at her husband and said, "If you are mad about something you should just say it, instead of making us all suffer."

Stone's brow creased, his frown deepened, and his slashes on the unfortunate stick became even more violent.

The women looked at me, as if I knew what Stone's problem was, but I only shrugged.

After a period of painful silence, there was a rustling in the darkness and Honeybee reappeared, looking as if she were about to burst into song. She sat next to Stone, and comparing the expressions of my two siblings was like comparing a sunflower to a bat.

We all sat silent, in bone-chilling tension, and it was not long before Honeybee could sense something was amiss and her bright smile dimmed. Like everyone else, she looked at me for some explanation for the evening's sudden bite.

My mother tried to change the mood. "Honeybee . . . he is such a nice boy," she said.

Honeybee's smile flickered on and off as she nodded. Her eyes glanced at Stone, finally realizing the direction of the cold wind.

"He is very polite," said my mother.

"He is a good hunter," Jade added.

At that Stone leaped to his feet and chucked his stick into the night with a mighty shout, making us all leap out of our skins. He sat back down, cracking his knuckles.

Cedar glared at him over the fire. "Stone, what is the matter with you?"

"You all act as if she is already going to marry him," he said loudly. Honeybee's face fell. I looked at the ground and I braced myself. I hated confrontation more than I hated anything in the entire world. It did not happen often in my family, but when it did, I pulled my head into my shoulders and tried to become a turtle.

"Well, it *is* a possibility," Mother said in a certain tone of voice we all understood well. A tone of voice I am sure she had not used with Stone since he was seven.

"What if Newt is not as wonderful as everyone thinks he is?"

"Stone, how can you say that?"

"I just think we should be careful. That is all."

"Newt comes from a good family. I've never heard anyone say anything bad about him. And you should not say things either. Especially in front of Honeybee. Look at her! You have ruined her happy day!"

Tears were starting to seep out of Honeybee's pretty eyes. I had to agree that Stone was overreacting.

"It is my duty to protect my family members," said Stone.

"Protect us from *what?*" my mother said, exasperated.

But Stone's jaw clinched shut. Instead of answering her, he turned to me and locked his eyes on mine. *Do not look at me*, I thought. *I am not a part of this.*

But then, as if Stone had tossed me a secret message with only his eyes, a grim possibility suggested itself to my mind. I blinked. I understood. And with that understanding, something hot and black smoldered in the center of my chest and my mild annoyance with Newt turned into wrath. I returned Stone's stare and gave a knowing nod.

"I can see that my opinion about Honeybee's future does not hold much weight," Stone said, breaking our gaze and glaring at the women. He stood. "Come, Jade, we are going home." He started to walk off into the darkness.

Reluctantly, Jade stood and followed him, but not before looking back at my mother and making a gesture that expressed her bafflement at Stone's behavior.

They had almost disappeared into the darkness when Stone turned and pointed at Honeybee, who was now in ruins, and said, "Think twice before you hang your hammock on a rotting tree, Honeybee." And with those parting words he took his wife and disappeared into the dark night.

My mother went to Honeybee, embracing her and wiping her tears. "Do not worry, little one. We all know Stone gets like this when he works too hard. The harvest must be more stressful for him than I had imagined. I am sure that when the time comes and Newt chooses you for a wife, Stone will be just as happy as everyone else."

But I knew better.

SANDPIPER

It has been two weeks since the kissing contest and now, finally, all of the corn has been harvested, and the cotton has been brought in and distributed among the women to be spun, dyed, and woven.

Our world was slowly going dry again, for the afternoon rains became less dependable, and the leaves fluttered from the trees like dying butterflies. The corn stalks were now parched and brittle in the sun's blazing heat. The milpa looked like organized neglect; like neat rows of thin, starving people. Children were free now to run through the rows of corn playing games and chasing each other, a luxury forbidden before. From late afternoon until twilight I could watch them from the window in the tree house. They spent much time in the corn.

The rain basin Lark had made for me stopped collecting water, and for the first time in four months I eventually had to make the walk to the cenote.

The cenote was unchanged since I had been there last, except the grass around it was taller and the trail was not as defined. The bucket still hung from the rope, though the entire scaffold looked weakened and precarious from the months of summer storms. I wondered who was responsible for fixing it.

On the day of the Naming Ceremony, I washed Feather in a basin of crystal clear water while the sunlight streamed through the trees in hazy beams.

Lark told me the Naming Ceremony was for all the children born that year. This was an extra special occasion for Lark's family since the tradition was to have the oldest member of the village bless the newest members of the village. The oldest member this year was Grandmother Vine.

When we arrived, Cedar was busy, like always, making food for everyone, and Jade, Honeybee, and I did our best to keep up with her.

While we worked, the other parents and brothers and sisters and cousins and aunts and uncles gradually arrived, and Lark introduced baby Feather to each of them, making her wave at the other babies ,who, he told me later, were not half as pretty as our Feather. Lark reluctantly let the extended relatives hold the baby, and as they bathed her in kisses and caresses he lingered anxiously, nervous that they might smother, drop, or steal her.

There were four babies born this year, and many families had come to celebrate their birthds together. When Cedar saw how the group continued to grow, she began cutting the limited number of tamales in half. When I caught a glimpse of Stone, I realized how important this ceremony must be, for he was dressed like a chief for the first time, wearing his father's jaguar cape and green-feathered headdress.

I brought platters of food out to serve the guests, and it made me happy to watch Lark, chatty as a parakeet. He had not stopped smiling since we arrived.

When I came back to get more food, Honeybee stopped me. "Have you seen Newt?" she whispered as she pulled the skins from the sweet potatoes and looked out at the crowd under the pavilion.

I shook my head. He probably would not be here—none of the babies being blessed today were in his family.

Honeybee still continued to search the faces. I understood her hope perfectly. I had felt that hope before.

Soon Stone broke away from the crowd and strode over to where we were working. "Mother, it is time to begin. You can finish the rest after the blessings are given."

With a sigh, Cedar pulled herself away from the food, wiping the sweat from her forehead with her arm since her fingers were sticky with sweet potatoes.

"Honeybee," she asked, "could you pour some water on my hands?"

Like a rabbit, Honeybee left her peeling and went to where the gourds sat in the shade by the lodge wall. But when Honeybee picked up a gourd it was empty. The next one was empty too. All four gourds were empty and dry.

"How can this be? I thought we filled all the gourds this morning," Cedar said.

"Do not worry Mother! I will get more water!" said Honeybee.

"No . . . it is all right, Honey, I will just wipe my hands on my apron and toss it aside. It will be fine."

But Honeybee already had two gourds in her hands and was headed toward the trail.

"I will be back soon!" she called over he shoulder.

"You will miss the blessing!" Cedar said.

"No—" she called back earnestly. "I will be fast!"

She bounded down the trail, braids swinging.

Jade leaned into me. "She only wants to get water because she will pass by Newt's hut on the way there and on the way back," she whispered in my ear. "Honeybee gets all the water lately . . . I do not think it was an accident that Cedar ran out." We looked at each other and grinned. I liked Newt, and I liked that Newt liked Honeybee.

Jade and I cleaned our hands the best we could on our aprons. Then we took off our aprons and followed Jade into the happy group of people.

"I want to hold my grandbaby," Cedar said as we approached Lark and he gently placed my daughter in her arms. "Think of it," she said proudly, "four generations of our family are here under this pavilion." She smiled at my baby who looked up at her, wide-eyed and alert. "What a lovely little dimple she has," she said as she touched the cleft in Feather's chin. "No one in our family has ever had a dimple like this. She must get it from your side of the family."

I shrugged and bit my lip.

I felt her eyes analyzing my smooth chin, and I wondered if she suspected anything. Fortunately Lark changed the direction of the conversation.

"It is lucky for us that Grandmother Vine is giving the blessings this year," he said to his mother. This statement immediately caused stress lines to appear on Cedar's forehead.

"Yes," she said. "I just hope she will not say anything . . . inappropriate. Sandpiper," she said, clutching my arm, "please do not think badly of us when my mother blesses your baby with the legs of a roadrunner."

"At least she will not be boring," Stone said, easing into a rare, relaxed smile.

Cedar's forehead remained furrowed and she cast an anxious glance at Grandmother Vine, who was seated under the pavilion in an enormous chair.

The chair was normally used by the chief for official village meetings and events. It was so big it made the old woman look like a hummingbird in an eagle's nest. Earlier Jade had fixed her hair in a silver braid around her head, decorated it with feathers and had fastened a feathered cape around her shoulders. She was wearing her best skirt and a new tunic that Cedar had made especially for the occasion. And even though she could not see anyone or anything, her countenance beamed, knowing that she was the person of honor.

Stone walked to Grandmother Vine and after touching her hand asked her if she was ready. She smiled, her lips curving around her toothless mouth. "I want to bless Lark's little baby first," I heard her say.

Stone nodded. He turned and welcomed everyone. Then he announced, "First, we will have the baby of Lark and Sandpiper."

I reached out to Cedar, ready to take my baby in my arms and bring her to Grandmother Vine, but Cedar held Feather close to her chest.

"We need to wait for Honeybee," she whispered loudly to Stone.

It was true. I did not want Honeybee to miss the blessing either. So instead Stone called a different couple forward and their little baby was placed in Grandmother Vine's arms. The mother of the baby whispered the name in her ear and Grandmother nodded. Everyone listened as Grandmother cleared her throat.

"This baby shall be known to all by the name of . . . Pumpkin." She projected her fragile voice as loudly as she could, but even then, there was a whispering among the people in the back who had to have the name repeated to them.

After a grand pause, waiting for the whispers to die down, she continued. The custom, Lark had told me, was for the blessing giver to bestow gifts upon the child that would help them throughout their life.

"I bless this baby—" She leaned toward the mother. "Is it a boy or a girl?" she asked.

The mother whispered back, and Grandmother Vine continued, "I bless this baby girl that she will live long. I bless her that she will be friendly, that she will not have big feet and that she will make excellent tortillas."

Cedar, who was still holding Feather, took one hand and pressed her fingertips to her forehead and closed her eyes.

The next baby was placed in Grandmother Vine's arms. Like the first, this mother also leaned over and whispered the name in Grandmother Vine's ear. Vine turned her head toward the woman and said in a loud voice, "Are you sure you want to name the baby *that*?"

Annoyed, the mother whispered again.

"Very well," Grandmother conceded. "It is, after all, your child. You are the one who will call him every day." Then to the audience she said, "This baby shall be known to all by the name of Salamander. I bless this baby boy that he will never anger his parents. He will do his work joyfully. Also, he will . . ."

As Grandmother continued, Cedar looked back to the trail. "Where is Honeybee?" she whispered anxiously. Lark and I shook our heads. "I thought she would be back by now. She is going to miss the entire ceremony."

". . . and he will be a very good finder of edible mushrooms." Grandmother finished.

The third child was brought to Grandmother Vine. "This child's name shall be Cottonflower," she said. "She shall always be honest and will weave beautiful cloth. She will always have a pleasant and delightful smell."

"Well," Lark whispered to me, "I think we can safely say that no one has ever received blessings like this before."

The baby was handed back to the mother, and it was Feather's turn.

"Is there any way we can wait?" Cedar asked. "Maybe we could have Feather's blessing later."

Then Jade spoke up. "What about Mosquito?" She said loud enough that everyone turned to look at her. "He has not been given his name."

"He was given his name last year," Stone said. "Was he not?"

"No," Cedar said thoughtfully. "Not in the ceremony, at least. Fern was too sick, and when she died we were worried more about keeping the child alive than naming him."

Jade smiled and pushed through the crowd to Grandmother Vine's chair. With great fanfare she set the toddler on the old woman's lap.

"My, my! This is a big baby!" said the surprised old woman.

"I want you to bless *my* son, Grandmother," Jade said, her head high and proud.

Grandmother recognized Jade's voice and smiled. "Of course, Jade . . . he is one of my favorites." She raised her voice, "This child shall be known to all as Mosquito."

Jade beamed.

"Mosquito shall be blessed with sound judgment, strong muscles, an excellent sense of smell and . . . a great fear of deep water." Out of the corner of my eye I saw Stone's mouth curve in a smile.

Jade picked up Mosquito, placed him on her hip, and kissed him.

"Mother, it is Feather's turn, now," said Stone. "We cannot wait any longer."

Cedar looked back at the trail once more before sighing and reluctantly placing Feather in my arms.

Holding my precious baby, I followed Lark through the crowd to Grandmother Vine's throne. Lark put his hand on Grandmother's shoulder and whispered, "Grandmother, it is us."

She nodded and smiled. "Oh, Lark, you dear boy. Of course it is you," she said. "Where is your lovely baby?"

I gently lowered Feather into her frail arms. Suddenly I became very nervous, for a thought had occurred to me. What if Grandmother Vine could somehow tell that Feather was not Lark's baby? Perhaps her blindness could give her some magic sense and she gave my baby some terrible curse or mentioned something out loud in front of all these people? I had a sudden desire to take the baby back, but Grandmother had already begun.

"This baby shall be known to all as Feather." Her voice was gentle and soft, as if she understood my daughter's temperament perfectly. My fears subsided, and I waited eagerly for what she would say.

"I bless this sweet baby—" But she stopped and her expression changed. Her face was alert and her mouth hung open. "Listen," she said. "I hear . . . Honeybee . . ."

At first I could hear nothing. But then we heard it, a wailing sound that pricked the hairs on my arms. Everyone under the pavilion looked around, trying to determine where the sound was coming from. It was long and mournful; the kind of sound that makes one feel black inside.

The moaning became louder and soon Honeybee emerged, walking toward the pavilion slowly and dragging her feet as if she were walking through deep sand. The gourds she had taken were nowhere to be seen.

Cedar was at her side in a moment, and as soon as Honeybee felt her mother's arms she folded to the ground.

No one said anything; no one could do anything but watch Honeybee's stricken face and tear-stained cheeks. "Newt," she said in between her loud sobs and gasps for air, "is in the cenote."

Instantly Stone bolted from the pavilion, sprinting down the trail so fast that dust flew from his feet and his green headdress fell to the ground. In his wake, the gasps and murmurs of the shocked villagers spread through the pavilion, followed by weeping and moaning, creating a chaotic din that muffled even Honeybee's sobs.

The sounds of suffering that filled the air made me instinctively turn toward my baby. But when I started to reach for her, Grandmother Vine was already cradling Feather protectively against her chest. With a quiet, steady voice, meant only for my baby to hear, she whispered her matriarchal blessing, "My dear child. I bless you to be a rope. A rope that will bind your family together so tightly that there will not be room enough for the beasts."

THE DRY SEASON

SANDPIPER

Newt's death cast a gloom over the village that lasted for many days. The women wept and the men brooded, though nothing was ever said out loud. It was maddening.

It was Cedar who suggested the hunting trip. She told Stone it would do all the men good to get away and change their routine. Stone, who had hardly eaten or spoken to anyone since Newt's death, was visibly relieved at the proposal. Everyone in the village soon embraced the idea of an excursion, for the men needed a release from village tension, and the women needed a release from the men.

I did not realize that Cedar had a hidden motive.

After a busy morning of preparation, they loaded their backs with weapons and provisions and vanished into the trees. Not long after they left, Cedar announced that there would be a meeting for all the women that afternoon at her lodge. A secret meeting.

I arrived early and heard voices from inside.

"I hope you are sure about this." It was the voice of Grandmother Vine. She sounded grim.

"I am sure," I heard Cedar say. "We have a crisis in our village, Mother, and sometimes a crisis cannot be solved until a woman steps in. Besides, if they can hold secret meetings, so can we."

The men had secret meetings? I knew I should not be listening to this conversation and I thought perhaps I should clear my throat and walk in. Or leave and come back in a while. But instead I leaned closer to the window.

"I think some things are better left unknown," Grandmother Vine muttered.

"Is it not our duty as wives and mothers to save our men?"

"I think the men are already doing their best to save themselves. I think it is better if we stay out of it."

"Mother, you surprise me. You are the one who always says we should say what we think and be more honest with ourselves and with others. This needs to be brought out into the open and discussed. You seem content to sit and keep watching our men drown themselves, but I am not."

"Humph. Cedar, if you do not like talking about tossing tassels in public, you are not going to want to talk about the cenote."

"What does tossing tassels have to do with the cenote?" Cedar asked.

"Maybe something. Maybe nothing. Maybe everything. Maybe we should ask Sandpiper."

"Ask Sandpiper?" said Cedar. "What are you talking about?"

How Grandmother Vine knew I was listening I will never know. I walked in, guilty.

"Oh, it is just you," said Cedar. "It does not matter what Sandpiper hears. She will not be telling anybody. Come help me clear some space for everyone to sit," she told me. "We have to squeeze a lot of women in this room."

I hope to bring you peace," Cedar said to each woman as she entered the lodge. "Thank you for coming." The women stepped around each other to find places to sit. We were knee-to-knee and hip-to-hip on the soft fur-lined floor. Cedar sent Honeybee to tend the children outside. I was glad, since her emotions were still fragile.

"Does everyone have a place to sit?" Cedar asked. I could feel her nervousness. I took a seat in the back corner of the lodge so I could observe.

"Why have you called us here?" asked Root. "Is it something important?"

Cedar was about to answer, but more women entered and the others had to scoot and squeeze, to adjust for the new bodies.

Finally things began to settle down. Gradually, each woman pulled out something to busy her hands; some began making lace for slips, some brought their mending, some nursed babies. Others brought pieces of clothing to embroider. I brought nothing since my hands were full with Feather. One woman, who was mending a torn tunic muttered, "How long will this take, anyway? I have work to do."

"Does this have to do with the festival next week?" asked someone else.

"No," Cedar said, finally securing the door. Taking a deep breath she turned and faced us. "I wanted to talk to you about . . . the cenote."

The busy hands paused, and every face looked up with guarded interest. A cautious voice asked, "Are we allowed to talk about the cenote?"

"Why not?" Cedar said, lifting her chin. "I think it is about time we discussed it freely." The women looked at each other with expressions of uncertainty. Then there was a moan.

"How could you bring up this awful subject when it is has only been a week since the death of my poor, sweet Newt?" The lament came from Newt's mother, a large, layered woman named Cabbage. "It is hateful that you want to talk about it. "

Cedar did not flinch. "I understand your feelings, but your son is precisely why I am bringing this up. He was special to our family as well. I cannot simply sit and do nothing as more of our sons and husbands are lost. Together maybe we can figure out what is happening to our men. There must be a reason. And if we can find out, then maybe we can stop it from happening again."

Nodding mournfully, Cabbage wiped her tears and blew her nose. The rest of us were silent, and no one offered any ideas. Some even picked up their needlework again. A baby began to whimper and was quickly offered a breast.

"Someone must know something . . . or at least have a suspicion," Cedar prodded. "Have you asked your husbands about it? Do they ever talk about it?"

A fly buzzed around the room while we waited for an answer. I knew everyone hoped for someone else to be the first to speak. At least no one expected me to say anything. Cedar glanced at Jade encouragingly, hoping she could at least say something to get the women talking. I wondered if Jade was remembering the pictures we found in the jungle, but she gave nothing away and her eyes stayed on her embroidery.

Finally a woman said, "My husband tells me it is harmless." She put down her lace and looked up. "But I do not believe him for a moment. I know there is something evil about that water."

Several women nodded their heads and grunted in agreement. "My husband gave me the same answer, and he was annoyed with me for asking about it."

"I think we all agree that there is something . . . " Cedar searched for the right word, ". . . *unnatural* about the cenote. But what is it?"

Except for a sneeze, and a few more flamboyant sniffs from Cabbage, it was silent. Someone yawned. I was beginning to think Cedar's plan would fail.

"How are we supposed to know anything when the men do not even talk to each other about it?" volunteered another woman. "I overheard my husband speaking with another man in the village. My husband said something about the cenote. The other man . . ." she paused, as if trying to decide whether or not to mention a name, ". . . told him that he should not speak of the cenote. He said something about a legend."

"A legend?" Cedar said hopefully. "Has anyone else heard them mention a legend?"

Everyone seemed mystified.

"I do not know anything about a legend," said one woman, "but I have always wondered what happens to the brains of the men who fall into the cenote. Have you ever looked closely at their heads? Inside it looks as empty as a calabash. It is as if their brains have been sucked out."

"It is from the vultures," someone said. "Everyone knows that."

"I did not think vultures could suck," said another.

"If you want to know what I think," ventured a woman named Rabbitfoot, "I think there are creatures in the water." Her comment drew chuckles from the others.

"Creatures?" Cedar asked dubiously.

"Yes, in the water. They live down there and they summon the men so that they can eat their brains."

There was more soft laughter, but Cedar did not dismiss her comment. "Anything is worth considering," she said.

"I do not think there are creatures," said another woman, "I think the men know exactly what they are doing. There is something in there that they want and they are trying to get it. Why else would they be so secretive?"

By now it was very hot in the lodge and many of the women glistened with perspiration. Some started to fan themselves. Some began flapping their blouses to circulate the air. Others shifted in their places or scratched insect bites.

"I know . . . that they can hear things," said Root, Turtleback's wife. Several other voices sounded in agreement.

"Yes, but do you know what they hear?" Cedar asked.

Root shifted uncomfortably and looked down at her hands. "I cannot say."

"Why can you not say?" Cedar pressed. "Do you know something that we do not?"

The woman's mouth closed and she continued to stare at her hands.

Cedar tried again, tempering her voice this time. "Root, this is important. Our men's lives depend on this. Please—tell us what you think they hear."

"I . . . I . . . cannot say," she said, and her chin quivered. "I have already said too much. I am sorry. It is so hot in here. I must leave." She stood, and the other women, surprised at her sudden showing of emotion, made a path for her. As she opened the door, I saw tears in her eyes.

We all listened to her footsteps fade away into the night. Cedar gently closed the door, and we all turned our bewildered faces toward each other. Root's reaction left us all puzzled. Why would she not tell us what she knew?

"I will speak to her on my own," Cedar reassured the many concerned faces. "Then perhaps she will tell me."

"She will not tell you," said a voice from behind Cedar. We

all looked to see Grandmother Vine's marbled eyes gazing at her daughter.

"I think she will when she realizes how important this is," Cedar insisted.

"She will not, Cedar."

"How do you know?"

"Because, Cedar," the old woman said solemnly, "she is ashamed."

"Ashamed? Why would she be ashamed?"

Grandmother Vine drew her lips in tightly and she looked as if she were deciding something. Then she slowly shook her head from side to side, hopelessly. "You are so close to understanding, and yet so far."

We all looked from Cedar to Grandmother Vine, suddenly feeling like eavesdroppers on a private conversation.

"Perhaps it is time you knew," she said, sighing heavily. "It would be a weight off my back, anyway, if I told you."

"Mother, what are you talking about?"

"Cedar, I still think it is going to do more harm than good, but I can see that you are determined to find out. Better that your innocence is crushed by me, I suppose, than one of the men. Of course this means I will have to tell you the legend, too, or you will think I am crazy."

"The legend? You know *the legend*?" Cedar exclaimed.

"The amount of things I know that you do not think I know would surprise you," she said, smiling wryly. "Now sit down and stop talking."

"But, Mother—"

"Cedar, sit."

We were astonished. No one ever spoke to Cedar that way. Yet Cedar remained standing and folded her arms.

"Very well," said Grandmother, sensing Cedar's disobedience. "Stand if you wish, just keep your mouth closed." She turned her head toward us. "Root left this hut because she is ashamed that her husband has secret desires."

"Secret . . . desires?" Jade choked, fanning her neck.

"Yes. Secret. Forbidden. Think about it. They are not going for a swim. They are not committing suicide. You all know that. They are

146

being seduced. They hear voices, Cedar. They hear the voices of beautiful women."

Jade and I glanced at each other, remembering the paintings.

"They . . . hear . . . what?" Cedar asked.

"They hear the voices of women, coming from inside the water of
the cenote. I know," she said, "because I hear them too."

Cedar finally sank to the floor and stared at her mother, dazed.

"Please . . . feel free to elaborate, Vine," said someone.

"One night, long ago, when I was a young girl, I overheard my
father tell my brother a strange legend . . . a legend that gave me night-
mares for many months." She lifted her face and surveyed the room as
if she were trying to look into our eyes. "I can tell you the legend, but
when I am finished you may wish you had never heard it. Are you sure
you want to continue?"

The room was silent. No one breathed. Hands were still. The nursing babies were either asleep or their mothers had smothered them with
their breasts.

"This was what you wanted, was it not? To discover the truth?"
Grandmother Vine said.

"I want to know," Cedar said.

"So do I," murmured other voices.

"Very well," Grandmother said. "I have always agreed with the
men of our village that this is something you are better off not knowing anything about. But the grief that the cenote has caused us for
so long, and the stubbornness of my daughter, makes me think that
perhaps it is time to tell you what I know. But I would warn you: if
you do not want to know of these horrors, I would advise you to leave
now."

A few women shifted uncomfortably, but no one budged.

"Are you certain?" she said, "This is your chance."

Everyone stayed where they were, their eyes fixed on the old
woman's face.

"Very well."

Each woman in the room took a deep breath and exhaled very
slowly. There was a strange feeling in the room at that moment, like

when one's hair stands on end before lightning strikes. We knew we were on the verge of a great and terrible revelation.

"You all are aware that long ago this mound was once a temple surrounded by a large city. We know that the Ancient Ones who lived here believed in many gods; gods of the sky and of the earth and of the animals and of the underworld.

"It was the peak of the dry season, so the story goes, when the strange women entered the city. They were beautiful women with large, deep eyes and skin as pale as bone. No one knew where they came from, for they just seemed to walk out of the jungle, without any origin or tribe or history.

"Everything about them was alluring, from the grace of their step to the arch of their brow, to the way they rested their cheek on their hand when they acted tired. They were charming and intelligent, and they dressed in fabrics the people had never before seen. Most of all, their musical voices were so lovely that one could listen to them speak and laugh and sing and never tire of the sounds that came from their velvet lips.

"Their arrival created a stir in the city, for everyone wanted to see them, to meet them, to talk with them. They were accepted quickly into the social circles, and the people called them 'the gossamer maidens' because of the sheer, iridescent fabrics they wore and their smooth black hair that was as fine as spider silk. From every corner of the city, the admiration of the gossamer maidens quickly turned to worship.

"An exquisite salon with its own courtyard was built especially for them and was furnished with tapestries and furniture so that the gossamer maidens could be comfortable and the people could sit around them on pillows and listen to them sing. Men and women alike, from every class of society, would bring them gifts of gold and jade and cups filled with melted chocolate.

"The maidens seemed indifferent to these gifts, however, and they never, it seemed, had the desire or need to eat. They also would never allow anyone to touch them, for, they said, they would lose their virtue, which made them all the more desirable.

"The maidens took a singular interest in the men, ignoring the city women who eagerly spent so much time and money imitating their dress and mannerisms. Coyly, the maidens begged and pleaded with the men to linger longer in their sumptuous sanctuary, and the men did, neglecting the other duties to which they were responsible.

"The disappearances were imperceptible at first. Hardly anyone noticed that the quiet, blind beggar who sat at the temple was absent from his corner. No one stopped to wonder why the man who always drank himself into a stupor disappeared. But slowly, one by one, husbands did not return from the quarries or the fields, and the fathers of small children vanished.

"Then, one morning before dawn, a hunter—who was never known to lie—came running into the city, waking people with news of a grizzly discovery. He had heard the maidens singing in the forest. Curious, he followed the music. He never found the maidens. Instead he found a cache of decaying bodies. He testified that the bodies were those of the missing men.

"The people laughed at him. They refused to believe that the delicate gossamer maidens had anything to do with the disappearances. They are harmless, they told him. They are here for us to enjoy and to give us pleasure. They took him to the maidens, thinking that he would never accuse them in public, but they were wrong, for he pointed at them with a trembling finger, telling everyone that they they were not women. They were beasts.

"The maidens, surrounded by their admirers, shook their heads as tears fell from their thickly-lashed eyes. How could this man say such hurtful things?

"Many people, touched by the sadness that shadowed the maidens' lovely faces, rushed to their defense. They told the man he was a coward for hurting their feelings. They told him he must apologize for his insulting accusations.

"But the three maidens shook their heads. Let him be, they told the people. For how was he to understand? He does not need to apologize. Perhaps all he needed was a little persuasion. And with that one of the maidens rose from her silken pillows and sauntered towards her accuser, humming.

"The other two joined her in a lilting harmony. The frightened man took a step back and paused. Smiling, the maiden beckoned to him, holding out her arms. Mesmerized, the people watched as the man, who only moment ago had called them beasts, walked willingly into her arms. The maiden embraced him, put her hands on his face, and kissed him.

"The man immediately relaxed. His arms came around her. His eyes closed. And then something strange began to happen. There was an unnatural tremble to his cheeks. His forehead rippled as if there was something crawling under his skin. His arms went limp, then his legs, and soon the people realized that the only thing that was keeping him standing upright was the maiden's ever-tightening grip on his head. When the maiden finally pulled away, she opened her eyes. Her lips, now wet, curved in a satisfied smile. Gently, she blew into the man's face and his eyelids fluttered open. But instead of eyes there was nothing but black holes. With unnatural strength, she threw his body aside, and when his head hit the ground it shattered like a clay pot. The people stared at the pieces of his skull in fascinated horror. There was nothing left inside his head. Everything had been sucked out.

"The maiden wiped her lips.

"Witnesses fled. They dispersed through the city, telling the tale to everyone they could find. Angry people came flocking to the place where the three maidens were and demanded that they leave. But the maidens with their satin smiles told the people that they were glad that the people of the city now knew of their insatiable craving, for they were always so hungry, and it was so very hard to go so long without nourishment. They asked if there were any other men who wanted to feel the softness of their lips.

"The maidens' calm and tender entreaties were like nothing the people had heard or felt, and their dark innocent eyes and pleading expressions melted the hearts of the people so that the initial feelings of disgust and revulsion changed to a perverted compassion. Instead of realizing that these women were creatures with no souls, many instead felt it impossible to think such lovely beings could be evil. That which would have normally been detestable became pitied. Beauty has a strange way of blinding people to the truth, and the people clung to their innocence like butterflies cling to carrion.

"Over the course of the next few days, some men avoided the maidens, but many others, tantalized with the thought of being caressed by their soft fingers, walked eagerly into their arms. What was certain was that any man who walked into their embrace never walked back out.

"Not everyone was overwhelmed by their charms, of course. Many could see them for what they were. When word reached the temple priests of what was happening, they ordered the maidens to leave the city.

"But the maidens refused, saying that they loved the city and its people, and they never wanted to leave. The priests and those who were not beguiled by the maiden's persuasive voices tried to force them out, but others stood in their way, telling them that it was not the maidens' fault, being the way they were, and that they should be protected.

"The priests would have none of this. They captured the maidens, and they killed them easily with spears.

"The people, as they observed the dead bodies of the three maidens were split on their emotions. Some wept over them, laying flowers on their corpses. Others spat on them and clung to their husbands, feeling an overwhelming relief that the beasts were gone. That night, the bodies were burned, and for the first time in many days, the city slept without fear.

"But the peace was brief. A few days later, the maidens again emerged from the forest, blinking like newly born fawns, only now there were *six*.

"The people were astonished. From the sound of their honeyed voices, they knew these women were the same species as the last. Immediately, the priests and those who would help them did what they could to kill the maidens. The delicate maidens offered no resistance, and destroying them was as easy as crushing a flower. The priests pushed aside the people who had fallen under the spell of their beauty; people who knelt between them and the priests' blades, offering their own lives to spare the monsters.

"But for every maiden that was killed, the next morning two more would take her place. The beasts were no longer discreet about when and where they embraced their victims. Sometimes several would overwhelm a single man at once, right in the middle of the street, leaving his hollow head gaping with holes.

"The priests did not know what to do. How could they rid themselves of these creatures before they killed every man in the city?

"Truly, these women were not human. They did not belong to this world but to the underworld. And if they belonged to the underworld, the priests proclaimed, they must be sent back.

"The next day the priests, armed with incense and holy amulets, surrounded the beasts, and drove them toward the crystal-clear cenote, believing it was an entrance to the underworld. They pushed them over the edge by the dozens until every last one sank beneath the water. Then they watched and waited.

"The creatures never resurfaced, and in the weeks and months that followed that horrific time, the women of the city seemed content that the beasts had been destroyed. But they had no idea that it was not over for the men. For them, the maiden's voices floated out of the cenote with alarming clarity. They kept this information secret, to avoid disturbing the peace of their wives and children.

"In the end, it did not matter, for after that the city started its descent into ruin. People refused to drink from the cenote, for it had become clouded and filthy. Yet men still came to circle the cenote and listen to the voices calling out to them. Sometimes they jumped in. People left the city by the hundreds, seeking a new place to live. Our ancestors were the few who remained, finding a way to survive by filtering the water of the cenote and by passing this secret story—as a warning—from father to son."

SANDPIPER

After she finished, we sat in silence. We were like blinking statues; the knitting and embroidery were relics of the past, part of another era. I heard someone swallow. Jade's eyes were so big and round I could see the white border around each dark iris.

"I told you they were creatures," whispered Rabbitfoot to no one in particular.

Grandmother Vine continued. "I used to think this was just a legend, until I became old and started to lose the power of my eyes. As my ears became more sensitive, I began hearing strange sounds. Sometimes like singing. At first I thought it was some of you, singing while you did your work. But the singing was so much more . . . captivating."

"What . . . are they saying? What are they singing about?" Cedar asked.

"They sing about their own beauty. They sing about being lonely and finding someone strong who will seek them out, comfort them, and hold them. Every now and then, they whisper how hungry they are."

"That is revolting," whispered Jade.

"Not to the men," said Grandmother Vine. "It pleases them to be desirable to them."

"Do the men have control over whether or not they hear the voices?"

"Hearing the voices? It is unlikely. But following the voices, yes. I do believe they have the power to choose whether or not they heed the voices . . . at least for a time. When they have gone to the cenote for too long, it becomes overwhelming and they eventually succumb."

Then Cabbage stood. "This is all a lie," she said fiercely. "I am disgusted that you believe this old woman and her morbid stories. Newt would never do something like this. He would never betray my family or this village. You are spreading lies, Cedar. You planned this whole meeting just so that you and your mother could frighten us. I will not sit here and listen to this."

Cedar quickly rose to her feet. "Please do not leave. What if it is true? I know it is too late to save your son, but think about the life of your husband."

Cabbage swelled. "How dare you, Cedar. Are you implying that my husband is involved in this? That he is being seduced by imaginary women? Are you saying that he would follow them and die rather than live with *me*?"

Out of respect for her feelings, no one answered her question.

"You are just feeding off each other's fears. The only thing we really need to worry about is if the cenote dries up. Then where would we be? And you should not believe one word of what old Vine says. She says strange things all the time. You remember the baby blessings? Her head is full of cornmeal."

Cabbage had gone too far. Cedar's chin came up and her eyes sparked. "If you are going to speak like that to the oldest and wisest woman in this village, then you may leave this lodge. Now."

The woman's face flushed purple with anger. Muttering under her breath, she made her way to the door, stepping on hands and knocking women over as she went. Cedar closed the door after her. Calmly, she turned and faced the women.

"Does anyone else believe my mother is lying?" she stated, her nostrils flared. "Because you are free to leave as well."

"There, there, Cedar," said Grandmother Vine with a smile, patting Cedar's hand. "No one should be forced to believe me. I wonder if I believe myself sometimes. . . . It is a very strange tale."

"Grandmother Vine," said Jade. "These women . . . do these women ever leave the cenote?"

"And do they have bodies?"

"Can they be touched?"

Vine shook her head. "I wish I knew the answers to your questions. I have often hoped their voices are more like listening to the ocean inside of a seashell . . . just echoes of something that is no longer there. I have hoped that when the priests pushed them into the cenote, they did die, and the sounds are only the remnants of their spirits."

"So they do not exist? Do the men understand that? That they do not exist?"

"No, they *do* exist. Vine did not say she was certain . . ."

"Does it matter? As long as the men think they exist, we have a problem."

At this the women began talking among themselves and Cedar leaned over to her mother.

"Why have you never told me about this before, Mother?" she whispered.

The old woman smiled. "It is never very wise to tell people you are hearing voices."

"You could have at least told me about the legend."

"And how would that have helped? What would you have done about it?"

"I . . . do not know," Cedar stammered.

"Worry. That is what you would have done. Now all these women are as frightened as rabbits. They will resort to desperate methods to keep the attentions of their husbands. Honorable men who have done their best to stay away from the cenote will be doubted. The women will be so obsessed with the voices that they will forget about the real needs of the men. You mark my words, Cedar. We have kicked the hornets' nest."

"But now that we know, there must be something we can do about it," someone said.

"Perhaps if we give it something. Like an offering to appease the maidens."

"We cannot give them something if they do not really exist."

"What if there was a way to fill up the cenote with earth?"

"Or drain it? Then we would know if they exist or not."

"And take away the only source of water we have during the dry season?"

"Perhaps the men who listen to the cenote should be marked with a sign of dishonor. We should put up their names on a sign so everyone knows who they are."

"We cannot do that. It would also bring shame to his wife. If my husband were lurking around the cenote, I would want to keep it a secret too."

The women all began to speak at once. The room filled with chatter until a loud voice spoke up.

"We could always leave."

The talking quickly died and for a few thoughts the women were silent.

After a while someone asked, "But . . . would we be able to persuade the men come with us?"

"Who needs the men? I say we tell them that it is either us or the cenote. If they decide to stay here and listen to the voices and drown themselves, so be it."

There was silence again. I knew we were all wondering if they might choose the cenote over us.

"I will not leave," said someone.

"And I will not leave without my husband," said Jade.

"No," Cedar sighed. "We cannot leave. This is our home. Our ancestors lived here. We have spent years clearing and cultivating the land for planting. We understand this place and it is part of us. We cannot leave."

"Then you will have to find a way to live with the voices," Grandmother Vine said sadly, "for I doubt they can be silenced."

SANDPIPER

"Well, this changes *everything*," Jade said the next day as we made baskets together, waiting for the men to return from their hunt. "Nod your head if you agree with me."

I nodded. Yes, this did change everything.

"Before Vine's delightful story, I actually felt sorry for Newt in his family, but not any more. That boy was exceedingly fortunate that I did not know his secret before he died, because if I had, I would have killed him with my bare hands. How dare he do this to someone as gentle and loving as Honeybee? How could he make her believe he was in love with her—make our whole family believe he was in love with her—and then give himself up to those—those—creatures? Any sadness or pity I felt for him when he drowned has died. What scum. What a liar. What a low, muddy, filthy, slimy worm. He was hardly worthy to be loathed. Nod your head if you agree with me."

I nodded. Vigorously.

"I do not think I will ever be able to make eye contact with any man again. Dishonest, disloyal, dis*gusting*. And where does this put us? What are we supposed to do about it? Thinking about it makes me ill. Of course, it is obvious that Stone is tempted by the voices. After all, he is a hunter! It is in his blood to pursue that which is difficult to obtain. And since he is always out in the forest, "hunting," it is a miracle that he comes home at all! Think about it, Sandpiper. Could there be a more virile man in existence? Nod your head if you agree with me!"

I paused, not sure if I should.

"Yes, he is! He is practically a beast himself! A beast that I love! Oh, Sandpiper, what will we do?"

157

I did not know. After the meeting, I did not even know if I could see Lark in the same way I did before. Did he hear the voices too? Perhaps. Somehow I just could not picture him being persuaded by anyone or anything . . . but me. I was certain his devotion to me was absolute. If there was a problem with our marriage it was on my end, not his. I believed that, for the most part, all the men in the village loved their wives and that they seemed to be doing everything in their power to stay away from the cenote.

Jade cried into her hands, and I put my arms around her, yearning to tell her my thoughts. *They are only voices*, I wanted to say. *We are women of flesh and blood. Surely that gives us an advantage.*

Later that day, I put Feather in the sling and accompanied Jade to fetch water from the cenote. While I pulled up the buckets Jade stood on the edge, holding Mosquito's hand and staring fiercely into the dark water, as if daring something to appear. When the gourds were full, I stood next to her. She hushed Mosquito and together we listened. There was a soft breeze, and the leaves on the banyan rustled. I heard bees and the shrill call of a bird, but other than that, I did not hear a thing.

I touched Jade's sleeve, indicating that we should go, but her lips were pinched together and her eyes were still narrowed and fixed on the water below. Before she turned to leave she leaned over the edge and shouted, "There are no secrets anymore!" Her voice bounced off the walls and echoed back at us. "We know you are down there!"

LARK

Something strange has happened to our women.

I first noticed it when we had dinner at my mother's lodge the night we arrived home from the hunting trip. It was a pleasant evening, and we sat around the fire roasting meat and vegetables on sticks and popping corn while watching the sky go from bluish to reddish to purplish to black. Stone retired to his hut early, Grandmother Vine was dozing in her hammock, and I sat outside with Jade, Piper, Honeybee, and my mother.

At first the conversation was normal enough. They asked me about my snares, and I told them some stories from the hunt, thinking I could make them laugh and shake off their unusually serious expressions. They listened politely but they seemed preoccupied.

At one point in my story, I paused because I could hear the croaking of a bird in the forest. I thought perhaps it was a toucan. Stone once said my nose resembled that of a toucan, which gave me certain kinship toward the bird, so I twisted my body in the direction of the sound to see if it really was, indeed a toucan.

I saw nothing but dark forest. When I turned back to face the fire I was surprised to see all three woman leaning forward, their eyes wide and bright, watching me with great interest.

Perhaps my story was more exciting than I had thought, and they were eagerly awaiting the conclusion, so I continued. When I did they relaxed and began eating their food again, but they chewed more slowly now, and kept glancing past me, into the jungle, toward the direction I had heard the toucan.

The bird croaked again, and again I turned to look for it. When I looked back the women had all stopped chewing and were watching me, just as before, as if I was about to say or do something that would endanger all of our lives. I said the only thing that came to my mind.

"Booga-booga-booga!" I shouted.

They all jumped. My mother yelped. "*Lark*," she scolded sharply.

"I was just wondering why you are all looking at me like that," I said, smiling.

They glanced at each other, their faces tense.

"It is . . . nothing," my mother said. She looked at her food as if she were being forced to eat someone's toes.

"It just seemed like . . . you were acting as if you heard something," said Jade.

"I did," I answered.

All heads came up again. Piper dropped her food in the dirt.

"What did you hear?" asked my mother anxiously.

"I heard a toucan. Surely you all heard it?"

"A toucan?" said my mother.

"Yes," I said.

"Just a toucan?"

"Uh-huh."

"Are you *sure* it was a toucan?" said Jade.

I nodded and filled my mouth full of food. "Pretty sure."

"What did the toucan sound like?"

I swallowed and thought for a moment. Then I opened my mouth. "Craaaooook . . . craaaaooook . . ." I cawed, mimicking the sound as best I could. I added a couple arm-flaps, to help them catch the vision. By the time I finished, I felt my toucan brothers would be proud.

But the women were not impressed. I could not even raise a corner of their serious, tightly drawn lips. They studied me in silence, their eyes penetrating my soul.

"Are you sure you did not hear anything else?" said my mother.

I squirmed under their heat of her stare. "Uh . . . insects?" I said, groping for the right answer.

"Hm" was the collective reply. They slowly nibbled at their food. It became very quiet. Only the forest was still alive with sound.

Suddenly Jade asked, "Could you tell if the toucan was female?"

Mother glared at Jade. Jade looked back at her with raised eyebrows and a shrug. Honeybee burst into tears and ran into the house. I looked to my wife for some explanation, but she was the most mysterious of all, just watching me with her big dark, doe eyes.

I heard the toucan again but dared not to say anything about it or look in its direction, fearing that I might make someone else cry. Perhaps there was something troubling about toucans that I was not aware of.

"Wait—wait—I think I hear it," my mother said, craning her neck like a goose. "Listen."

The bird called again.

"There. Did you hear it?"

I nodded cautiously, but she was not asking me. She was asking the other two.

"I did!" said Jade, triumphant.

"Did you?" she asked Piper, as if our lives depended whether or not Piper had heard it.

Fortunately for us all, Piper nodded.

They began eating again, and my mother heaved a long sigh.

Things were still odd the next day when I passed through the village. Gone were the traditional white slips that our women wore. Instead, they had ripped the seams in their skirts so that I could glimpse their bare legs as they walked. Some had designs painted on their faces and arms. Instead of the long braids our women usually wore, their hair was all bunched up on top of their heads, tied with colorful strings and feathers. Some of them had even pierced their ears. We men discussed these changes furtively amongst ourselves, joking that the woman looked as if they were preparing for war.

The only one who seemed unchanged was my sweet Piper. I shared with her my observations and asked if she knew anything about their strange behavior. She just sighed and shook her head.

SANDPIPER

The week after the hunt, there was wedding for a young girl called Chrysanthemum to the young man called Red Owl. We women came together for the first time since the secret meeting to give her gifts and advice, just as they did for me when I was married. I marveled at how the advice had altered.

"Always make sure you look attractive for your husband."

"Do your hair neatly every day."

"Do not let yourself get too skinny."

"Do not let yourself get too fat."

"Pinch your cheeks and bite your lip before he comes home every day so that you look fresh and appealing."

"Speak with a voice that is soft and smooth, never raise your voice at him."

"If you cannot sing, do not try."

Even when Grandmother Vine gave her advice about tossing tassels, Cedar did not protest. The old woman did not, however, reveal to us what the most important body part was, though I was still not sure I wanted to know.

The last piece of advice Chrysanthemum received was from a bold woman who made even me feel queasy when she hissed, "Just remember, if your husband falls into the cenote, it is your *own fault*."

LARK

I discovered, to my dismay, that a large animal had destroyed one of my best snares. I gathered the bundle of sticks and twisted rope and brought it back to my yard to see if I could fix the damage or if I would have to make a new one. Sandpiper and Feather left earlier that morning to gather berries, so I was alone.

Or so I thought.

As I began untangling the twine from the sticks I remembered the scaffold by the cenote. It was in urgent need of repair. In my mind I made a list of the supplies that I would need to strengthen the structure.

Then, without any warning, a figure came swooping out of nowhere and sat next to me, nearly scaring every hair off my head. The creature had bright red lips and blue eyelids. Her hair towered on her head, and she had a belt cinched so tight it almost cut her in half. The hem of her skirt shortened when she sat and I could see the tops of her knees.

It was Jade.

"Lark," she said, breathlessly. "Do you think I am pretty?"

"I—ah—well—"

"Well, do you?" repeated the red lips.

"I—I do not know," I stammered.

"What do you mean you do not know? You can see, can you not?"

I surveyed her anxious expression, the gaudy face paint and her wide eyes and said the only thing I could.

"Of course you are pretty. But—I—I thought you knew that already."

"*I* know I am pretty. I want to know if *you* do."

"Me? Me in particular?" I said, inching away from my sister-in-law.

"No, you in general. I mean men in general. The men in the village. I want to know what the men in this village really desire. What is it that attracts a man to a woman?"

"Well . . ." I began, trying to think of something safe. "It helps if she is nice."

"No, no, no . . . that is not what I mean. I mean in the way she looks."

"Hmmm . . . I like women who smile a lot. I am not so keen on women who eat with their mouth full, and head lice is always a turn-off."

"Ugh, I am getting nowhere with you," she said, throwing her hands up in exasperation.

"Why do you not ask Stone if he thinks you are pretty?"

"I did," she said, looking down.

"And?"

"He said, 'what happened to your lips? You look like you got hit in the face with a tree branch.'" She sniffed and wiped a tear from her eye, making a big smear across her cheek.

I put my snare on the ground and faced her. "What is this really about, Jade?"

Her expression became desperate. "How can I make Stone like me more?"

"What are you saying? Stone loves you. You do not need all of this paint for him to like you more. He thinks you are the most beautiful woman that ever breathed air."

"That ever breathed air? Verses a woman who breathes, I do not know, maybe water?"

My eyes narrowed. "What do you mean by that, exactly?"

"Oh, nothing, nothing. Do you really think he thinks I am beautiful?" Her voice was filled with doubt.

"I know it. He worships you."

"Then why does he not tell me? I cannot remember one time our entire marriage that he has said anything about my hair or my clothes. The only time he ever tells me he thinks I am pretty is when I am wearing absolutely nothing."

I could not stop myself. I laughed out loud.

"This is not funny," she pouted.

"Believe me, Jade, he thinks you are beautiful. But it is not always about how you look. Sandpiper loves me, and my shirt is not exactly ripping open with muscles."

"What does it have to do with?"

"I do not know exactly. It has a lot to do with how you feel about yourself. I do not think beauty is something you can put on and take off. It is always with you. It is displayed by the way you act and speak. Any woman who feels good about herself is a beautiful woman. And for a man, feeling needed, wanted, and desired by a woman with that kind of beauty, well, that is a very powerful thing."

"If I told Stone that I needed, wanted, and desired him, he would run away."

"I highly doubt that. But you do not have to say it. You show it. It is not really something you have to talk about."

Jade heaved a loud sigh. "Men never talk about their problems."

I smiled and picked up my snare and started working on it again. "That is because we do not have any."

I thought she would laugh at this, but she did not, so we sat in silence for a few thoughts. Then she said, "Why does Stone get up at night and leave and then come back?"

"He does?" I asked, trying to not sound concerned. "How often?"

"Not every night. Just every now and then."

I shrugged. "I do not know. Maybe he has to do his yellow waters."

"Hm," she said. I am not sure my answer satisfied her, but at least she finally left.

Our conversation made me uneasy. Did she know? But how could she? No man would ever tell her, I was sure of that.

SANDPIPER

One morning, Lark took a machete and was gone all day. When he came back, he had a huge load of agave leaves strapped to his back. He dumped them in a pile at the foot of the tree house where they tumbled to the ground like pile of green spears.

"I need you to make more rope," he said. He told me he wanted one very long, thick rope. One that was strong and would last a long time. "Start with these," he said. "I will go and get more."

So I did. Using rocks, I pounded the thick leaves until my hands ached and blood seeped from my knuckles. I smoothed away the pulp and hung the dripping fibers to dry on wooden racks that Lark had erected in a sunny part of our yard.

Lark brought the second load, and this time we crushed the leaves together, adding more fibers to the drying racks until they looked like they were layered with piles of soggy yellow hair. That night we both went to bed exhausted.

Two days later, the fibers were dry. I showed Lark how to separate the strongest fibers from the weakest by whipping the fibers against spikes and yanking them toward me. As I did this, the weak strands broke off and the strongest strands remained in my hands. When I was finished, I had a handful of straight, smooth, strong fibers, ready to be twisted into rope.

To begin weaving, I held the end of my rope down with my foot and twisted up. When it was long enough I looped it around a tree and continued twisting, adding more fibers into the rope as I went, using the tree to keep it taut. I twisted like this for an incredibly long time, adding more and more fibers and wrapping the finished sections of rope around the tree like a great spool, stopping only to crack my stiff knuckles. After a while, Lark came to inspect it. He unwrapped it from the tree, measured it with the span of his arms and said, "It needs to be longer."

By now, Feather had awakened and was crying pathetically on her blanket in the shade. I sat down to feed her and examined my red, stinging palms. Lark brought a gourd and sat down next to me and we both took turns drinking the cool water.

When Feather was full and happy again, I returned her to the blanket and added more fibers to the rope.

After a while Lark stood behind me and watched me with a worried countenance. "Piper," he said, "I believe we now have more than enough for length, but I think it needs to be thicker."

I nodded. *Do not worry, Lark*, I thought. Right now the rope was the thickness of two of my fingers, but I had a plan, and it would be four fingers thick when we were through. Instead of starting over, I continued to twist and add more fibers until I had twice as much rope as Lark wanted and the tree trunk bulged like a giant skein of yarn.

We unwrapped the rope and put one end through the crotch of a tree and pulled until the lengths were even. Then, with Lark holding one side of the rope and me holding the other, I showed him how to twist and wrap the rope around itself, doubling the thickness. It took both of us on each side to keep it taut, to keep it twisted, and to wrap at the same time. Eventually, we moved into a rhythm; he would twist and I would duck under his rope as he stepped over mine. If someone were watching us they would think we were doing a strange little dance as we twisted and ducked, over and over, fusing our cords together.

We finished just before the sun slipped behind the trees. Our separate cords were now combined into one long, thick rope. That evening, as we sat by the fire eating, we admired the magnificent rope coiled between us, and we knew that this rope would be strong enough to lift five men and thick enough last a hundred years.

In the morning Lark left early, carrying long poles and a heavy bag on his back, the contents of which were unknown to me. Before long, he returned for a second load, and I helped him coil our rope around his shoulders and fill his arms with various tools. Where he was going or what he was doing I had no idea, for he never said, and as usual, I did not ask. He was about to leave once more on his mysterious errand when he turned around and said, "Will you come with me?"

The tone of his voice was meek and imploring, like the voice a child would use to a parent before walking out into a dark night. It made me stop what I was doing and gaze into his soft eyes for a moment and nod. *Of course I will, Lark.*

I loaded Feather in the sling and followed him.

It seemed we were headed toward the temple mound at first, but instead of going up the trail to the mound, he turned on the water trail. We were going to the cenote.

We came out of the forest and into the clearing where everything always seemed quieter. I listened, as I always did now, for the voices, but I heard nothing but faraway mating calls of birds and distant monkeys.

Before long, we entered the shady thicket that surrounded the cenote. Lark walked up to the dilapidated scaffold, whistling softly. I noticed the pile of poles and the bag he had left with that morning were already here. He set down the tools and the rope.

"You can sit down and make yourself comfortable," he said. "We will be here for a while."

I sat among the plants, making sure I did not encroach on the territory of any snakes or fire ant mounds and wished I had brought a mat to sit on and a fan to wave. Feather was becoming fussy, so I let her nurse while I watched my husband work.

Lark wrapped his arms around the great ceramic pot. Straining, he slowly eased it onto his chest, slid it out of the scaffold, and lowered it to the ground. Then he tipped it on its side, and with his hands he began to pull out rocks and debris and black sludge, making a dark pile on the ground that gave off a strong, rotting odor. Once the entire pot was empty and scraped clean, Lark set it aside and began to work on the scaffold.

As he pried off the loose and weak poles from the scaffold and lashed the new ones in their places, I realized how much I enjoyed watching Lark work. Even though he was small, he was strong, and it was clear he had done this before. I could not help admiring the way he moved and measured and pounded with the masculine efficiency that eludes even the sturdiest woman.

I slapped a mosquito on my cheek and waved two more away from my baby.

I thought back to the women's meeting and the fearful countenances of the women who were so terrified that their husbands would succumb to the cenote. I was anxious too, at first. But it did not take me long to realize how silly it was to worry about Lark. Perhaps it was because every night, he would take me in his arms and tell me over and over that I was the most beautiful thing he had ever laid eyes on. Part of me disregarded his praises, for I knew I was not a beauty. But it made me happy that at least I pleased Lark. Sometimes I wondered if he was lying; just telling me all of those nice things because he wanted me to feel good. But I knew Lark, and I knew he could not and would not lie.

As soon as the scaffold was fit with the new poles, it took on a younger, healthier appearance. Lark stood back to examine his work, giving it an approving nod. He then lifted the pot back up to its place in the scaffold.

He opened up his mysterious bag. He pulled out some large stones, and with them in his arms he hoisted himself up the side until he could see into the top of the ceramic pot. He lowered the stones inside and they clattered at the bottom. Then from his bag he added smaller rocks, then sand, then what looked like charcoal from our yard fire. He layered these materials over and over until the pot was filled up to its wide brim.

Lark climbed down and brushed the rock dust and charcoal soot off his hands. He took out his machete, and with the tip he pulled the hanging bucket toward him. Once he had a grip on the bucket, he sliced through the frayed rope, and set the bucket down in the grass. He unwrapped the old rope from the spool and tossed it aside in one great heap. Then, taking the new rope we had made, he tied it around the spool. Turning the handle, he coiled the rope around and around, watching as the spool thickened. He turned to me and smiled. "Now comes the tricky part."

Hoisting the remainder of the rope around his shoulder, he put his hands on the scaffold. He was not going to climb all the way up to the pulley, was he? My eyes studied each pole in the structure. He had not replaced all the poles, just the ones that looked like they were on the verge of collapse. Although it was an improvement, I still did not think it looked strong enough hold a man even Lark's size.

But Lark did not seem concerned. Nimbly he climbed up the side of the scaffold. When he got to the top, he lay across the ramp and scooted himself out over the cenote. As he did this the scaffold creaked.

I bit my lip, took a deep breath in through my nose and held it. What if the arm broke and he fell? How would I get him out? Perhaps the women were wrong . . . maybe the men were not dying because of voices but merely because they were trying to change the rope.

It suddenly seemed quiet and I realized that Lark had stopped whistling. Instead his tongue poked out of the side of his mouth as he scooted further out the end of the arm toward the pulley. Sweat dripped from his forehead, chin, and nose. When he reached the pulley, he took the end of the rope and threaded it into the pulley and pushed the rest through until the rope, from the pulley down to the spool, was more or less taut, and the excess hung down into the hole of the cenote. Then he slowly slid himself backwards until he could find a foothold to climb down. It was not until his feet finally hit the ground that I exhaled.

Resuming his whistling, he picked up the bucket and walked over to the edge of the cenote. Again with his machete, he coaxed the new rope to him and tied the end securely to the bucket. He set the bucket on the ground amid the coils of new rope and turned the handle on the spool. The coils slowly unraveled and traveled up to the pulley like a strange, obedient snake. The bucket followed until all of the rope was on the spool and the bucket dangled at the top of the scaffold.

"Shall we test it?" Lark said.

He turned the handle the other way and the bucket lowered down into the cenote. He stopped whistling and listened. I scrutinized his countenance, wondering if he was hearing *them*. But soon we heard the sound of water being punctured. The rope slacked while the bucket filled. Then Lark drew the bucket up and when it appeared, it was wet and shining and dripping with water.

Lark pulled it to the top and let the water tip out and run down the ramp and into the pot. It trickled through the filter much quicker than before, sounding like rain and reminding me of the feeling I felt in my breasts every time my milk came in. When it came out the bottom, it flowed much faster and freer than before, and would make filling gourds far less time-consuming.

Satisfied, Lark bent over to collect his tools and hoisted the old rope onto his shoulder. I regarded him with silent awe. How could anyone think that Lark was a man who listened to the voices of the cenote? He was not a listener of the voices; he was our ally against them.

Just when I expected Lark to rise and walk with me back to our hut, he crouched lower to the earth, examining something on the ground. He put down his tools and began picking things out of the dirt. He put them carefully in his pocket. Then he again gathered his tools and stood.

"Shall we be off?" he said with a troubled smile.

I nodded and followed him away from the cenote, pretending I had not seen the black beads he had placed in his pocket.

LARK

The bad news first.

The bad news was that I found Stone's bracelet at the cenote. I picked up the beads so that none of the other women would find them and wonder. As always, I hoped Stone was being careful.

The good news was that the traders arrived in the village today.

The traders always come around this time of year. They came in a large caravan; men, women, and even children, each carrying large bundles and poles on their backs. After speaking with Stone for permission, they set up their tents and hammocks, creating a temporary village on the Grassy Top. In the center of this village, they rolled out their carpets and blankets and set up their wares for all to come and browse.

We never knew what they would bring until they arrived. Sometimes they sold spices and fabrics, sometimes furs and pearls. As I walked past the colorful blankets laid out on the earth, I saw that this year they had a greater variety of trinkets than ever before, with everything from feathers to baskets to pottery. One man was gathering an audience as he displayed a smooth flat stone that flashed as bright as sunlight on water. He called it a mirror.

As I meandered, I knew that Sandpiper would enjoy seeing this spectacle. Perhaps there was even something she would want. I was about to turn and head back down to the tree house when something caught my eye. At the end of the row was a tall man selling jewelry. I walked closer. Displayed on the blanket were necklaces and bracelets and armbands. There was a bowl of pure white pearls and a pot with colored feathers springing forth out of it. The trader sat, his long legs straddling a three-legged stool, watching me anxiously. When I stooped down to get a closer look, he picked up several necklaces and dangled them under my nose.

"Some beautiful necklaces for the woman of your heart?" he said. The necklaces glittered in the sun and one caught my eye as it swung from his finger. I put my hand under it and looked more closely. It was made of smooth red stones. Sandpiper liked red.

"That is an excellent choice," said the trader enthusiastically. "Very beautiful. Those stones come from the western deserts and are very difficult to obtain."

I looked at the necklace again. "How much?"

"Make me an offer," he said.

"Ah . . . I have some rabbit pelts," I said.

He rolled his eyes and shook his head. "I have mountains of rabbit pelts. Trade me something I do not already have."

I thought again, my mind's eye searching the inside of the tree house for something this man would find valuable.

"I will have to look and see what I have," I said finally.

"I understand, I understand," he said, not at all trying to hide his obvious disappointment and pulling the necklace from my hand. He carefully set it down on his blanket as gently as if it were made of little red eggs. "Remember that we will only be in this village for one day, one day only . . . and my jewelry sells quick"—he clapped his hands—"like lightning. This is the only red necklace I have, and I do not expect to keep it for long."

We both stood. He was much taller than me, unusual looking, burly and dark with a prominent cleft in his chin and bright red feathers tied in his hair.

"You are a married man, yes?" he said.

"Yes," I said.

"And you are buying this for your wife?"

"I was thinking of doing that," I said, trying not to sound too committed.

"Then go get your pretty wife and bring her to see it. It is good to get the wife's opinion on things like this, is it not? Find something to trade, bring your wife, and we shall bargain."

I ran down the mound to fetch her. On our way back up we passed Stone's hut, and I asked Jade if she could take the baby while we bartered with the traders.

By the time we returned, the Grassy Top had transformed into a crowded, colorful flurry of selling and trading, for news spread quickly that the traders would only be here for one day. I strode forward, looking into the crowd for the man selling necklaces, but I soon found I was walking alone. I looked back and Piper was standing at the trailhead, still as a deer.

"Come, Piper. I want to show you something," I said, taking her by her hand. I worried that if we did not make speed, the necklace I had seen would be taken by someone else. I pulled Piper into the melee of basket-holding villagers. Everywhere people were talking and laughing and haggling, and their bodies buffeted us as we passed through.

I could only glimpse the top of the head of the man selling necklaces, sitting on his stool, showing his wares to other potential buyers. I held tight to Piper's hand as we waited for our turn. Peering around the other villagers, I was relieved to see the necklace of red stones still lying on the blanket. Finally, the couple in front of us finished their trade and the man looked up at Piper and me.

"You have returned," he said, smiling broadly.

And at that moment, without any warning, Sandpiper collapsed.

I would have liked to have caught her, but I did not. Instead I knelt beside her limp body and lifted her head off the ground. Her eyes fluttered open, looking at me and then over at the trader.

Slowly I maneuvered her into a sitting position. The trader offered her some water from his own flask. Then he turned his attention to other costumers while I helped Piper wake up. She kept looking at the trader and rubbing her eyes. Finally, when the blood came back into her face and she seemed more alert I pointed to the necklace. "See that? Do you like it? Do you think it is pretty?" But Piper was still in a daze. She did not look at the necklace at all, but just watched the trader as he traded an armband for a beaded leather bag.

The trader turned to us. "Are you feeling better now?" he asked Piper. Piper buried her face in my tunic, obviously embarrassed and nodded.

"This is my wife," I said, patting her on the back.

"She is enchanting," said the trader. "Did you bring something to trade?"

I nodded and presented my ocelot pelt.

SANDPIPER

I never thought I would see him again.

I do not know why I did not think of it, not even when Lark came and told me that traders had come. It was only when I came up to the top of the mound and saw their blankets and their poles fixed with flags that I remembered those days, a year ago now, when the traders came to my island.

The moment I realized who these people were, the blood in my body stopped flowing. I could not have moved my legs even if I had wanted to, but to my horror Lark pulled me forward into the mass of people anyway. "I want to show you something," he said.

But what if he is here? And will he recognize me? What will I do if he does? What will I say? I would not say anything, of course, at least not now. Not like this, not with Lark at my side. I tried to pull away, but Lark would not let me go.

He dragged me into the crowd, and I kept my head low, my eyes on the ground. Surely he was not here. There are probably many groups of traders that come and go on the mainland. Lark towed me past the blankets of clothing, the blankets of nuts and spices, blankets of knives, and the men with parrots on their shoulders. Then I saw him.

At first I would not believe it, but with every step Lark was taking me closer and closer to him, and the dread coiled inside me like a viper and I wished I could evaporate into the steamy air.

In a blink we were there, standing right above his blanket, watching those scarlet feathers dangle in his soft shining hair that hung down his naked brown back. I knew how soft that hair was. I knew how smooth that back was. Fear and desire fought inside of me like animals trying to claim territory over my heart. *What will he do when he sees me? When he looks in my eyes?*

Then, he turned to us and said, "You have returned," and everything started waving around. Every sound and shape around me lost depth and texture, blurring into only muted colors and muffled words, as if I had been jerked underwater.

The next thing I knew I was on my back, staring up into his coal-black eyes as he filled my mouth with cool water. I looked in those eyes for any kind of recognition; a secret nod, or a lingering gaze, but he acted like he had never seen me before. His eyes did not remain on my face any longer than they would on the face of any old woman or a child. It took many thoughts before I realized why. It was my hair. He could not see the one part of me that made me different from anyone else . . . unforgettable, even. Without it, I was just another face in another village. He turned and answered questions of other customers, handing Lark the flask. Lark continued to try and pour water down my throat, but I coughed it out and groped my way into a sitting position. I did not want Lark to help me. I did not want Lark to touch me. I wanted Lark to disappear.

I watched him as he displayed the necklaces. I listened to his voice, deep and smooth as chocolate. His profile was just as I had remembered, as was the curving lines around his mouth when he smiled. And this did not make me feel relieved but rather like crying. I hid my face in the folds of Larks tunic and listened to Lark's voice vibrate from the chambers of his chest until the deal was done and I could escape. I was not even sure why Lark had brought me there or what he wanted to buy from this man of my past.

On the way back to our home Lark handed me a necklace of red stones. "What do you think? Do you like it?" he asked.

I nodded vaguely. My fingers wrapped around it and I dropped my arm to the side. I just wanted to be left alone for a while so that I could absorb all of this. I had to figure out what I was going to do. Lark suddenly cut in front of me.

"I will help you put it on," he said. I nodded. *If it makes you happy.* He fastened the stones around my throat and stood back and looked at me. "That looks nice," he said. "Too bad they are leaving in the morning. If I had more pelts I could get you something else."

For the first time that afternoon, I looked into Lark's face. The traders would be leaving in the morning?

That afternoon, I took a basin and filled it halfway with water that I had heated over the fire. Then I took another gourd of cool water and poured it into the basin. When it was not too hot and not too cold, I dipped little Feather's toes in the water, and her eyes became big and she curled up her legs. With one arm around her soft body, I poured in more cool water. And tested it with my elbow. Slowly I lowered her into the water, her spanking place first. She was tense and looked up into my face in apprehension, but I smiled, and when I smiled so did she, showing me her pink gums.

I soaked a clean white cloth, and after squeezing almost all the water out, I gently cleaned her face. I started on her forehead and gently glided down over each eye. I filled up the cloth with water again and squeezed it across her glossy brown tummy and fat brown legs. Slowly she began to relax. I washed under her arms and around her neck, making her giggle. I cleaned each hand and in between each finger and the bottoms of her pink feet. Finally, I scrubbed her hair. I pulled her out, dripping wet and wrapped her in my clean apron. Then I sat down, holding her on my lap and working my apron into every fold of soft baby fat so that she would not get a rash. When she was dry, I held her close to my nose and breathed in her sweet smell and rocked her back and forth like it was just her and me in a little canoe.

"You must be clean and look your best," I told her, "for tonight there is someone I want you to meet."

SANDPIPER

The evening was cool.

Stone and Jade came to the tree house to meet us, for we planned to walk up to the mound together. I finished feeding Feather and set her gently in the sling across my chest. Then I unwrapped my hair, letting it burst out into its natural shape and used the wrap instead for a cape around my shoulders. Lark gazed at me approvingly and said, "I like your hair, Piper. I am glad you uncovered it. I think it is beautiful."

Jade looked from Lark to me, her countenance stormier than usual. But I did not care what Jade or Lark thought about my hair, for I was not unwrapping my hair for either of them. I had plans tonight, and if this was going to work, he would need to know who I was.

Music and laughter floated down from the temple mound as the four of us walked up the trail, passing empty huts as we went. Everyone must be there. When we came to the Grassy Top, we found the place ablaze with torches and drums and festivities. There were bonfires, tables piled with food, and dancing. How villages celebrate when the traders come!

My eyes searched through faces and shadows. He was there, somewhere in this gathering. I could feel it. I just had to find a way to get away from Lark.

Lark guided us through the crowd, exchanging greetings and smiles and holding my hand. I smiled when I needed to, I hugged when it was required, but all the time I was looking for those red feathers set in ebony hair.

At last I saw him. Or, rather, he saw me. I turned from a conversation Lark was having with Stone and there he was, through a gap in the crowd, leaning up against the post of the pavilion, looking at me with those same intense eyes that I remembered.

For a few moments, my breath ceased and my knees trembled. If I had not grabbed Lark's arm I would have again fallen to the earth.

"Piper?" he asked. "Are you all right? Are you feeling dizzy again? Here, come and sit down."

I sat on a bench, knowing that his eyes were still watching me.

Lark squatted and looked into my face. "Stay right here. I am going to get you some water."

I nodded and rubbed my hand against Feather who slept soundly in the sling under my cape.

As soon as Lark was gone, I stood up and left the bench. The crowd had shifted and I could no longer see him. I slowly walked around the group, searching faces and heads, trying to see where he had gone.

Then I saw him, sitting at a fireside, the glow of the flames illuminating his countenance. My heart beat faster. A voice inside of me said, *leave things the way they are.* Lark was good to me, even dear to me. I was, after all, the only one who knew the truth, and perhaps it was better if it stayed that way.

But as I watched Red talking and laughing, and I saw the outline of his profile against the fire's blaze, a desperate, forbidden hope surged in my chest, and I did not fight the urge to move toward him. *Leave things the way they are,* came the voice again, but with each step, the tinier the voice became until I could not hear it at all.

Soon the compulsion to go to him overpowered me, as if I were caught in a current. Vaguely, I knew there might be consequences, but I did not care. At this moment, Lark was smaller than a grain of sand on the seashore. Nothing else mattered more than the invisible connection between me and this man from my past, and it was pulling me toward him like an insect to a brilliant, flashing flame.

I saw him look at me out of the corner of his eye and smile. He knew I had been watching him. I walked toward the fire, knowing the language I could speak that would make him come to me, even in my muted state. To a man, there is nothing quite so loud as a touch.

I passed behind him, slowly running my fingertips across his back, shoulder to shoulder. Then, I walked toward the dark forest, rolling my hips from side to side, knowing, with complete confidence, that he would follow.

He wasted no time.

As soon as we exchanged the light of the fire for the light of the moon, he grabbed my hand. A warm thrill rippled through my body, for I had forgotten how my hand felt so small in his. For the first time in a long time I felt tiny.

"I did not expect to see you here," he said, his eyes glittering like obsidian. "I remember you. You are the girl from the village on the island where the houses are on stilts. The Fish People. I remember your hair."

He remembered me. My heart danced!

"You remember going swimming?" I asked, savoring the ease of speech.

He stepped closer. "Of course I do."

"And . . . you remember the mango grove?"

"How could I forget?" he whispered, glancing at my mouth.

I had told myself to be calm and not to get too excited, but my delight that he remembered me was overwhelming. I could not refrain from diving in. "I kept my promise," I said.

"Promise?" he said, eyebrows raising slightly, "What promise?"

"You told me to never forget you, and I never have. Look." I pulled the scarlet ibis feather out of my pocket. "I still have this." It was just as perfect and resplendent as it was the day he left me.

Perplexed, he looked down at the feather and then back at my face. "What . . . is . . . that?"

"You gave it to me just before you left. You took it from your hair."

"Ah . . . yes," he said, "of course. It is unfortunate we only had one night."

"You gave me a gift that night, do you remember?"

"A . . . gift? You mean . . . besides the feather? You will have to remind me."

"Here it is. I brought her with me."

"Ah . . . her?" he said.

I lifted up my cape to reveal the sling strapped across my chest. I moved back the fabric so the moonlight could shine on Feather's exquisite, sleeping face.

Instantly, he jumped back as if I had just revealed a tarantula. "No, no, no—I think you have me mixed up with some other man."

"But you just told me you remembered my island. You remembered swimming, and the mango grove."

"Keep away, woman." His face twisted like he had just bitten a bad fruit. "I do not know you. I have never been to an island with stilt houses. I cannot swim, and mangoes give me hives."

For a moment no words came from my mouth. How could he deny something like this? How could he refuse the responsibility of this perfectly formed child? I studied his face, desperately searching for understanding. Then I stepped away from him and swallowed hard. "You are lying," I said, trying to sound stronger than I felt. "I know you, and I know this is our baby. Do you not see? She has your chin."

But he refused to even glance at her. "I would never. Not with someone like you. You are too tall, and your hair is like a . . ." He searched for the word, ". . . like a rat's nest."

If I were a butterfly and he had just ripped off my wing, it would not have hurt so much. "You—you said you liked my hair."

"I hate your hair. It is ugly."

"You said you thought I was brave, Red."

The name escaped my mouth before I could stop it, and off it floated into the night air. Embarrassment flooded me. I longed to grab the word and swallow it back up. I had called him that so many times in my mind that I had forgotten I did not really know his name.

"What did you just say? Why did you call me that?" he said. " 'Red'—was that it? Do you think that is my name? My name is Roach. Now I know you have me confused with someone else. Get away from me, woman. Go find someone else to blame your problems on."

I could see now how stupid I was to come here. What had I expected? I had not wanted much. I only wanted to offer him a glimpse of our love's fruit, and now I was being plucked apart petal by petal. Tears stung my eyes. "It does not matter what your name is. I know who you are, and you are the father of my child," I said, even though I was even having my own doubts now. This horrible person could never be the father of such a sweet baby. I narrowed my eyes. "I do not remember you being so rude before."

"I do not remember changing," he said, spitting.

I stepped back in disgust. This was not the man I had fallen in love with. What happened to that man I had spent countless nights dreaming about? What happened to the man who made me think he would come for me, marry me, and be the father of my children if I had stayed on the island? I shook my head in disbelief. He was a mirage. It was all a mirage. I realized now that my mother had been right. He never would have come back for me. I was just another girl on another island. Red was a fantasy I dreamed up that had this man's face. As this realization sunk in, the mists of infatuation fell from my eyes and I saw things clearly. I had fallen in love with an image of someone who did not even exist.

Suddenly there was a sound of crunching leaves in the forest, and we both froze.

"Who's there?" the man named Roach said. "Who are you? Show yourself."

Bushes and plants shook. "Hello?" came a familiar voice. "Piper? Is that you?"

My blood turned cold, and I wanted to melt into the earth. *Please not him*, I begged. *Anyone but him.*

"Oh, there you are!" said Lark appearing out of the bushes, smiling and looking relieved. "I have been looking all over for you!"

His eyes traveled to the other man and his smile died.

"Who—?" Lark said, looking back and forth between us both. "Who are you? Are you not the jewelry trader? And . . . what are you doing out here . . . with my wife? Sandpiper, are you crying?"

"This is your wife?" said Roach, his eyebrows raised in surprise. There was a dreadful, sickening moment while I stood there, not knowing whether to defend myself or to run, to speak or to be silent. I wanted to make myself small. Small as a pebble. Small as a bead. Small as an aphid, safe and quiet on the underside of some dark leaf. Then Roach began to laugh, and I knew that from that moment on, nothing would turn out well.

"Yes, she is," Lark said, moving toward me protectively. "My wife and my child."

"Your wife and your . . . ?" Roach could not even say the last word. He threw his head back and laughed again. I watched his neck-stone jerk up and down.

Lark stood straight and tall. "I do not understand what is so funny."

"Do you know what she just told me?" Roach wheezed, wiping tears from his eyes.

Lark pointed at me. "What she just told you?" He looked utterly confused. "You must have that wrong, because my wife does not speak."

I cringed. This was getting worse and worse. *Please, gods, strike me down before this man says the words that will ruin me.*

The man stopped laughing and looked at Lark like he was an idiot. "We are both talking about the same woman, are we not? This woman, standing here? With the crazy hair?"

Lark looked at me and nodded his head. "Yes. This woman. My woman. And she does not speak."

A low rumbling laugh sounded in Roach's throat and became louder and louder until he was howling so hard I thought the whole village might come running to see what was happening. I watched him with growing hatred. When he finally gained control of himself he turned his head to me and a cruel, crooked smile slowly spread all the way up to his ears.

"Shall you tell him, Rat Nest, or shall I?" he said pleasantly.

But I was paralyzed. My mind was as hollow as a coconut. I stood in powerless agony, knowing that there was nothing I could do but stand there and witness the breaking of my husband's heart.

"Tell me what?" said Lark.

"How well do you really know your wife, my friend? Did you know that the two of us were just having a nice little conversation together? And she told me the strangest thing. She just told me that this baby she has at her chest is not yours but mine. Now, just to reassure you, brother, it wasn't me. That is important for you to understand. But I would venture to guess that the baby is not yours, either. I am sorry to be the one to share this nugget of truth with you, but you have made a marriage oath to a woman with a roving heart. You have my pity." He chuckled and looked at me. "There. I told him who you really are. Defend yourself, you who cannot speak." He spat the last word in my face.

How had I ever found this man attractive? With each vile word that came from his mouth he became uglier and uglier to me until I could hardly stand looking at his revolting countenance. It was enough that he was insulting to me, but to treat Lark, who would never say an unkind word to any living thing, made me livid. What did I ever see in this repulsive, disgusting man?

Lark stared at Roach, his countenance fixed and unbelieving. "Come, Piper. Let's go home. We do not have to waste our time with men who tell lies." Lark turned back to the distant lights of the festival, his arm around my shoulders.

As much as I wanted to go with him and escape from this pit I had dug for myself, I could not move. I stood, immobile as a pole in the ground, glaring at the man I had spent the last year of my life fantasizing about, wishing I could claw his eyes out with my fingernails.

I pushed away from Lark. "He is right," I said.

Lark blinked at me in surprise. "Piper?" he whispered.

"He is right, Lark. Everything he said."

"Piper . . ." Lark whispered, his mouth open and his eyes blinking in surprise, "Piper . . . you . . . speak!" As if that was all that mattered at that moment.

"I told you! I told you!" Roach snorted, dancing around us and hissing in Lark's ear, "Now who is the liar?"

Anger burned hot in my chest and my fists became tight. Lark looked up at the man who towered over him and with a cool, steady voice said, "I do not know who you are or where you came from, but this has nothing to do with you, and you better get as far away from us as possible, for if you do not," Lark's voice wavered. "I will be forced—I will be forced—to—to—"

But he was too late. By the time he finished his threat I had already sunk my fist in the dead center of my former lover's lying throat.

LARK

"So tell me the truth."

It was the next day. The traders were gone. The party was packed up. Most people were still sleeping off last night's revelries. For everyone else in the village, life would quickly settle back into its normal order and routine, but for me life was breaking apart into little pieces. I was not sure about anything, and a great, suffocating heaviness pressed down on my chest.

Last night, after Sandpiper had knocked the air out of the trader and we left him gasping for breath on the forest floor, we walked back home. Not a word was spoken. Sandpiper climbed up into the tree house, I stayed below, pacing around the fire until it was just smoke and ashes. Then I walked up the mound, passing the empty huts and listening to the merrymaking up on the Grassy Top. When the festivities finally came to an end, I folded myself among the shadows as the laughing villagers made their way to their huts. Then I walked up to my mother's dark, quiet lodge and paced around it. I went everywhere I could think of as long as I could just keep moving. All night long in my mind, I could see Piper on some beach with that man. I could see Piper whispering to him in the dark. I could see Piper . . . I shook my head and began pacing again.

In the morning I went back to the tree house. Piper was there. She had restarted the fire, and she sat close to it, on a little stool, nursing the baby. When she saw me she had an anxious look on her face, as if she expected me to yell at her. I was not going to yell at her. "When you are finished," I said, "we will go for a walk."

We walked a long way into the forest to a place where I used to go when I needed to think. It was a little meadow that was always green, even in the dry season. It was filled with ferns, moss-covered logs and plants with blue flowers and heart-shaped leaves. There was something about how the sunlight filtered through the trees here that always made me feel at peace. It was a place that I had often come before I was married, when I felt alone. It had helped me through hard times. But there never was a time as hard as this.

I sat down on one of the logs, feeling tired and as heavy as stone. Sandpiper remained standing, her hands stroking the little lump in the sling. If only I knew what she was thinking, and if only when I asked her what she was thinking she would tell me the truth. That is all I wanted, simply the truth.

"Sit down," I said. "Sit down here, next to me."

Cautiously, as if I might suddenly bite, she sat, straight and primly, next to me on the log.

"Let me hold the baby," I said.

She obediently took the baby from the sling and handed her to me. She put her own hands in her lap.

The baby's skin was brown and warm and she gurgled sleepily when she saw me. I sat her on my knees, facing me, and let her grab my face with her little hands. She looked up at me, blinking her dark, starry eyes and giving me a gummy smile. She seemed disappointed when I did not smile back.

"So tell me the truth," I said as I caressed her tiny hand with my thumb and ran one finger over the dimple in her chin. "Is she mine?" My voice cracked on the last word.

There was a pause. "No," said Piper softly.

I swallowed hard, and my eyes began to sting. Somewhere deep in my chest I felt a sharp pain. I turned Feather around so she could lean against my body. She always seemed so content and happy in my arms. I rested my lips on her soft hair as the tears rolled down my cheeks. Perhaps if I held her there for a while, the pain would go away.

Even though she was right there on my lap, I felt as if some bond between us, like an unseen umbilical cord between father and daughter had been severed. She was not mine. My blood did not pump through her veins. There was no part of this beautiful little person that was from me. It was a loss that stung like nothing I had felt before.

Piper was still and silent.

Finally, sniffing and clearing my throat, I looked at her. Her face was wet with tears too, and her eyes red.

"Why did you pretend you could not speak?" I asked.

"I . . . I do not know . . ." she started. "I was angry . . . at first."

"Angry?"

"About getting married. About taking the oath with someone I had just met."

"Oh," I said quietly.

"And I . . . I . . . did not want anyone to know that I was with child. I thought . . . I thought I could keep it a secret better if I did not speak. Everything was new to me, all the people and the customs and the place, and I just wanted to observe. But then people started thinking I could not talk at all, and then . . . it became who I was."

You could have talked to me, I wanted to say. I would have understood. But would I have understood? And would I have taken an oath of marriage with a woman who was carrying another man's baby? Never. Never could a woman who had touched another man become my wife. Yet I did take the oath with her, and the past year had been the happiest of my life. The pain in my chest swelled. It was almost more than I could bear. I closed my eyes and shook my head.

"I am so sorry, Lark," she said. "I did not mean to deceive you."

We were silent for a long time. Had she ever wanted to be married to me? I wondered. I loved her so much, and the whole time I had loved her, she had hidden another man in her heart. How often did she think of him? I shook the thought from my mind, stopping myself before I started asking too many questions that I did not want answered.

"Perhaps," she said, "you no longer want me."

I swallowed.

"Perhaps . . . I should go back to my island," she said.

This cut me to the heart. I was confused about a lot of things at the moment, but I knew for certain that if she left, it would kill me. But I did not tell her that. Instead, speaking slowly and carefully so that my voice would not crack again, I said, "I will have to think about this."

I slid Feather back into Piper's arms and left them there in the sunlit ferns.

SANDPIPER

After Lark left, I walked home feeling miserable and ashamed. Accomplishing even small tasks that day, like watering the garden or threading a needle seemed extraordinarily difficult and pointless. The last thing I wanted was to return to my island by myself with a baby.

I did not see Lark the entire day. In the evening, I climbed up the tree house ladder with Feather secured to my back and sat down on the mat to feed her as the light around us gradually grew gray. When it was so dark that I could not see my hand before my face and the insects hummed their night songs, I lay down and tried to sleep as the tears ran down my face. This would be my second night without Lark by my side.

But then the tree house creaked, and I could feel that someone was climbing the ladder. He climbed higher, his hands making squeaks as he gripped the rungs. I could tell from the breathing that it was Lark, and the gratitude I felt that he had returned was almost overwhelming. My heart beat faster. I wiped the tears from my face and sat up.

Something red and glowing appeared in the doorway. It was a stick that he must have pulled out of the fire. Through its faint light I could see Lark's face, lit like a ruby as he held the stick in his teeth. He entered the tree house and sat across from me. Taking the stick from his mouth, he lit a candle. The tree house became bright enough for us to see each other and our shadows spread onto the walls. He set the candle between us and the scent of melting beeswax filled the air.

"You wondered if you should go back to your island," he said.

I nodded and held my breath.

"Perhaps you should."

A chill swept through my body like a cold wind on wet skin. I lowered my eyes to the flickering candle as tears again started to fall. My heart was crushed. I had not expected those words to make me feel so sad.

"But I have been thinking about this all day," he continued cautiously, "and I believe that it might be possible that there are more reasons we should be together than apart. For example," he took something that looked like a white stone out of his tunic and stood, his shadow mimicking his every action. He reached his arm above his head, and with the stone he drew a line as long as my smallest finger on the wood boards of the ceiling. He then drew another line, crossing the first. He continued to draw lines through the center point and as he did he spoke. "One reason we should stay together is that you have started speaking. I find this method of communicating much easier than hand signals and scratching with sticks in the dirt." By now he had finished drawing lines and he lowered his hand. He had created a star on our ceiling. "I am anxious to know what it is like to be married to a wife who speaks."

"Another reason," he said thoughtfully, looking up and beginning a new star, "is that I think we work well together. Our talents are complementary, and we both accomplish our tasks the best we can."

He finished making marks, and his hand came down again. Now there were two stars on the ceiling.

Then he crouched down. He took my hand, cupped in his, and placed the stone inside. "Sandpiper," he said quietly, "can you think of any reason we should be married?"

I held the stone in my hand and searched his gentle, earnest countenance. His eyes were red and his cheeks had a slight puffiness to them. Had he been crying too? I closed my fingers around the stone and rose to my feet. I reached up and line by line, I drew a star. "For Feather," I said. "We should stay together for her sake."

A slight, relieved smile formed on his face. He stood. "May I?" he asked, holding his hand out for the stone. I placed it in his hand and he drew another star. "We should stay together because I do not know how to cook."

"Neither do I," I said. "Have I not burned or spoiled almost everything I have made for you?"

"Yes, but I do not think it is your fault. I think it is our pans and pots. They must be broken."

"All of them?" I said with a weak smile. I took the stone and drew another star. "We should stay together because I do not want to go back to my island with a baby and no husband."

"Why not? Would your family not take care of you?"

"I would shame them."

He nodded, and I handed him the stone. He drew another star. "I think we should stay together because you are the only woman I know in this village who does not nag." He got halfway through drawing the star and then stopped. His face peeked around his arm, and he raised his eyebrows. "But perhaps that will change now that you can speak," he said.

"You will have to wait and find out." I said, smiling. He narrowed his eyes at me and then finished the star. My turn again.

I bit my lip as I tried to think of another reason. "I think . . . I think we should stay together because I am the only woman who can tolerate your singing."

"That is perhaps the best reason so far," he said with a sober voice and sparkling eyes.

I smiled and handed him the stone. Our collection of stars was growing.

"I think we should stay together because . . . because we are a bird."

"We are a bird?" I asked. "What does that mean?"

He smiled and lowered his arm. "Sandpiper, I just cannot get over how wonderful your voice is."

His words and the way he was gazing at me made my cheeks warm.

"You know," he said, finishing his star, "I knew you could talk."

"You did? How?"

"You spoke in your dreams."

"Oh," I said. This made me nervous. I had no desire to know what I said in my dreams, especially at this moment when my marriage was hanging by threads. "Tell me what you meant when you said 'we are a bird.'"

"Do you remember the bird they released when we were married on the beach?"

"Yes . . . but I do not remember what they said about it."

"They said that marriage was like a bird. They never told us how our marriage was like a bird. But I have thought a lot about that since, and I think I know. A bird cannot fly with only one wing. It must have two to get off the ground. You are one wing and I am the other. We depend on each other."

I had never thought of this.

Then he added another star, skipping my turn. "I think that if you left, I would be the loneliest man in the world."

"You could get married again."

"No, I could not."

"But you lived just fine without me before."

"That is just because I did not know what I was missing. It would be like . . . like only eating tortillas your entire life and then someone gives you a tortilla with meat in it. You cannot go back to eating plain tortillas again."

I frowned. "So you are saying I am your meat?"

"I am saying you are my everything," he said solemnly. "Most of all, Sandpiper, I made an oath. I promised you I would be your husband, to love you and to take care of you. Now," he said. "Look up at the stars." I looked up at our crude cluster of stars on the ceiling. "We will stop for tonight, but we will keep drawing stars when we think of reasons we should stay together. Then," he paused and lifted his lips in a half smile, "when the time comes that we can no longer think of any more reasons, I give you permission to dissolve our oath. You can leave, and I will go back to eating meatless tortillas for the rest of my life."

LARK

bsolutely delicious," I said the next day when we were sitting in the shade of the tree house eating slightly burned beans and very burned corn cakes.

"Good. Then you can have mine," Sandpiper said with a smile as she passed me her plate.

"I would not dream of depriving you of the experience," I said, pushing it back to her.

Our banter was interrupted by the sound of light footsteps coming down the trail, and Honeybee appeared out of the forest, carrying a bowl. I smiled and gave Sandpiper a wink, "Now we shall have some fun," I said. She looked confused, so I held up one finger over my mouth. "Do not speak," I whispered.

"Ho, Lark. Ho, Sandpiper. I hope to bring you peace!" Honeybee said as she walked toward us.

"Ho, Honeybee," I replied. "I hope to bring you honor."

Sandpiper nodded and waved in her usual silent way.

"I brought a new tonic for you, Sandpiper," Honeybee said. She showed us a calabash bowl filled with something that looked like monkey entrails and smelled like death. "This one will surely make you speak again." Her timing could not have been more perfect.

I peered in the bowl. "What is it?"

"Animal throats," she said proudly. "But do not worry, they are cooked. I have been saving them up. There are some turkey throats, rabbit throats and one throat of a dog. It took me a while to gather them, and they started to smell, so I added a lot of chili pepper to hide the odor."

The odor was stomach wrenching. One whiff would kill a small squirrel.

"Does it take several doses to work, or will one do the trick?" I asked.

"I am not sure," she said, solemnly. "I have decided that Sandpiper's ailment is very difficult to heal. She may need to drink a little every day for the rest of her life. However, there is a chance this could be potent enough to make some improvement after just one dose."

"Impressive," I said, with a nod. "So . . . are you going to try it, Piper?"

Sandpiper smiled like a sunflower and nodded eagerly as if she had been waiting for this moment her entire life. Her enthusiasm pleased Honeybee and she handed her the bowl.

With great suspense, Honeybee and I watched Sandpiper tip the bowl of watery, chunky soup up to her face and "sip."

Then, she licked her lips and set the bowl down. She made a long, deliberate swallow. Honeybee watched, her face eager and hopeful. I folded my arms and leaned against a tree, trying to suppress my laughter at Sandpiper's excellent acting.

Sandpiper cleared her throat several times. Then she said in her beautiful new voice, "I . . . I . . . think you forgot the honey."

Honeybee's jaw unhinged. She stared at Sandpiper, gaping in astonishment.

"Careful not to hold your mouth open like that for too long, little sister," I said, "bugs might fly in."

Honeybee closed her mouth with a click. She looked from Sandpiper to the bowl and back to Sandpiper again. "It worked," she whispered, her hands coming to her heart. "I cannot believe it worked. Sandpiper . . . you . . . you can . . . you are talking!" She flew at Sandpiper, embracing her in a tight hug. Then she stepped back, grasped Sandpiper's hands and said, "Everyone is going to be so surprised! Can I tell them?"

Sandpiper nodded. "If you want."

Honeybee squealed and bounded off into the jungle, shouting, "Jade! Stone! You are never going to believe this!"

When she was gone I turned to Sandpiper. "There is another reason," I said.

"What do you mean?" she asked.

"Another reason for us to stay together. Another star."

She seemed doubtful. "We should stay together to play tricks on people?" I could tell she was feeling a little forlorn about fooling sweet, believing Honeybee.

"Do not worry about her, I will tell her later that it was my idea. I was actually thinking that the reason we should stay together was that my family will now be able to know the true you. I am not the only one who loves you, Piper."

The miracle of speech transformed our marriage. Being able to ask Sandpiper any question I wanted and get a thoughtfully articulated answer was more than I could have ever hoped for. I always knew Sandpiper was smart, but I did not know how observant she was, nor did I realize how funny she was. I also did not realize how much she cared for the people in my family. We talked all day about every topic. I was able to answer questions she had been wondering about for a long time. Throughout the following days it was easy to come up with more reasons why we should stay together, and each night more stars were added to the ceiling. At night I would say, "Lie down next to me, Sandpiper, and look at the stars. Look at all the reasons we should be together." When the ceiling was filled, we started drawing stars on the walls. The more we thought about it, the more the reasons seemed limitless.

All was not perfect between us, but at least I had convinced her to stay. That was all I cared about. We had traveled through the darkest place in our marriage, and our marriage survived. Nothing could ever come between us again.

SANDPIPER

A rainstorm came during the night. In the morning, I woke to Feather's cries and discovered she was shivering. It was unusually chilly, and tiny bumps spread all over my cold arms too. Lark was still sleeping. After I filled Feather's tummy with warm milk, I put her on my back and we came down out of the tree house into the damp world. The ashes were wet and there was not a warm coal left in the fire. Worse than that, all the wood around was wet. Making a fire this morning was not going to be easy.

I wish I had known it was going to rain. During the rainy season we always took care to protect the firewood, but in the dry season, it hardly ever rained. If I had had some kind of warning I would have at least covered the coals with something or protected a few pieces of kindling. Now I had to figure out how to get the fire started from scratch.

I remember my father once told me that I could make a fire in any place, in any situation if I simply pretended I was a mother bird making a nest.

I scanned my yard, trying to see with the eyes of a bird who was about to bring several defenseless, naked, featherless chicks into the world. I spied some old rope left under the table, a patch of dry leaves beneath the tree house, and found some dry cornhusks under a basket. I piled these next to the fire pit.

I scooped out the wet ashes and cleared a space for my nest. First I shredded the rope and cornhusks, making them as fluffy and as nest-like as I could. Then I crumpled the leaves inside the nest. I felt like it needed something more, so I retrieved a handful of cotton from the tree house, formed it into a little cup, and tucked it in the center of my nest. This would be the cradle for my ember.

After a diligent search in the forest, I found several dry sticks. I broke them and arranged them in piles, smallest to largest beside the fire pit.

When everything was ready, I took my flint and began making sparks. Because my nest was soft and dry, it did not take long for an ember to appear in the cotton cradle. Gently, I blew on the ember and it glowed bright red, like a tiny beating heart. Gathering the entire nest in my hands, I lifted it toward the sky so that I could blow on the ember without breathing in smoke. After a few steady breaths, smoke billowed out of the nest, and I could feel the heat coming close to my fingers. I set it back down in the fire pit. The smoke was thick now, and flames flickered from the nest. Quickly, I added the smallest sticks around the burning flames and worked in the larger sticks one at a time until my crackling fire had a life of its own.

I leaned back and watched my creation flash and wave, enjoying the warm heat on my face and hands. I took Feather from my back and held her in my arms so that she could feel the warmth of the flames.

I thought how this fire was very much like my situation with Lark. What fragile flames we had developed at the beginning of our marriage were wiped out by the revelation of my dishonesty. After that, it was as if everything around us was too wet to even think of kindling a fire. Lark's idea of drawing stars in the tree house ceiling was like starting a spark. But the spark he cast would not grow into an ember if it did not have a soft place to land.

Lark was right when he said our marriage was like a bird; and right now it was a bird with one broken wing, floundering in the grass. I was the broken wing, and if the bird had any chance of flying, I needed to improve. I had hurt him deeply, and this caused me more pain than I had expected.

Lark had a deep heart to forgive me. Deeper than any heart I had ever known. I vowed to myself that I would work harder, that I would be a better wife. It was my duty then, I decided, to make the nest soft. It was up to me to use whatever skills and talents I possessed to make Lark happy again.

Hello, Grandmother Vine. I hope to bring you peace," I said as I entered the dark lodge.

"And peace to you too. But who is that voice? I do not recognize it."

"It is me. Sandpiper."

"Sandpiper?" her face brightened. "Honeybee was buzzing about you and a miracle. So it is true, then? You can speak now?"

"I always could speak," I admitted as I sat down next to her. "I just did not have anything important to say."

"I doubt that," she said smiling. She reached out her fragile hand for mine. I grasped it lightly. Her skin was as smooth and delicate as a bat's ear. I was afraid if I pressed too hard I might bruise her. "So tell me, was it really Honeybee's tonic? She has been trying to smear slime on my eyes for months."

I smiled. "No, it was not Honeybee's tonic. . . . Grandmother," I said changing the subject. "I need some advice."

She chuckled. "Oh, you have come to the right place. I have lots of that. More women should be like you and come to their grannies for help. Tell me what you want to know and I will joyfully share all my great wisdom."

"Do you remember the advice you gave me during my bride's circle? About . . . ah, tossing tassels?"

"You mean about sex?" she said cheerfully, louder than I wanted.

"Yes," I whispered.

She smiled. "Of course, my child! You know—" she lowered her voice. "My husband used to tell me I was an expert. You must still be wondering what the most important body part is. There are many people out there that will tell you a lot of strange things, but I was married for thirty years before my husband died, and believe me, I know what I am talking about."

I thought for a moment that this was too weird and I should leave, but she was holding my hand, and before I could escape she continued.

"When it comes to making love with your husband, the most important body part is . . . right here." She tapped the side of her forehead.

"I do not understand," I said.

"It is your brain, Sandpiper. You might feel love coming from your heart, and heat coming from your hips, but the source that feeds these passions comes from your brain. Nothing that happens in bed is as powerful as what is happening in your mind."

Her words struck me like a hammer, and I sat there numbly as I reviewed my past thoughts and actions and measured them against this new idea. After a while Grandmother Vine patted my hand the way one would wake someone from a dream. "Is there something else you were wondering? Something else that is troubling you?"

Her words brought me blinking back into the present. Yes. There was something else that I wondered about, but I felt it was too rude to ask.

"Ask, Sandpiper."

Timidly, I spoke. "Is it true what you said about the voices? That you only started hearing them when you began to go blind? Or . . . "

Grandmother Vine relaxed back into her chair and smiled. "Ah. Now this question is a little harder to answer. It is true that the voices became louder when I became blind. But even as a young girl I could always hear them. That is why the legend frightened me so much. Some of us are born with gifts, some of us are born with curses. I suppose mine is a little of each. In the end, it does not matter so much who can hear the voices, Sandpiper. What matters is whether or not we choose to seek them out."

LARK

"How long do we have to wait here?" I whispered.

"Hush," Stone murmured, peering through the leaves.

"But this is taking forever. I do not think there are any deer in this part of the forest."

"You must have the patience of a wolf if you want the heart of a deer. Look there, I think I see one coming."

I sighed and readjusted my crouching position. There was nothing I enjoyed more than being shoulder to shoulder with my sweaty brother all cozy in a dark section of the forest where scorpions hid under rocks and ants swarmed around my sandals and sweat dripped from my nose and at any moment a jaguar could pounce on us and no one would find us for days. Truly, this was one of my favorite activities. But I was hungry. I reached in my bag for some dried fruit, but instead my hand felt something else. I pulled it out.

"I believe this is yours," I whispered.

"What is it?" he asked without taking his eyes from his prey.

"Your bracelet."

"Many thanks, brother. Honeybee has been pestering me about that." He took the beads and slid them into his pocket. "Now if you will please close your mouth so I can get a good shot at this buck . . ." He took an arrow and fit the end to his bowstring.

"I found it at the cenote," I whispered.

"Hush." Stone pulled back the string and aimed.

I held my tongue to let him concentrate. Stone started a slow inhale, and I knew from experience that on the exhale, he would let the arrow fly. The deer's heart was destined for only a few more beats. But then, the deer took a step, moving its most vulnerable organs behind a tree and Stone's exhale brought a low growl instead of a kill. He lowered his bow.

"You found what at the cenote?" He whispered, still watching the deer with hawk-eyes.

"The bracelet."

"So?"

"I just hope you are being careful."

"I am." The deer stepped back into position. Stone lifted his bow again, fingered the string and pulled back.

"I saw your hammock in your yard. You have taken to sleeping outside at nights now?"

"I can hear better outside," he whispered. The deer leisurely nibbled at the grass, taking one step at a time. Stone followed it with the tip of his arrow.

"And . . . what is it that you are listening to?"

"Are you accusing me of something?" he hissed, lowering his bow as the deer stepped behind another tree. "I sleep outside so I can hear if anyone is on the trails at night. I am doing my duty, Lark. If you remember, Newt died on my watch. I will not let it happen again."

"It is also your duty to break promises to your father?"

"What are you talking about?" Finally, Stone looked at me. His whisper was quite loud now. My heart started to beat, but it was too late to turn back.

"I believe some of the women know."

"And you think I told them?" Stone roared. The deer we had been stalking bleated and bounded out of sight.

Stone frowned deeply as he watched it go. He stood and threw down his bow. "And that is why you will never be a hunter!" Stone proclaimed to the entire forest. "That could have fed both of our families for a week," he said in disgust. "And as far as the cenote goes, why would it be so bad if the women knew? It would be a weight off my shoulders. No one in this village is trying as hard as I am to keep people from dying. Sometimes I feel like I am the only one who can do anything. You cannot help me, the other men cannot help me, the women cannot help me. I am the only one."

"Oh," I said. "So everything depends on you?"

"Seems that way."

I shook my head. "You are always acting like you are better than everyone else. Just because you are the chief does not mean you have some immunity from the cenote. No one does."

"That is what I am saying, but no one else will help me."

"No, you are saying that no one else is as worthy as you are."

"That is a lie," he said. "I do not think that."

"Well, sometimes you act like it."

"And what makes you think I broke the oath? Any other man might have told them. Or you."

"Because, unlike you, the rest of us do not want the women to know."

Stone shoved his arrow back into his quiver. "Why would it matter to you? You are not a Listener. At least—" he glanced at me. "Not anymore."

"I would prefer to not talk about it."

"Then why did you bring it up?" he growled.

"Never mind," I said. "Forget about it."

Stone picked up his bow and turned toward the forest. "Go home, Lark," he said over his shoulder. "I have a family to feed."

SANDPIPER

It is so much easier to talk to you now," Jade told me. "It is as if you are a real person, instead of a tree trunk."

She had come to teach me how to make tamales, even though when I first asked her she rolled her eyes and sighed like I had just asked her to remove all the grains of sand on the floor of my hut with her teeth. But I knew that Lark loved Jade's tamales, and I was still on a quest to make my nest soft and please Lark in whatever way I could.

"Making tamales takes many hands . . . or many hours," she had said with her startlingly bright red lips that commanded my whole attention. I knew it was rude to stare, but I positively could not look any place else. "But," she said with a heavy sigh, "I shall teach you."

This red paint had recently become very popular among the village women, and they were wearing it all sorts of ways. Jade told me that she was the one who discovered it, and then her paint was stolen, passed around, and exploited. She explained to me in great detail the pains it took for her to make herself some new paint and how now she kept it in the pocket of her apron at all times.

I thought the red paint looked silly. And desperate. But I understood their thinking. I knew they were just trying to do what was in their power turn the men's heads away from the cenote. The red paint, in addition to the mirrors the traders had brought, had created a sort of beauty frenzy among the women. I did not think the men were impressed by the changes they had made or with the amount of time they spent looking in their mirrors. Nor did I think that simply modifying one's appearance was the answer. I knew I was not numbered among the village beauties—one glance in Jade's mirror confirmed that—but Lark constantly reassured me a thousand times how much he loved me just the way I was. I did not feel the need to change anything about my appearance. In fact, it seemed that it was the one thing I had in my favor. There were other things I needed to improve. Becoming trustworthy, for instance.

Making the tamales took two days. On the first day, we had to grind the corn and mix it with lime to make the corn masa paste. Jade taught me how to sort, clean, and soften the cornhusks, and pound the dried chilies into a coarse powder.

The next day we started cooking the meat early, letting it roast for most of the morning. Then, when it was so tender and juicy that the meat fell from the bone, we made a sauce with the chilies and mixed it into meat with our hands.

All the while, Feather sat quietly on a blanket watching us and Mosquito toddled around, sticking sticks in the earth. He started making piles of little rocks and then throwing them into the forest until he became bored and decided to throw them at Feather, but Jade put that to a stop.

Feather was not hurt—I do not even think she knew she was in danger—but Jade scolded Mosquito, and he cried until finally Jade offered him the corner of her apron, which he gratefully and vigorously began to suck. Meanwhile I climbed up into the tree house and went to my box on the shelf. I took out the little animals Lark had made, and brought them down.

Mosquito was still stricken and tear-streaked from Jade's reprimand, and he watched me with large, suspicious eyes as he leaned against her leg and sucked on her apron. I crouched down and set the jaguar on the earth. After the jaguar, I put the coati and the deer, and then the turkey, rabbit, and tapir so that they were all following each other in a little line. When I looked up, Mosquito had stopped sucking and was staring, his mouth open, his eyes bright. I motioned for him to come and play with the animals. He needed no second invitation.

First he knocked them all down. I stood and walked back to my place with Jade, letting him play the way he wanted to. But after a few moments I looked over my shoulder and he had lined them up carefully again, just as I had done. Now he was moving each one forward, little by little, as if they were moving over a plain like they were all part of the same family. Feather watched him with mounting curiosity and even made some attempts to crawl to him on her belly, looking more like an iguana than a baby girl.

Finally, Jade and I had everything ready, and all we had to do was assemble the tamales. We stood next to each other; I spread the pasty masa flour on the softened husk and passed it to her. She filled it with the meat and chilies, wrapped it in the corn husk and placed it in the bottom of the pot.

"Tell me about where you came from, Sandpiper," she said. "What was your island like? What did you do there?"

I shrugged. "It was just an island. Lots of sand and ocean. Most people fished. My family made nets. That is about all."

"Do you ever miss your family?"

I paused. Yes, I missed my family. I yearned for them. Every day I wondered if my mother thought of me. I realized she had been right about Red, but in my heart I still could not forgive her for sending me away. And so every day when those feelings of longing rose up in my chest, I pushed them back down by reminding myself that she was the one who made me leave, and she was the one missing out on my life. "No," I said. "I do not miss them. This is my family now."

"Do you miss the island?"

"Yes. I miss that. It was not as hot there. I miss the breeze; I miss the sound of the ocean. I miss swimming."

Jade sighed. "I bet there was not a cenote on your island to worry about."

"No . . . no cenote."

There was a long silence while we folded more tamales. It made me smile to remember how much this food disgusted me when I first came, but now the smell of the meat and the sauce made my mouth water. I could not wait for them to be finished. Lark would be so surprised.

"Do you think Stone will be happy that you made tamales today?"

She shrugged. "He probably will not even notice."

"What do you mean?"

"All Stone cares about is hunting. Sometimes the only way I feel like I can get any attention from him would be if I tied antlers to my head."

"That could be dangerous. He might put an arrow in you," I said, smiling. But she did not smile.

"Sometimes I just get so tired of worrying about it, Sandpiper."

"About what?"

She lowered her voice. "The cenote."

"Oh," I frowned. We were back to that. I remembered the black beads that Lark picked up when we went to change the filters, but I could not bring myself to mention it to Jade. I thought it better to pretend I knew nothing and find out what she knew first. "Do you think Stone . . . ?" I asked, purposely leaving my question unfinished.

"Is it not obvious?" said Jade bitterly.

There was silence for a while. I looked at Feather and saw that Mosquito was marching the animals toward her.

"He is never around to help me with my tasks," Jade said as she folded another tamal. "He never takes Mosquito anywhere. Every day he seems more and more distant and distracted, like he does not even know I exist." She dropped the tamal she was making and she growled as she gingerly wiped the dirt off the outside and then put it in the pot. "The other day I cornered him and asked if he ever visited the cenote."

"You did? What did he say?"

"He became serious and started asking me all kinds of questions like, why did you ask me that? What do you know about the cenote? Do you ever follow me? And then he acted like he had a headache and stormed off."

"Does he . . . toss the tassels with you?" I asked.

She shook her head as tears welled in her eyes. "He sleeps in a hammock."

I bit my lip in dismay. It must be true then. It must be true that Stone was a Listener after all. I was stunned. If Stone listens to the cenote, what hope was there for the rest of the men? Was anyone strong enough to resist it?

"But you know what I did?" Jade continued, wiping her tears away on her sleeve, "I set up my own hammock inside the hut." She smiled triumphantly through her tears. "Besides, I have done a lot of things on my own without Stone around to help me, and if I cannot do it on my own, there is always another man in the village willing to help me. I could be an independent woman if I wanted to. I would not fall apart like Fern did. I have decided that if he wants to throw himself into the cenote, let him. I can provide for myself. I do not need him."

Her attitude surprised me. "If Lark decided to jump, I would not feel that way," I said.

"Why not?" asked Jade. "Would you not feel betrayed? Abandoned? Worthless?"

"No," I said as I smeared paste onto a husk and handed it to her. I took another husk skin and loaded it with masa, searching for the right way to express my feeling. "I do not think I would feel that way because . . . because . . . he is . . . he is Lark." I finally finished. There was really no other way to say it. "He is just Lark. There is no one like him."

"That is the truth," she said in a way that did not sound like a compliment.

"Besides, I think it would hurt Lark's feelings if he thought I suspected him."

"Feelings?" She snorted. "Men do not have feelings, Sandpiper. They only have urges."

When we were finished and my tamales were steaming over the fire, I understood why we only had them at festivals and celebrations. Making them took a lot of time. I was completely exhausted.

Jade lined up the rest of the uncooked tamales in her basket. They looked like little sleeping babies.

"Thank you for your help," I said.

Jade just waved her hand. "You are my sister," she said. "It is not a problem." She turned to her son. "It is time to go now, Mosquito. Give the animals back to Aunt Piper, " Jade said.

Mosquito gave them all back but the jaguar, which he clutched under his chin.

"That is not yours, Mosquito. It is baby Feather's. Now give it back," Jade said, more sternly.

"Do not worry," I said. "Let him take it home. He can keep it. Lark would be happy that he likes it so much."

Jade sighed, too worn out to insist.

They headed up the trail, Mosquito at Jade's heels with one hand clutching the jaguar, the other holding her apron.

"I am grateful for you, Jade!" I called. "I hope to bring you peace!"

She looked back, smiled weakly and waved her hand again. "Peace," she said.

I cleaned up. I washed out the bowls and utensils with as little of my precious water as I could; I was not going to the cenote today. I took off my soiled apron and put on a clean one. Then I gathered the wooden animals and put them in my apron pockets and picked up my baby. It was time for a rest.

I climbed up to the tree house, with Feather on my back, looking forward to the day when Feather would be able to climb up on her own. I was in the habit of putting Feather down on the floor of the tree house, since she had always stayed in one place. Now that she could scoot around, I always made sure I was between her and the open doorway. I set her on the soft sleeping mat, covered with a rainbow-colored blanket Cedar had woven for her. Then I sat down and played little games with her toes and tickled under her chin until she laughed so hard she could not breathe. She might have Roach's chin, but she had Lark's disposition.

I was about to lie down next to her, but the wooden animals in my pocket were uncomfortable. I rose to my feet to put them away. I stepped over to the shelf and lifted the animals from my pockets to the box. They made a happy clattering noise as they fell in, as if they were glad to be home.

Just as I was about to close the lid, I saw the old red feather. I looked back at my baby, sitting on the blanket. She was busy testing each of her fingers as if trying to decide which tasted the best. She gave a yawn that was so big for her little face that it gave her two double chins. I had a few more moments to spare and turned my back.

I took out the feather and twirled it around in my fingers and smiled, for I knew that this part of me was finished. I was not in love with that man anymore. I had grown up. I was learning from Lark what real love was.

However, just having the feather in my hand brought back so many memories that, for a moment, I allowed myself the luxury of remembering, once more, that night so long ago under the moon. I remember that it looked as big and round as pot filled with silver, and I could still smell the gardenia and plumeria that floated on the warm breeze, folding through my hair. It was a magical night that I would never forget, yet I knew better than to dwell on it now. I thought I was in love with him, but I had only been in love with a feeling. I knew that Red was a myth and Roach was the reality.

I opened my eyes and looked again at the feather. For a moment I considered throwing it away. But I did not.

Instead I put it back into the box.

It was just as I was closing the lid that a warning flashed through my core and I remembered my baby. I felt panicked, for somehow I knew what I would see before I even turned around.

The blanket was empty. I glanced to the doorway just in time to see Feather's body disappear off the edge.

LARK

I had just finished visiting Grandmother and was headed for the trail when I saw the figure of my mother coming toward me.

"Hello, Mother!" I called out, grinning. "I hope to bring you honor!"

I expected a salutation from her in return. A wave, a greeting, a smile. When she did nothing but march toward me, I decided that it was a pity that not everyone could be as jolly as I was on that beautiful evening. The setting sun lit the outline of her hair and dress in a soft amber glow, a fitting halo for such a warm, wonderful woman. What an exceptional mother she is, I thought. What a glorious life I have. I am utterly spoiled.

We met at the pavilion. "Lark," my mother finally said with uncharacteristic weariness. "I hope to bring you—" but she did not finish the greeting. Instead she put her hands on her face and cried.

I stepped forward and folded myself around her. "Oh, Mother," I said gently. "Why are you sad? Why do you cry so hard?"

"I cannot say. I cannot say," she moaned.

I held her back to look in her face. There, in her eyes I could see something that made my blood go cold. My grin disappeared, and I became still. "What is wrong, mother? What has happened?"

She struggled to control her voice. "There . . . has been an accident."

I swallowed. "Sandpiper?" I asked.

"No."

I closed my eyes and exhaled.

"Stone?" I said. "Jade? Honeybee? Who is it? What happened? Tell me, Mother. I do not want to play a guessing game."

But we both knew there was only one name left. She looked up at me and I saw it in her eyes.

"Feather?" I whispered, swallowed hard.

She nodded and looked away. "She fell . . . "

". . . from the tree house," I finished.

I released my mother and turned away. Something in my throat started to swell, and I felt as if I could neither swallow nor breathe. This could not be happening. I had Feather in my arms that morning. I pressed my fingers against my eyes hard, as if trying to push them out the back of my head. "No." I said. "No-no-no-no-no." I felt as if an arrow had pierced my chest and I sank to my knees. "Mother," I breathed through my hands. "What have I done? What have I done?"

She knelt beside me and pulled me to her. "You have done nothing, Lark. It was an accident."

My mother was silent for a long time, stroking my back. "Lark," she said as she gently pushed me up. "You are bleeding." I opened my eyes and her apron was covered in blood.

She took off the apron and I held it against my nose. Then she held me until the sun pulled its warm golden arms of light away and left us in cold darkness.

When we reached my home, Jade and Mosquito were there, as was Honeybee, and everything was lit with torches, as if we were hosting a party. I thought I had seen Stone, too, pacing beyond the circle of light in the shadows. Sandpiper would not even look at me and was curled up like a snail on the ground. Next to her, lying on a mat was a small, still bundle, wrapped in a rainbow blanket.

Above us loomed the tree house.

I dared not look at it. I never wanted to see it again. How stupid I was to build something like that. How did I think that would ever benefit my family? I had created the greatest snare the village had ever known. I had caught and killed my own child.

I went to the bundle and took her in my arms. She was not quite stiff. I unwrapped the blanket and held her in my lap. Her face was exquisite and beautiful, her delicate black eyelashes closed and peaceful.

I had never really noticed the shape of her lips before, as supple and perfect as a blossom.

I found one of her little hands and I examined it closely. It was so small in my hand, barely bigger than my thumb, and there were dimples where her knuckles would one day be. It was so soft and smooth. It was beautiful, a tiny miracle of creation, this little hand. Why had I never noticed how amazing it was? I thought of all the times I had put my finger in her hand and she closed this little hand around it, as if it gave her great safety and security to be with her father. Now the hand was limp and would never close around my finger again. I pressed her tiny fingers to my lips. "Forgive me," I whispered for just her to hear. "Please forgive me, my daughter."

I rocked her in my arms, putting her to sleep one last time. The night was endless. All night I held her. All night Sandpiper cried.

In the morning, Stone came and dug a hole and we buried her. And then my family went home.

Never had I known such heaviness and such pain. My heart felt crushed between stones.

Sandpiper and I only spoke once when I asked her to get the animals I had carved, for I knew I would never set foot in the tree house again. She climbed up and brought them down to me without a word. I put them in a sack and left Piper alone. I could not bring myself to look at her, for I was afraid I would see the blame in her eyes. But that was not even my worst fear. What I feared most was that she would leave, for now she could return to her village without a baby and without shame. I had no hold on her anymore. Now that Feather was gone, there was nothing to keep her here. I would be back at the beginning again. Silly, sad, awkward Lark, unwanted and alone.

I slowly walked up the path and to Stone's hut. My mother was there, talking with Jade, but when they saw me they stood as still as trees. I entered the yard and held out the bag to Jade.

"Here. These are for Mosquito," I said, without looking in her eyes.

She wiped her hands on her apron, took the bag, and pressed it to her chest. "Thank you, Lark."

I turned down the path, eager to get away from the pity that radiated from their faces. My mother caught up with me.

"Can I walk with you?" she asked.

I sighed. "If you want."

"How is Sandpiper?"

I shrugged. How could I answer such a horrible question?

"Come to my house tonight for dinner. You and Sandpiper. We will take care of you. This is too hard to bear by yourself, Lark. Nothing is as hard as losing one's child."

I stopped and faced her, my soul burning. "Why?" I asked her. "Why should this be hard? She was not even mine, Mother." The words cut like barbs.

A sudden sadness broke out on her face and tears filled her eyes, yet she showed no surprise at the revelation. My outburst only confirmed what she already knew.

"Do you understand what I am saying?" I wiped the tears fiercely from my cheeks. "Feather was not mine! So why should this be hard?" I said through my teeth and pounding my fist against my chest.

"Because you loved her, Lark. And love makes things hard. Love also makes things right. Feather was, and always will be yours."

She reached for me, but I shouldered her away and headed for the forest.

"Lark, where are you going?" she said.

"I do not know, and I do not care." All I knew was that I did not want to be held. I did not want to be babied. The only thing I wanted to do was walk. I would walk and walk, until I could no longer feel the scorpions in my chest.

SANDPIPER

Sweat dripped off my face as I leaned over and pressed my breast between my hands. A dark spot appeared on the earth as the milk seeped out, drop by drop. It might as well have been blood for the agony it took to discharge it from my swollen breasts, for they were still trying to make food for a baby that no longer existed. Any movement, even the act of lifting my chest to breathe sent flashes of white pain up through my scalp and down to my curled toes. It seemed that no matter how many drops I was able to release, the searing pain was still there, the rock hard pressure was still there, and I could do no other work but try to relieve myself of this agony. Now the ground beneath me was stained in drops. Drops of milk, drops of sweat, and drops of tears.

Every day either Cedar or Jade brought food, but I did not desire it, and I did nothing to protect it, and it was left on the table and eaten by birds and animals.

My in-laws took turns staying with me at night, but they could not stay with me during the day, for they had their other duties to attend to. They begged for me to come and stay in their homes where I would not be alone and where they could watch over me, but I would not leave this place where my baby's heart was last beating. My heart felt open and turned over, raw and ragged, like a field that has been plowed through.

If only I had turned around sooner. If only I had not put her down. If only I had not picked up the feather. Oh, my daughter, what have I done? I was your protector and guardian! I had never meant for this to happen!

I had robbed myself. Robbed of seeing her at two, five, and ten. Robbed of seeing her grow in to a beautiful young woman and teaching her about the world. I would never take her to the ocean or see her fall in love and marry. And suddenly, for the first time since I left my island, I realized how my mother must have felt when she sent me away. She, too, was robbed. She knew she would never see me pregnant or help me deliver my child or be there to hold my baby or see me grow and flourish as a mother. But she sacrificed it so that I could have a second chance.

At night I could hear Feather crying for me to come to her. Once the crying was so real I got up and searched for her in the night only to wake up the next morning, lying in the forest with nothing but engorged breasts and a broken heart.

It was in the evening of the third that they came and found me sitting on a stump, sweat dripping from my face, trying to relieve the pressure in my breasts by hand. But by this time, no milk came from my breasts, only pus. Hands felt my forehead and other hands made me lie down on blankets in the shade. Hands covered my breasts with wet leaves and set steaming hot cloths over the leaves. The heat seeped into my chest like an iron. Slowly, very slowly, I could feel the hard knots in my breasts untangle, relax, and melt away.

Hands washed my hair and bathed me with sponges, and the cool water ran over my skin like a balm. Hands lifted my head and put food in my mouth.

I dared not to open my eyes to see their faces, to see the looks of pity or disapproval in their eyes, for they all know it is my fault. I became a mother by mistake, and this proved I was unfit to be a mother in the first place. Lark told me to make a net under the tree house, but I never did. He was right to worry. I was wrong for not listening to him. My world was broken up, and trying to put it back together was as hopeless as trying to fix a crushed egg.

Over and over I asked them where Lark was. Cedar told me he was at her lodge, "where you should be, too," she said. She told me we should be together during this time, not apart. But how could we when I had made such a horrible mistake? They tried to get me to come with them, but I refused. They set up a hammock under the tree house for me and I fell asleep.

I slept for years.

In my dreams I saw a bird with both wings broken, floundering in

216

the dirt. It fluttered its wings in vain, succeeding only in stirring up the dirt around it and drawing more attention to its plight. Exhausted, it finally stopped trying. I could see its breast heaving frantically up and down while it turned its head this way and that in panic. Beyond the dying bird, in the forest, the eyes of some unknown creature lit up like embers.

Days went by. Dark days. Lonely days when my chest was tight as a drum and my tears watered my cheeks like rain. I did not want to sleep, afraid the dream of the bird with the broken wings would repeat itself, but I did not want to be awake, for then I had to remember the depth of my misery. There was no state of being that I could live in that gave me peace or comfort.

The only thing I felt would give me hope was to see Lark again. To have him tell me all of those things he used to tell me and to have confidence in me, to reassure me, to forgive me.

But Lark never came.

More days passed, and still the heaviness of my soul did not lift.

Slowly I started to do things again. I gathered firewood for myself. I started a fire. I cooked something. I cleaned a bowl. I repaired a basket. Sometimes I would just sit and stare into the forest, wondering when Lark would finally come home.

One day, after I made the fire, my eyes stopped on the young ceiba tree in my yard. I knew by the spines on its trunk that it was the same species of tree as the one up on the Grassy Top, the tree that Lark called The-Tree-Under-Which-Prayers-Are-Heard.

A tiny piece of hope glittered in my heart like a speck of gold at the bottom of a well. I crawled over to the tree and knelt beside it. Closing my eyes I pictured Lark in my mind. With an inward voice of desperate hope I prayed to whatever gods would listen that I needed him. Bring him back to me, I pleaded. Help him to forgive me. Bring him back so we can be together again, so that there will be someone who will help me bear this heavy grief, for I cannot do it alone.

I opened my eyes and looked up at the ceiba's leaves, waiting and hopeful. But I felt nothing and I saw nothing.

The next day, I sprinkled corn on the metate, took the stone mano in both hands, and crushed the kernels into cornmeal. I spread more corn, leaned over the metate and put all of my strength into smashing and grinding the corn, back and forth, back and forth.

After a while I stopped to stretch, and when I did my eyes lit upon the open door of the tree house.

I gazed back down at the tiny bits of meal that I had ground, finer than sand, then looked up at the tree house again, and when I did an idea struck me with such great force that I wondered why it had not occurred to me before. I realized what I needed to do. Driven with a sense of purpose I had not felt in many days, I strode to the ladder and climbed. When I reached the top my eyes spied the wooden box and I walked straight to it, without glancing at anything else in the room. I grasped it in my hands, my heart quickening. I opened it, reached in and pinched the horrid red feather in my fingers. Carrying it like it was something poisonous I climbed back down and set the feather on the metate. Then I lifted the mano and without hesitation, I crushed it.

I crushed it and pounded it and ground it. "Never, never, never," I repeated with each stroke as I thrust the mano across the stone, obliterating the feather. "Never—ever—again."

Never again would I waste a thought on that man. Never again would I wish for anyone but Lark. When I finished the feather was nothing but dust.

I blew it off the metate. Then I stood, wiped my sweaty hands on my apron, and with the confidence of a child who knows she is worthy of an answer, I again approached the ceiba tree and fell to my knees.

I prayed for a long time. When I was finished, I let out a deep, shuddering sigh. Then, I opened my eyes, looked up into the branches of the tree, and saw something that took my breath away.

It was a sandpiper.

It fluttered down upon the dirt in front of me, and I gazed at it in childlike wonder. I had never seen a sandpiper in this place. Sandpipers are sea birds that love to leave their tracks in damp sand and wet their wing tips in salt water. The jungle was not this bird's home.

"What are you doing here?" I whispered. The little creature leaped about in front of me, showing off its spotted breast and blinking at me with its bright curious eyes.

It hopped in a circle and fluttered its wings, and then flew to a nearby bush.

I went to the metate and scooped cornmeal into my hand.

"Please stay," I said, stepping softly toward the sandpiper. "Look. I have some food for you." Crouching, I held out my hand and offered him the meal.

The bird opened up its beak and chirped, "Twee wee wee!" It flew a little farther and landed on the trail that led toward the temple mound. It turned around, cocked its head, and blinked at me again.

I walked toward it, bent over, my hand open. Sandpipers are not the most graceful fliers; instead, they liked to dash along wet beaches, dodging incoming waves while searching for insects in the sand. This one ran in long ovals on the path, cheeping "twee wee wee" and stopping only to look at me curiously with its merry black eyes as it coaxed me further along. Several times it let me get very close, so close I could have touched it. Even as a child who lived on the beach, I had never come so close to a sandpiper before.

Its familiar, simple beauty fascinated me. The head and top feathers were nut-brown and its underside was white as popped corn and speckled with dark spots. Around its neck it had a dainty brown collar. How delicate the little creature's legs were, and how exquisite were its wings! The bird seemed so breakable. It would not take much to injure it. I marveled at its smooth black beak and the way its soft feathers folded into each other in perfect order.

"You are not an ugly bird at all," I said in surprise.

The sandpiper flew up to a low branch and cheeped, "Twee wee wee!" as if my compliment annoyed him. But even if I had offended it, it still did not fly away to where I could not follow. It was my namesake, and for now my only friend. I wanted to know where its nest was, and if there was a little family of sandpipers displaced and hidden somewhere in this foreign forest. My misery was for the moment forgotten, and following this little creature was my life's only desire.

219

I tagged after it along the trail, never bothering to wonder where we were going or how far we had come. Then the bird flew off the trail into the dense forest, and I stood on the path and sighed, thinking our journey was finished. But then I heard it cheep again, "Twee wee wee!" and peering into the trees I saw it, perched on a vine, blinking at me with its glittering eyes. It still wanted me to follow, and for some reason I felt it was vitally important that I did. I left the trail and stepped into the dappled forest.

The bird traveled more slowly now, waiting for me to step over fallen trees and navigate around thorny bushes. I almost grabbed a bright green snake on accident, thinking it was a vine. I was more careful after that, checking before each step for ant mounds and thistles, all the while brushing away mosquitos and trying to keep one eye on the little bird who was always just out of reach. I tripped over a root and landed against a tree trunk, disturbing dozens of yellow butterflies. They fluttered around me in a cloud of sunny petals, brushing my skin with their wings and face before landing back on the tree, closing their wings and becoming invisible again. Always, the little sandpiper was there, watching me, waiting to lead me on.

Finally, the bird landed on a branch a few paces away, level with my face. Beyond the branch, past the leaves and vines, I could see patches of blue sky and I knew we were near the opening of a clearing. The bird did not move as I came closer, and even though I had long ago dropped the handful of cornmeal in my stumblings through the jungle, I felt confident that I might coax it to land on my finger. Slowly, I reached out until my hand was so close that all I had to do was straighten my fingers to caress its breast. But just as I did, the bird flew away, leaving the branch. My eyes refocused, and in the place where the bird had perched a moment ago, there was now a man.

The man was standing off in the clearing, but the manner in which he was standing, and the position of the trembling branch from which the bird had just flown made the man seem like he was perched on the branch. Even from far away I knew immediately that it was Lark.

"Thank you," I whispered up toward the canopy. "Thank you for helping me find him."

My whole spirit swelled with hope. The very sight of his familiar figure and disheveled hair started my heart beating like the wings of a hummingbird. I ducked under the branch and left the forest, stepping into the brightness of the clearing, beneath the dome of cloudless blue sky. Cupping my hands around my mouth I called out to Lark, but he did not hear me, and I began to walk forward, smiling, my heart pounding.

This place seemed so familiar, as if I had been here before. I tried to get a sense of where I was. All around me were grasses that came to my knees. Looking out into the clearing, beyond Lark, I saw a cluster of green plants surrounding a tall banyan tree.

Then I stopped. I knew where we were now.

We were at the cenote.

SANDPIPER

I called to Lark again, but he did not turn around. Instead he disappeared into the green fronds that concealed the pool.

"No," I whispered as my stomach folded in upon itself. "Not you."

My body went numb and my heart beat so hard it hurt. *No, I thought. Please, not him too. Not now. I must be mistaken.* It could not be Lark. The cenote did not affect Lark. Lark was . . . immune. Besides, Lark never came to the cenote without me, and Lark would be whistling, and this man was not. Lark is stronger than the cenote voices, or at least he loves me more than them. Did he not tell me I was everything he ever desired? Did he not tell others that I was his ideal? Did he not? It cannot be Lark. It must be someone else.

I tried to think of logical reasons he might be there. Perhaps he was cleaning the filter or making sure the scaffold was sound. Or perhaps he was getting water. But none of these reasons made sense, since the scaffold was on the opposite side of the cenote. I could not think of any other reason he could be there.

Except one.

I was surprised at how quickly the anger came. A few moments ago I was ready to fly across the grass, embrace my husband, and tell him everything was going to be all right.

But now . . .

A breeze blew across the clearing. I could hear it weave through the grasses as they gracefully bent toward me. The breeze was cool and wet and smelled of water. It ruffled my blouse and moved up the back of my shirt, making me shudder. To me it only sounded like the wind, but I knew that to him, it sounded like so much more. What was he doing at that moment? Was he closing his dark eyes, imagining their curving bodies and flowing hair? How did his countenance appear? Was he pleased? Intrigued? Was he leaning forward?

The thought repulsed me and I turned back into the forest. I wanted to get as far away from him as I could. I climbed through the jungle, thorns scratching my legs and catching on my skirt and slip, ripping the lace. I did not know where I was going, but soon I stumbled up on a path and I started running, my face hot, my heart smoldering with anger. I came around a bend I did not even notice the man until I ran straight into his chest.

"Stone!"

"Sandpiper," he said, holding me away from him by my shoulders. "I have been looking for you." His voice was calm and steady. Hearing Stone's voice did something to the muscles in my body. Here was a brother, a friend, someone strong and stable. I melted against him, and the tears came. Sobs heaved out of my body and fluids poured from my noise. I should have felt embarrassed but I could not stop the sadness that emptied out of me like water from a gourd. It kept coming and coming and he stood there for a long time. Eventually, I felt his arms come around me, light and brotherly.

I curled up in his chest. He did not push me away but he did not he tighten the embrace, either. After a while I realized how awkward this was, for being held by him was like cuddling up to a boulder, so I composed myself and stepped back. Stone's arms left me and hung at his sides.

"I apologize," I said, sniffing and wiping my eyes with my sleeve. "I am sorry. I just need to get back to my home." I tried to move around him, but he stepped in my way. I looked up, expecting to see sympathy, but his countenance was unreadable.

"Sandpiper," he said. "What are you going to do?"

"I told you. I am going home." I sniffed. I tried to get around him again but he grabbed my arm. Now his expression was unmistakably stern and as he held me the breeze came through the trees and rustled the leaves above.

He looked over my shoulder, toward the cenote. His jaw tightened and his nostrils flared. When he looked back into my eyes he said, "Sandpiper, do you know where Lark is?"

"Lark?" I said, my voice pleasant yet sharp. "Perhaps." I glared at my brother-in-law. I wanted to hear a man say it. I wanted to hear one of them admit that they were being called to the cenote. "Do you know, brother?"

I could see the muscles in Stone's jaw ripple as he chose his words. "Yes," he said finally. "And he is . . . in trouble."

My eyes narrowed. "Yes, he is. Because when he gets home I am going to hit his head with the biggest stick I can find."

"Sandpiper, his life is in danger."

I pressed my lips together and wrenched my arm from his grasp.

"He will not listen to me, Sandpiper," Stone said as I turned away. "I have been out there three times to bring him back, but . . . he will not listen."

Three times? I suddenly felt weak. The only thing that kept me on my feet now was my anger. "If you cannot get him to come back, what makes you think I can? And what makes you think I even want to? Why should I go to him? Can you not see that he is the one who is betraying me? I went to find him, to bring him home, but he is the one who is staring into the cenote, listening to them."

I expected Stone to deny it. Instead he stepped towards me, grasped my shoulders, and with an expression of great astonishment he whispered, "You know?"

"Yes, I know," I said crisply. "I know everything. I know the legend. I know about the women. I know that they call you . . ."

With these words Stone turned crazy. Shaking me like a sapling he said, "How do you know? Did Lark tell you?"

"Does it matter?"

"No, it does not. I . . . I . . . am just so . . . grateful!" Releasing me, he stepped back and raised his hands above him. "She knows!" He shouted at the sky.

"You are grateful?" I snapped.

"Yes, Sandpiper! I am grateful and so relieved! Because now you can help!"

"Help?" I blinked. "Help?! I am not going to help. He got himself into this mess."

The joy melted from Stone's face. "But Lark is . . . confused . . . and he is hurting."

"I am hurting too."

"I know. I am not making excuses for him."

"You are," I said.

"There is no excuse for what he is doing. It is wrong. We both know that. But he is my brother. More important, he is your husband. Do you not see, Sandpiper? He is ours, not theirs. We cannot let them take him away from us. I have done everything I can to make him come back, but I do not have as much power as you do. He does not love me the way he loves you."

"If he loved me he would not do this!" I shouted. "He made me an oath!"

"And you made an oath to him." Stone's voice remained steady. "You both promised to take care of each other. To help each other when the other was in trouble. If that vow is not honored at a time like this, what good are vows and oaths in the first place?"

I was silent. I did not care to say more to this man who was twisting my words in favor of his brother.

"Besides. You are not the only one who made an oath with Lark."

I stared at him. "What are you talking about?"

"Years ago, when we were much younger, Lark and I wanted to end the deaths in the village. We made a promise that we would try protect the village from the cenote in whatever way we could. We never told our father, of course. He would not have permitted it. We would put cotton in our ears to help block out the sound of the cenote and took turns patrolling the village at night, checking to see if anyone had gone . . . out. We would confront them and persuade them to come home. Sometimes we were successful. Sometimes we were not.

"But then the scaffold broke. The scaffold had been there as long as anyone could remember. No one wanted to fix it—for fear of the voices. Besides, everyone knew Lark was the only one with the skills. For days, people hinted that Lark should be the one to fix the scaffold. Lark was reluctant. But the need for clean water was getting desperate and the women complained to us, asking us why we could not get out there and repair the most vital structure in our village. The pressure became great. He was forced to volunteer.

"He took cotton for his ears and was out there for several days. When he finished the scaffold, it was better than it had ever been before. But the experience had damaged him. The voices had seeped into his heart. It was not long before he began visiting the cenote on his own."

My eyes closed, and I shook my head. I could not believe what I was hearing. Why had no one told me this before?

"I knew he was going and I stopped him. I reminded him of his duty not only to his family but also to his future family, even though he had given up hope that he would ever marry. When he met you, everything changed."

"Everything changed," I said. "Until now."

"You must hear me. Lark knows the danger better than anyone, but his spirit is weak now. He does not have the will to stop himself. He needs a reason to turn around."

"So what are you saying I should do? Try singing to him to make him come back to me? Strip off all of my clothes and run out there naked to see if he will follow? If you think that is what I should do then you shame yourself, Stone. This is not a contest between them and me. I will not do that. This is Lark's problem, not mine."

He turned his back to me and dug his fingers into his hair in frustration. "Listen to me, Sandpiper," he said, facing me again. "I do not know what you can do. But I know that a man like Lark does not come to the cenote without cause."

Flames flared up inside me. "Are you saying that this is my fault?"

"No, no . . . I am not saying that," Stone said quickly. "You have become Jade's sister. I know Jade talks about me to you, so you know that I have a lot to learn when it comes to husband and wife relations. I know I am not perfect. But I will tell you this. The only thing a husband really wants is to be accepted by the woman he loves. That is all. If he knows that you still love him, I believe he will come back. I believe you are the only one who can turn him around. You are the only one he will listen to. You are his only hope." Stone looked deep into my eyes. For the first time, I saw fear in face.

"It is not your fault," he continued, his voice soft, "but when a man is discouraged and alone, the voices are so much louder. Believe me, I know. The voices have found him again, and they want him. They will not let him go until he jumps."

I tried to keep the tears down, but holding them in was so painful.

"I know you must feel betrayed. But we both know him well, and we know he is not a bad person. He blames himself for what happened to Feather. He loves you more than anything on this earth and I know he will come back. He will come back if he knows there is a reason."

I closed my eyes and pressed the tears out.

"Please, Sandpiper, we all make mistakes," he said, his voice trembling. "I am begging you. At the very least, remember your oath."

Instantly my tears sizzled and dried like drops of water in a hot pan. "I may have made an oath, but that does not take away my choice."

Stone was silenced. There was a large rock beside the path and he sank down on it. He put his head in his hands, pressing hard against his temples as if he wanted to crush his head. After a while he lifted his chin, but kept his elbows on his knees, as if he just lost a very long race. "I am sorry," he acknowledged, his voice broken. "I understand the burden of an unwanted oath. Make your choice, Sandpiper. Just make it quickly."

I left him, deteriorating on that rock. And as I turned my back, I heard him start to cry.

Cedar found me sitting alone, below the tree house, staring into the forest. I could hear her coming, but I did not move, even when she placed her hand on my shoulder and invited me, once again, to come with her to her lodge for the night.

Would you like to know where your son is? I wanted to ask her.

She crouched down and took my hands in hers. "Sandpiper, please come with me. Stay with us until Lark comes home."

The tremor in her voice gave her away. She knew. And she was afraid.

I looked directly into her eyes ". . . until Lark comes home." I echoed, my voice cloaked in doubt.

She took my hand and helped me stand. I clung to her arm as we walked up the trail. "It is not your fault, Sandpiper. Do not blame yourself." She repeated over and over. But her advice only soured my heart, for now I could sense in her words a double meaning.

By the time we arrived at the lodge it was twilight. When Honeybee saw us, she embraced me and led me to a place to sit by Grandmother Vine. I slumped into my seat and stared at the fire that crackled cheerfully, mocking us all. Cedar set a bowl of food in my lap. I never even looked to see what it was. All of us were as somber as the grave.

They ate in silence. After a while, Stone appeared, followed by Jade and Mosquito. They sat down on a log next to each other. I saw Stone reach for Jade's free hand, and at that moment I hated them.

I stared back at the fire, fighting the anger inside of me. The silence was unbearable.

"I wish Lark was here," sighed Honeybee.

"He will come back. When he feels better," Cedar said, her smile forced. "He just needs some time alone."

I could feel Stone looking at me, and I knew he was trying to get my attention. I ignored him.

"Yes," said Jade, "he will be back. Perhaps he will smell Cedar's wonderful food and come walking in any moment."

They all perked up expectantly, as if Jade had said the magic words that would somehow make Lark suddenly materialize out of the darkness at that precise moment. When he did not, there was a mutual sigh.

Honeybee was sitting with her elbows on her knees, and her chin in her hands, looking more like a child than ever. She frowned. "Lark always makes everything better."

"Yes," murmured Cedar, "he is a good son."

"And a good brother," added Honeybee.

Jade held Mosquito tight. "And a good father."

I still had not touched one morsel of food in my bowl. Again I could feel Stone watching me, yearning for me to look up at him.

"Stone," Cedar said. "Eat up. I did not fix this food so that it would be wasted."

Stone took his plate and set it on the ground. "I am not hungry, Mother."

Finally I lifted my chin and met Stone's gaze with unsmiling coldness. Stone parted his lips and mouthed the word "please."

I wanted to scream.

By now Jade had noticed Stone's behavior and she looked back and forth between us, suspicious. Meanwhile Cedar tried to start a conversation about planting this season, and though she was the only one speaking, she was only background noise to the silent conversations going on around her.

I had had enough. I stood and handed my untouched food to Cedar. I left the fire and let the darkness of the night swallow me whole.

I had not planned on walking out on the family, but I could not sit there any longer and listen to them talk about Lark while Stone tried to make me feel guilty.

I wanted to be alone. I walked toward the pavilion, thinking I would sit there for a while. The moon was almost full, and the further I walked away from the bright fire, the better my night eyes could see the moonlit world.

I remembered when I first came to this village and how patient Lark had been with me. My thoughts had been so absorbed in thinking about being pregnant that I hardly appreciated the many kindnesses he had done for me. I remembered the many avocados he brought to me. I thought about his willingness to go along with my silence when he knew all the while that I could speak. I remembered the ocelot pelt that he was so proud of but traded for that necklace that I never wore.

I remembered all the times he had complimented the food I had made, even when I knew hungry dogs would have passed it over. And all the hours he had filled the empty space between us with kind words and funny stories, while I refused to speak. I thought of the days and days he had spent in the forest, building me that stupid tree house. I thought of the day Feather was born and how he stayed with me in the cornfield, even though the rain pounded on our heads, and even though he did not have to because it was a woman's job.

I stopped under the ceiba tree and felt the cool night breeze blow against my skin. For the second time that day, I was under a praying tree, but I did not feel like praying now. Something rustled above me and I cast my eyes up to see the white ribbons fluttering in the branches, waving like little flags against the black sky. For many months, I wondered what these white ribbons were for until I saw Cedar tie one around a branch the day Newt was found in the cenote.

Would there be another ribbon on that tree tomorrow?

I started walking.

I thought of the nights Lark had been away doing guard duty in the corn milpa and came back with all those little animals for Feather. Memories of him holding Feather flooded into my mind and I knew he was the only person on the earth who loved that baby as much as I did, even after he knew she was not his.

I was the girl who got pregnant. I was the wife who lied to her husband. I was the one who fantasized about another man. I was the mother who turned her back on her baby. What was it that Stone had said? Everyone makes mistakes.

I walked faster.

I had been so outraged that Lark had let himself listen to the voices of the cenote, but had I been true to him? All those nights when he made love to me and my mind was elsewhere, thinking about Roach and his revolting face. . . . The words of Grandmother Vine pounded in my ears: The most important body part is the brain. Were the dead men who gave up their brains to the cenote any different than what I had done in my own mind?

I remembered Lark's face when he saw me with Roach in the forest. I remembered afterward how I waited for him to yell at me, to abandon me, to publicly humiliate me like I deserved, but he had not done any those things. Instead, he had talked to me, listened to me. He came up with a plan for us to stay together. We all make mistakes.

I began to run.

My mother's words sounded in my mind: *You know nothing about love.* And now I knew she was right. I had always thought love came easy, that it did not involve suffering or sacrifice or pain. I thought that love was about good smells, soft skin, moonlit nights, and hopeful promises. But what good was a promise that was never kept? If love gave up and died when things became difficult, then what good was love for? And if love leaves when life becomes hard, was it even love in the first place?

I was on the balls of my feet now, flying down the black path as the tears wet my face. When I reached the bottom of the temple mound, I took the trail to the cenote. Here the trail was darker and each step looked as though I were stepping into a bottomless crevasse. I was forced to go more slowly, carefully picking safe places to land my feet, trusting the white stones that bordered the path. I heard pounding footsteps behind me, and I wiped the tears from my face as Stone jogged up to my side.

"I know this is between you and Lark," he panted and pushed something white into his ears. "But I will be here if you need me."

I said nothing, still deciding whether to be annoyed or grateful that he had come. No one knew what to prepare for tonight.

The silver moon shone through the trees ahead of us, and I could hear the breeze filter through the leaves above. We were almost there. Hold on, Lark. Stay right where you are.

Then, just as we came to the clearing I heard a sound that stopped my heart. I clutched Stone's sleeve.

"What—?" he began.

"Shhh," I said. For a moment we both stood still as deer. I held my breath and tried to listen past my pulse that throbbed in my ears. Had I imagined it?

"What is it?" asked Stone after a few thoughts had passed. "Did you hear something?"

I nodded. "I heard a splash."

Stone took off at a sprint, dashing through the grassy, gray-blue clearing. By the time he entered into the trees, I had caught up to him. Together, we approached the rim of the cenote and Stone stared down into the black hole.

"You were wrong," he said in between breaths. "If he had jumped he would be splashing or yelling for help."

I shook my head. Stone may know more about the cenote than I did, but I knew more about water than him. When someone drowns, there is very little noise, if any at all. A water death is a silent death.

Stone turned his back to the cenote and shouted Lark's name, but I continued to peer down in to the dark hole, my heart pounding against my chest like a trapped animal. The surface of the water was darkly iridescent in the moonlight, and undulated gently, as if I were looking down on thousands of glimmering beetles. I knew that water would not move like that unless it had been disturbed. Something had breached the surface. There was only one thing to do.

"Lark!" Stone was still shouting.

I put my hand on his arm. "Stop, Stone," I murmured.

"I am sure he will hear me and come out of the bushes," Stone said. "He is probably ashamed that we are here and that we know he has been—"

I shook my head. "He cannot hear you."

"What makes you think that?"

"Because he is down there," I said, looking into the hole.

Stone's countenance became haggard. "How do you know?"

"I do not know—for certain. But I know how to find out." I pulled off my blouse and unwrapped my skirt, dropping them in the grass. I stepped to the edge, wearing only my long white slip.

Stone took a step back. "What are you doing?" he said.

"I am going down."

"Are you crazy? You will drown!"

"I will not drown. I am an experienced swimmer."

Stone grabbed my arm and pulled me back. "I will not let you. It is my duty to keep the people in this village safe. Lark would kill me if I let any harm come to you."

"Lark will not be able to kill you if he is dead. Let go of me, Stone. We are wasting time. You cannot stop me from—" Just then I heard voices coming toward us in the darkness. I turned around and saw dark shapes moving through the grasses. They called to us.

232

"Stone! Sandpiper! Is that you?"

The dark silhouettes of Cedar and Honeybee and Jade appeared from behind the leaves.

"We thought you might be here," Cedar panted.

"Sandpiper," said Jade slowly. "Why are you standing on the edge of the cenote next to my husband without your clothes?"

"She thinks she is going down to get Lark," said Stone, still gripping my arm.

"What do you mean?" gasped Cedar. "Where is Lark?"

"He is down there," said Stone pointing into the cenote. "She thinks he is, anyway." Honeybee started to cry and Cedar wilted against a tree.

"Sandpiper, you are insane if you think you can rescue him," said Jade. "No one has ever come out alive. How do you even know Lark is down there?"

Before I could answer Stone released me and peeled off his tunic. "I am coming with you," he said, tossing his shirt aside.

"No you are not." I said.

"No, you are not!" said Jade, moving between us and putting her finger in Stone's chest. "You are not going anywhere."

This was making me crazy. "Enough!" I said in a tone that surprised even myself. Jade and Stone stopped arguing and everyone looked at me. "I will go down, and I will do it alone. Besides," I added, "I am the only one here who can swim."

This silenced them.

I turned around to the cenote and was about to dive when Honeybee's quiet voice asked, "How will you get out?"

I stopped. She was right. There was no point going in if there was not a way back out. I looked around desperately at my options. My eyes landed on the scaffold.

"The rope," I said.

Immediately Stone unsheathed his knife and went to the scaffold. He sliced through the rope and the bucket dropped into the dark pit with a dull splash. While he unraveled it from the spool, I looked down into the cenote. I had never been frightened about anything before, but now I was so scared I could not stop shaking. It was not the dive I feared; but what I might find down there in that dark water. Desperately I hoped that the women of the legend were not real. They are only the echo of something that happened a long time ago, I repeated to myself, like the sound of the ocean in an empty shell.

Stone handed me the end of the rope. "I do not know if this is strong enough," he said.

"It is strong enough." I knew it was. Lark and I had made this rope.

"I will give you plenty of slack. If you need more, tug one time. When you want to be pulled out, tug twice."

I nodded. I stepped to the edge of the cenote, winding the end of the rope several times around my hand and looked down into the water, black as oil. A wind coming up from the cenote ruffled my slip and every part of my body shook.

I turned and took one last look at Lark's family. They were huddled together, their countenances pale and ghostly in the moonlight, their eyes wide and fearful.

"If it is as you say, and my son is down there," whispered Cedar, "then make speed, Sandpiper."

Clutching the end of the rope, I closed my eyes and tried to breathe. Then I tucked my chin, lifted my trembling arms, and sprang off the edge, dropping headfirst into nothing.

When I plunged into the water I was consumed in a terrible, cold blackness. Like an arrow, I sped downwards, deep into the belly of the cenote. When I finally slowed, I began stroking through the muffled silence, still holding tight to the rope.

The water weighed heavily on my body, and the only sounds were the groggy strokes of my hands. It was too dark to know if my eyes were open or shut. I groped through the darkness for something, anything— but I could only feel empty water, all around.

My lungs burned. It had been a long time since I had held my breath like this. I had to go up. I pumped my legs like a frog till my face broke the surface and I breathed in the cool night air. Then I took in a great gulp before going back down into the silence.

My slip billowed against my legs as I kicked downwards and pushed myself deeper and deeper into the water. I was just about to come back up for air when I felt something brush past my arm. It was hair and I grabbed it.

I pulled it closer to me and felt down the round head. A hand weakly grasped my arm and I could feel Honeybee's bracelet around Lark's wrist. Immediately, I unwound the rope from my arm and threaded it under his shoulders, tying it at the back. I tugged the rope twice, as hard as I could, and Lark started to glide upwards. Putting my arms under his shoulders, I kicked my legs, helping him rise faster. Above me, I could see the pale fuzzy circle of the moon far beyond us. We were moving upwards, moving up and out of the cenote. My lungs were near collapse, but my heart was lit up like a torch. Lark was not completely lost. Perhaps we could still bring him back.

We were not far from the surface when Lark's body stopped moving, as if the people above had decided to take a break. I quickly swam to the surface and gasped for air. I wiped the water from my eyes and mouth and shouted up, "Pull harder! I have him on the rope! He is almost out!" My voice bounced off the walls of the cenote, wavy and dreamlike. I wondered if they could even hear me.

The faint answer came back from somewhere above. "We are pulling! But the rope is caught!"

The rope is caught? Caught on what?

Then something grasped my ankle yanked me under the water.

The moment my ears filled with liquid I could hear them. At first, it was like a hundred whispers. The whispers grew louder like distant seagulls and quickly became so piercing and shrill I felt like someone was sticking a knife through my ears and into my brain.

Their voices surrounded me. Some seemed far away, some seemed right behind me. They were indeed the voices of women, but the sounds were not beautiful; they were hideous. It was not music at all but whining screams, and the sounds filled my entire body with terror. I could see nothing as I was slowly pulled deeper. Then, gradually, like the moon coming out from behind a cloud, they revealed themselves. I could see them all around me.

Silver and pale, the curving shapes of women drifted in a wide ring around Lark's limp body. There were legions of them swimming, patient and shark-like. Their long hair flowed behind their faceless heads like the tentacles of jellyfish. They did not kick with their legs nor stroke with their arms, yet they glided around Lark and me as if the mere bending of their fingers and the curling of their toes propelled them.

The thing that gripped my ankle tightened its knife-like fingers and continued to drag me down through the circling, swimming figures. As I was pulled past Lark's torso I could see some of the women clutching his chest and legs with their slender white arms. Two more brushed against me and floated up to Lark's head, where they gripped his face and neck with their long fingers and nuzzled their strange faces into his hair. Seeing them clinging to my husband like leeches, keeping him from escaping to freedom and air, made me livid.

I could not release my foot from the grasp of the woman below me, but my hands were free, and I reached up and grabbed the flowing black hair of the women holding Lark and wrenched back their heads. Surprised, they instantly they released Lark and his body began to move upwards again. I tried to kick free of the hand that still held my ankle, but it only held me tighter, cutting into my skin. I looked up desperately as Lark's body disappeared above me, toward the distant light, toward the surface, toward our family. The silhouettes around me screamed and howled in anger, and I thought their shrieks would destroy me with their intensity.

Lark was safe, but the rope was gone.

Then, as if commanded by an invisible leader, they all calmed and the shrieking and wailing diminished to a low purr. The voices drummed, soft and constant, smooth and low, like clicking cicadas on a summer night. One of the shadows floated before my face. Her hair smoked around my head like incense and caressed my cheek. When I looked into the place where her face should have been I only saw a hollow, dark space, void of expression, void of countenance. The figure spoke.

Do not be afraid.

The words came not through my ears but through my mind. Her voice was so pleasant, so gentle, and her lilting accent was like the music of some forgotten primeval tongue.

You must be very noble to sacrifice yourself for him, she said, touching my cheek. *But your efforts were unnecessary. . . . All we really wanted was his mind; we would have given the rest of him back to you.*

The figure swam a tight circle around me.

We are not as strong as we once were. . . . Our ancient bodies do not need as much nourishment as we once did to survive. . . . But you see, we still get hungry . . .

Part of me wanted to paddle upward, to get out of this place. But part of me wanted to linger, for her voice was so soft and beseeching. Perhaps, I thought, these women were not evil after all. Perhaps they were also miserable victims.

She hovered close and I peered into her dark, featureless face.

You are pretty, she said. *So very pretty.*

No, I am not.

You are, she said, reading my mind. *You are pretty like us.*

I knew that if we were not in the water, then I would be able to smell her. What would she smell like? As her voice swirled around me I thought she must smell like the forest after the rain, or blooming gardenias or the sea breeze coming off the waves in the morning.

Stay with us, she whispered. *Be our sister.*

My lungs relaxed, and the fierce desire for air was fading. I could feel my mind closing in around itself, folding and shrinking like a scarf tucked into a pocket. It would be the easiest thing to just take a breath of water . . . How beautiful they all were, swirling around me like mermaids, breathing the water, in and out, as easily as fishes.

It will not hurt. Just relax. . . . We will do the rest. It will surprise you how peaceful it feels to surrender . . .

Her hands came to my face. Everything began to dim and darken. I could feel my blood slow and I closed my eyes.

Come to us, sister . . .

I heard a faint plunging sound above me and when I opened my eyes I saw the women scatter like a school of fish. I was amazed that they could move so quickly when I felt so dazed and weak. A large rock came dropping down before my face.

Tied to the rock was the rope. My rope.

Somewhere deep in the confusion of my mind something awakened. I remembered that I did not belong here. I knew that I must grab this rope; that every hope depended on it. But my hands felt so awkward and slow, as heavy as logs. Only with great and painful concentration could I lift them, maneuver them through the water and close my fingers around the fibers.

The women reappeared from their hiding places shrieking and pulling their hair as I started to rise swiftly upward. They tried to grasp me, to pull me back down but their fingers slipped off my skin as the rope carried me up toward the beautiful white light of the blurred moon.

When my face broke out of the water, I could still feel their fingers clinging to my body, but their hands dripped off of me like sludge as I was pulled out into the cold night air. My arms were weak, and the foul, rancid water heaved from my mouth and nose, but nothing would make me let go of the rope. With each choking breath, I could feel my strength return, and I gripped the rope harder. I will never know how they pulled me out of that pit or how I held on, for my mind was still trying to untangle what around me was real and what was not. When I came to the top, I could feel the warm wonderful hands of my family on my skin, grasping me, holding me, pulling my shivering, trembling body out of the hole.

"Are you all right, Sandpiper?" someone said. But all I could think about was the delicious night air that filled my lungs and the beautiful, concerned voices that surrounded me. How real their voices sounded! How familiar and genuine! I tried to move, to sit up, to speak, to thank, but my body ignored my brain and lay as lifeless as a corpse. Instead, hands lifted me.

"Carry her over here . . . gently."

"Careful, now . . . good . . . "

"Next to Lark."

"You should have seen him, Sandpiper. Stone pushed all the water out of Lark, and he is breathing. He is breathing, Sandpiper! Did you hear that? And you saved him!"

I could hear Honeybee's voice fluttering above me somewhere, but everything was indistinct and faint. Someone took my hand and placed it in Lark's.

Then, I rested.

SANDPIPER

The cracks and snaps of the fire woke me, and I opened my eyes to see its warm soothing glow. Cautiously, I sat up, aware of a hundred fresh points of pain, and as I did, a blanket slid from my shoulders revealing my slip, still damp. Lark lay next to me, covered with a blanket and breathing soundly. On the other side of the fire sat Stone.

Where were we? I looked around, seeing no hut or tree. I realized they must have pulled us out to the clearing. I looked down at the blanket and fingered it in wonder.

"Cedar brought the blankets," Stone said, reading my thoughts.

I adjusted my position and pain shot up from my foot. I moved the blanket to see my ankle, neatly wrapped in a clean bandage.

"Who—"

"Honeybee," said Stone.

"Where are they all now?" I asked.

"Cedar took Honeybee home to sleep. Jade went home to be with Mosquito."

"And you stayed here. All night."

He nodded.

"What about the cenote? Can . . . can you hear them?"

Stone smiled. "They are silent, for now. I think you have thoroughly humiliated them."

"And Lark?"

Stone stirred the fire. "He will recover."

"How far into the night are we?"

"The birds will start singing soon."

I pulled the blanket back around me, finally content.

We were silent for many thoughts. Eventually, the crackling fire died down to glowing coals, and I looked up to study the sky. The moon had gone down and the sky was spread, horizon to horizon, with the brightest stars I had ever seen.

"Thank you, Stone," I said, "for everything. You have done so much for us tonight."

He nodded his head.

"Can I ask you something?" I said, casting my eyes back up the sky.

He waited.

"Can you leave us?"

Stone looked at me for a long time. "How will you get home?"

"Oh, we will find a way."

He took deep breath, sat up straight, arched his shoulders back and stretched. "I suppose so. You know where to find me if you need me?"

"I know."

"Is there anything I can do before I go? Do you want me to put another log on the fire?"

"No. Thank you, Stone. We will be fine."

Stone looked doubtful. "Are you sure?"

"Go," I said.

"Very well," Stone said as he stood. "I hope to bring you honor, Sandpiper."

"I hope to bring you peace."

Stone's eyes met mine and he gave a brief nod, "You have."

When Stone's dark figure finally disappeared into the trees I rolled over.

"Lark," I whispered.

No response.

I moved closer to him and pulled his blanket down. His tunic was torn and wet. His matted hair clung to his forehead in thick damp locks. He had fingernail marks all over his body, scars he would carry the rest of his life.

"Lark."

No response. A silver rim of starlight tipped the ridges of his profile.

For a long time I just watched his torso rise up and down and marveled at the miracle of breath and life.

"Lark," I said again. This time he squeezed my hand.

I crawled closer to him and put my head on his chest. I could hear the drum of his heart.

"Piper . . .," he murmured, laying a hand on my head. "You are here."

"Yes, Lark," I said.

"I have the strangest feeling that in the very recent past I was in a dark hole, surrounded by women who were trying to eat me alive. Tell, me, Piper, was this a dream?"

"No."

He moaned. "I was afraid you would say that."

He rolled away for a moment and coughed out some water. I patted him on the back. When he rolled back he said my name again.

"Piper."

"Yes?"

"I did something terrible."

"I know," I said.

"I am so sorry."

"I know."

"It is unforgivable."

I pulled myself close to his face and put my hand on his cheek. "No, it is not."

"I could not stop myself, Piper. After I fell in, they were all around me, pulling me down. I could not get out. I have never felt so alone and terrified. I . . ."

"We do not need to speak of that right now," I said, pushing the hair away from his face. How had I never noticed how beautiful he was? His eyes, his lips, his chin . . . He was the most perfectly formed human I had ever seen. Had it always been so? I stroked his cheek again. "It is over, Lark, and now you are safe."

"Piper, I know . . . I know you cannot want me after what I have done. You probably never want to see me again. Why are you even here? Why did you not let me drown? You should have let me drown."

I smiled. "You sound disappointed. Do you want me to push you back in?"

He squeezed my hand and tried to laugh, but the air came out in wheezes. When he could finally speak he whispered, "Sandpiper, what would I do without you?"

"It was not just me. I had a lot of help. I am not the only one who loves you, Lark," I said as my tears dropped on his cheek.

He closed his eyes and gave a weak grin. "You are using my own words against me."

"How could I let you die, Lark? Do you not remember that we decided that we are better together than apart? There are far too many reasons for us to be together." I rolled over on my back. "Look up, Lark. Look up at the stars."

We cast our eyes on the heavens. The stars scattered across the black sky, millions of them, thick as sand on a beach.

"Do you see them, Lark? See all the reasons we should be together?"

Lark was silent. After a long time he spoke. "I doubt there are that many reasons," he said, trying to sound lighthearted, but failing to conceal the crack in his voice.

I laughed softly. "I think there are." I turned to face him. "I believe there are reasons that we do not even know about yet, and that we will never know if we do not stay together."

The tears rolled out of his eyes, and I kissed him; on his cheeks, on his lips, on his chin . . . and the more I kissed him the more he cried. He knew I was right.

Beyond us in the forest, we heard a bird. Then another, and soon all the birds joined in, heralding the rim of blue that tipped the eastern horizon. Carefully, we sat up. My arms were rubbery and lifeless, and my head felt dizzy and strange, like it might roll off my neck. Gently, carefully, we stood. Leaning against each other, we staggered toward the temple mound, our legs shaking and weak, like children learning to walk all over again.

Lark cleaved to me and I cleaved to him. I thought at any moment, we would both go tumbling to the earth, but it was no matter. We were out of the water, and we were under the stars.

"Piper," he said, "you need to take me away from this place."

"Yes, I do," I answered as I held him steady. I had already been thinking that, and I knew the perfect spot.

Above us, the gods must have looked down and thought how awkward and clumsy we seemed, shivering and leaning against each other for support, our legs trembling with the weight of our bodies as we walked beneath their purple starlit canopy. But if they were wise gods, they could see that our strength was not in our legs, or our arms; it was in our hearts. We were strong because we were together. And leaning against each other, we were stronger than we ever had been. After all, we were not meant to walk, Lark and I. We were meant to fly.

EPILOGUE

Later Jade and Honeybee told me the rest of the story.

While Lark and I were struggling in the water, the family stood in a line, holding the rope, waiting in suspense for my signal. As soon as they felt the two tugs they hoisted Lark out of the cenote. He was limp and lifeless, and by the time they dragged him into the clearing, it was clear to everyone that Lark's spirit had passed from this life.

"Clear to everyone, that is, except Stone," Jade said, flashing her beautiful smile. I had noticed, since our night at the cenote, that Jade's bright red face paint, flamboyant clothes and hairdo had disappeared. Now she was back to her old self again, and she seemed even more beautiful than the first day we met.

She explained how Stone had slammed Lark's chest with his fists, shouting out "You will breathe, brother! You will breathe!" over and over again.

"It sounded similar to the growing songs we sing to the corn," Honeybee added thoughtfully, "only much more terrifying."

"But we were absolutely stricken that you had not come out of the water with Lark," Jade continued.

"That is when I came up with the idea for the rock." Honeybee beamed.

They found a large stone and lashed the end of the rope to it and hefted it into the water. Since Stone would not leave Lark's side, the women pulled me out on their own. "We were not going to let you drown," said Honeybee. I knew they told the truth, for I could see the evidence burned into the palms of their hands.

Jade told me that she and Stone talked for a long time that night, and spoke of things they had never discussed. He told her everything. She was relieved to know that Stone had never been a Listener after all, but had been trying to protect others.

"So I suppose you two are not sleeping in hammocks anymore," I said.

"Yes, we are," Jade replied, "Just not two."

When Lark told Honeybee we were leaving, she cried for three days straight. "I cannot live without you," she wept.

One of Honeybee's friends, Crocus, would marry in a few days. Honeybee begged Lark and me to stay for the wedding, but he was eager to be on our way.

"There will always be another reason to stay," he told me. But for Honeybee's sake, we stayed long enough for me to attend the bride's circle. Besides, I had already made Crocus a gift. Every bride ought to have her own rope. I even braided in some strands of fiber that were dyed in Jade's bright red dye, so that my gift had purpose and beauty.

Jade and I arrived late. It was not my intention to disrupt the meeting, but everyone watched us as we squeezed in next to Honeybee, and the women did nothing to conceal their whispers.

The whispering made me uncomfortable, and I wished that I could blend in the way I used to, with my hair wrapped up and my voice muted. I expected the whispering to die down.

When it did not, Jade cleared her throat, "Thank you for your attention, everyone," she said, "but let Sandpiper be. Turn the focus back to Crocus." Reluctantly, the woman obeyed.

The women continued their advice. Crocus blushed and smiled and thanked each woman in the most appropriate way for their gifts and words of wisdom, while I mulled over what I could say when it came to my turn. This was the first bride's circle where I would actually get to say something. But what? What advice could I give, seeing how I had done almost everything you were not supposed to do in a marriage?

Honeybee leaned into me and whispered in my ear. "Sandpiper, do you know what they have been saying about you?"

I looked at her and shook my head. Did I want to know?

"They are calling you and Lark the couple that survived. You have done a great and brave thing. Everyone has a great respect for you now, Sandpiper, and they are saying that your heart is deep, even deeper than the cenote. Now there is a new legend for the cenote, and it is a story everyone will know."

My cheeks became hot, and I lowered my eyes. Was that really what people were saying? Now what kind of advice was I supposed to give?

My mind raced. I could tell them that it was important to be honest. No one could argue with that. Or I could tell the new bride to forgive her husband for his weaknesses, for we all make mistakes. I could tell her to always remember the oath she made and to honor it. Or I could tell her to "make the nest soft" and cook good foods and keep a clean yard and take good care of the children.

All of those things were important, it was true, but I still did not believe it was sufficient. There was so much more to a marriage than that. I truly felt that I had just been lucky. I had happened to marry someone who was extraordinary, a man that was so special that I would accomplish the impossible for him. I knew Lark was not the perfect man, but he was the perfect man for me. If I was completely truthful, the best advice I could think of to be happy in a marriage was to simply marry Lark. But I could not say that.

Then it was my turn. There was a hushed silence as every face turned toward me, their ears perked and their eyes wide like dozens of curious owls, waiting to hear what words of wisdom would lift from my lips.

But wisdom has never come easy to me, and my mouth was dry and empty. After all this time, and after all that I learned, I was at the beginning again, dumb and silent as the temple ruins.

Jade nudged me in the ribs. "You have a voice, Sandpiper. Use it."

I cleared my throat and the owls leaned forward.

"Just . . . love him," I said.

The owls sat back and frowned, disappointed at my statement. "Of course," mumbled one woman, "but it is not that simple."

No, it is not simple, I thought. *It is not simple at all. But it is true.* They were truest words I had ever spoken.

Lark and I said goodbye to Cedar, Jade, Mosquito, and Honeybee, and it was not long before Lark became so emotional that his nose started bleeding all over everybody. I ripped off a strip of fabric and handed it to him and he promptly stuffed it up his nostril.

We promised everyone we would come back someday, "bringing all twelve of our children," Lark added.

Stone was the last to say good-bye. He clasped Lark in a strong embrace. Then he turned to me. He took off one of his necklaces and lowered it over my head. "I have never known anyone so brave," he said, looking into my eyes. "I am honored to be called your brother."

Then it was time to go. We pulled our packs on to our backs and headed in the direction of the distant sea.

As we made our journey, I thought of the many stories we tell around our campfires and how they are all about the courageous things people do to win the heart of the person they will marry. But what about after the marriage? Now I knew that the deepest, most powerful love stories did not happen before the wedding but after. Perhaps we do not hear those stories because they are far more sacred and only meant for two hearts. That was something else I could have said to Crocus. I would have to remember that and tell her someday.

But I was anxious to see my mother and to tell her all that had happened to me in the past year and a half. I was anxious for her to meet Lark. But most of all, I wanted to show her what I had learned about love.

This bird was flying home.

DISCUSSION QUESTIONS

1. Why didn't the men want the women to know about the voices?
2. The cenote was a necessary source of life for the village, but it also harbored a great evil. What do we have in today's world that is like the water from the cenote?
3. The Ancient Ones mutilated their bodies to make themselves more beautiful. Do we do that today? Where is the line between beauty and mutilation?
4. What good came from the women opening up a discussion on the cenote? What bad came of it? Was it worth it?
5. How did the news that the men could hear voices of women change the attitudes that the women had about themselves?
6. After the women knew the truth, they *still* didn't open up communication with the men. Why not? How did silence make the situation worse?
7. There were three bride circles. How did the advice change as the women grew through their experiences? What advice would you give a young bride?
8. One woman's advice at the bride's circle was that if your husband falls into the cenote it is your own fault. Do you believe that is true?
9. How do you think things might be different in the village now that Stone is no longer bound to his oath?
10. Is there a point when a man has visited the cenote so many times that he shouldn't be saved?

ACKNOWLEDGMENTS

This book is the result of many beautiful minds, the first being my children who came up with the imaginary game that I overheard as I washed the dishes that inspired the crux of the plot.

I had many readers who graciously swam through my murky drafts, including Holly Dyreng Penrod, Kaylene Peets, Debbie Bagley, Kathleen Brown, Trisha Bagley Kunz, Shan'tel Nelson Christianson, Liza Wilson, Mandy Al-Bajaly, Shelly Dyreng, Michelle Dyreng, Angie Kelly, Leon Nelson, Connor Kunz, and Patsy Bagley Brunson. Their suggestions and insights were invaluable and each has their fingerprint somewhere in this story.

I also want to thank Suzanne Warr for writing advice, Helene Brown for her honest initial critiques, Ryan Kunz for his detailed edits, and Nicole Empey for her helpful brainstorming sessions. Thank you to Gwen Holt and Katie Hamstead Teller for helping me fine-tune the book before it was accepted at Cedar Fort. Thank you to Vanessa Garnick Boshoff for answering my impromptu questions about indigenous peoples, and to Jessica Bagley Heath for being excited about my first chapters and for never letting that enthusiasm waiver.

I am indebted to the people at Cedar Fort: Emma Parker, Lyle Mortimer, Kelly Martinez, Greg Martin, Justin Greer, Michelle May and Shawnda Craig.

I owe much of my sanity to my fellow mothers at the Moonlight Bookreader's Guild. You are champions. May your children grow up to be kind, courageous, and lice-free.

This book would still be a pile of papers under my bed without the efforts of Korinne Bagley Nelson who only paused in her relentless enthusiasm to let me have a baby, and for Liza Wilson who took Korinne and me on the adventure of our lives in the Yucatán, Mexico.

Most of all, I am grateful for two parents who excelled at star-counting, and a very good husband who made breakfast every morning for the kids while I typed away in my bedroom, and who is the inspiration of everything that is good about this novel.

ABOUT THE AUTHOR

Chelsea Bagley Dyreng was born in Jackson Hole, Wyoming, and is the daughter of a fireworks salesman and Miss Malibu. She earned her BA at Brigham Young University, worked as a librarian, and then moved to North Carolina, where she and her husband are currently raising five God-fearing, book-loving, adventure-seeking kids.